What the critics wrote about
Joanne Harris

'If Joanne Harris didn't exist, someone would have to invent her'
Sunday Express

'Witty, moving and thought-provoking'
Time Out

'Tantalising and suggestive, and leaves us wanting more'
Sunday Times

'Harris's prose reads like poetry, and it's a physical
experience to fall into her imagery'
Philadelphia Inquirer

'One of Britain's most popular novelists'
Daily Mail

'Harris is a writer of tremendous charm, who creates a winning
blend of fairy-tale morality and gritty realism'
Independent

'Sensuous and thought-provoking . . . subtle and brilliant'
Daily Telegraph

'Harris writes with verve and charm . . . serious delight'
New Yorker

'She is so terrific, she can write about anywhere, anything,
anyone'
Daily Telegraph

'A writer of tremendous charm'
The Time

The novels of Joanne Harris – have you read them all?

CHOCOLAT

When the exotic Vianne Rocher arrives in the French village of Lansquenet and opens a sinful chocolate boutique directly opposite the church at the start of Lent, the villagers are split into opposing camps.

'Mouthwatering . . . A feelgood book of the first order'
Observer

BLACKBERRY WINE

A bottle of home-brewed wine left to him by a past friend provides the key to an old mystery and a terrible secret for Jay Mackintosh.

'Touching, funny and clever'
Daily Telegraph

FIVE QUARTERS OF THE ORANGE

A tragic childhood in Occupied France comes back to haunt a secretive widow.

'Vastly enjoyable, utterly gripping'
The Times

COASTLINERS

On a tiny Breton island, Mado returns after a ten-year absence to fight the tides and attempt to bring a dying community back to life.

'A writer of tremendous charm, who creates a winning blend of fairy-tale morality and gritty realism'
Independent

HOLY FOOLS

In seventeenth-century France, Juliette takes the veil, only to find that a man from her past returns to haunt her behind the convent walls.

'With this bold, inventive book, Harris confirms her position as one of Britain's most popular novelists'
Daily Mail

SLEEP, PALE SISTER

A blackly gothic evocation of Victorian artistic life: Joanne Harris's second novel, first published before she won worldwide recognition.

'A hauntingly evocative laudanum-dream of a novel'
Time Out

GENTLEMEN & PLAYERS

At St Oswald's, a Northern boys' grammar school, a dark
undercurrent stirs, of obsession and revenge.

'A gripping psychological thriller . . . with pace,
wit and acute observation'
Daily Express

THE LOLLIPOP SHOES

Vianne Rocher seeks refuge in Paris with her two daughters,
but encounters a dangerous adversary.

'*Chocolat* was a hard act to follow but Harris has managed it in style'
Daily Express

THE EVIL SEED

Joanne Harris's haunting debut novel, a gothic vampire story.

'A dark, gothic romance filled with mystery, jealousy,
and violence . . . a thrilling read'
Style

BLUEEYEDBOY

A dark tale of a poisonously dysfunctional family, a psychological
thriller that makes creative use of all the disguise and mind
games that are offered by life on the internet.

'Delivers an almighty twist in the tale . . . brilliantly
atmospheric and at times heartbreaking'
The Times

PEACHES FOR MONSIEUR LE CURÉ

When Vianne Rocher receives a letter from beyond the grave, she has
no choice but to follow the wind back to Lansquenet, the French village
where, eight years ago, she opened up a chocolate shop.

'Immerses the reader in a bath of seductive imagery'
Sunday Times

RUNEMARKS

Five hundred years after the End of the World, a young girl
born with a runemark on her hand must find the old gods.
An epic tale inspired by Norse myth.

'If you liked Philip Pullman's *Northern Lights*, try this'
Heat

RUNELIGHT

Two girls. With new runes. And the end of the world is coming. Again.

'One of my favourites . . . The author's wonderful
imagination is showcased to great effect'
The Sun

Other books by Joanne Harris

JIGS & REELS

Joanne Harris's first collection of short stories: sly, funny, sometimes provocative.

'Tantalising and suggestive, and leaves us wanting more'
Sunday Times

A CAT, A HAT, AND A PIECE OF STRING

Joanne Harris's second collection of short stories: sensuous, mischievous, uproarious and wry.

'A moreish collection . . . comical, scary, sad and surreal'
Independent

THE FRENCH KITCHEN (with Fran Warde)

A beautifully illustrated cookery book of Joanne Harris's French family receipes.

'Simple yet stylish recipes from the heart of a French family'
Sunday Telegraph

THE FRENCH MARKET (with Fran Warde)

A mouth-watering collection of recipes . . . inspired by fresh, seasonal French market produce.

'Crammed with authentic local recipes . . . A glossy, uplifting book'
Sunday Tribune

A CAT, A HAT AND A PIECE OF STRING

Stories by
Joanne Harris

BLACK SWAN

TRANSWORLD PUBLISHERS
61–63 Uxbridge Road, London W5 5SA
A Random House Group Company
www.transworldbooks.co.uk

**A CAT, A HAT AND A PIECE OF STRING
A BLACK SWAN BOOK: 9780552778794**

First published in Great Britain
in 2012 by Doubleday
an imprint of Transworld Publishers
Black Swan edition published 2014

'Faith and Hope Fly South' first appeared in the PiggybankKids anthology *Journey to the Sea*, published by Ebury Press, 2005; 'There's No Such Place as Bedford Falls' in the *Sunday Telegraph* supplement 'Seven' on 23 December 2007; 'Would You Like to Reconnect?' was broadcast on Radio 4; 'Rainy Days and Mondays' appeared in *My Weekly* magazine on 26 April 2008; 'Harry Stone and the 24-Hour Church of Elvis' in the PiggybankKids anthology *Mums: A Celebration of Motherhood*, published by Ebury Press, 2007; 'The Ghosts of Christmas Present' in *Harpers & Queen*, December 2005; 'Wildfire in Manhattan' in *Stories – All-New Tales*, ed. Neil Garman and Al Sarrantonio, published by Headline Review, 2010; 'Road Song' in Plan UK's anthology *Because I'm a Girl*, published by Vintage, 2010.

A CIP catalogue record for this book
is available from the British Library.

Addresses for Random House Group Ltd companies outside the UK
can be found at: www.randomhouse.co.uk
The Random House Group Ltd Reg. No. 954009

The Random House Group Limited supports the Forest Stewardship Council© (FSC®), the leading international forest-certification organisation. Our books carrying the FSC label are printed on FSC®-certified paper. FSC is the only forest-certification scheme supported by the leading environmental organisations, including Greenpeace. Our paper procurement policy can be found at www.randomhouse.co.uk/environment

Typeset in Goudy by
Kestrel Data, Exeter, Devon.
Printed and bound by
CPI Group (UK) Ltd, Croydon, CR0 4YY.

2 4 6 8 10 9 7 5 3 1

MIX
Paper from
responsible sources
FSC® C016897

To Chris
whose stories always draw blood

Contents

Introduction

An interviewer once asked me this question: *If you were to be stranded on a desert island, what three items would you take?*

I gave this frivolous answer: *A cat, a hat and a piece of string.* Partly because I liked the jaunty, careless bounce of the phrase, and partly because each item has many potential uses, on its own or separately, which makes my choice more than the sum of its parts.

I'd bring the cat for company. The hat for shelter from the sun. The piece of string has multiple purposes, including to amuse the cat, or to keep the hat on in a high wind. There's also a scenario in which I use the hat and the piece of string to make a simple fish-trap (presumably to feed the cat); or a less appealing one in which I strangle the cat with the piece of string and cook it for lunch, using the hat as a makeshift tureen. (To be fair, I can't imagine myself ever wanting to eat a cat, but who knows what might happen if you were stranded for long enough on a desert island?) It occurred to me that I could probably think up a hundred similar stories featuring just those three items.

The stories in this collection are a little like that too. Though seemingly unconnected at first, you'll find they are linked in all kinds of ways to each other and to my novels. Some take place in locations you may recognize; others feature characters with whom you may be familiar. Some stand alone – for the present, at least – which does not mean that they always will. Stories are often so much more than the sum of their individual parts; to me, they exist like unfinished maps to as-yet-undiscovered worlds; waiting for someone to pencil in the connections as they find them.

As I said in *Jigs & Reels*, short stories do not always come easily to me. Sometimes they drift like flotsam to the shores of that desert island; at other times I bring them home from my travels around the world; or sometimes they rattle inside my head for months – and sometimes years – on end, like coins trapped inside a vacuum cleaner, waiting for me to release them.

In any case, I hope that these may take you a little further into that unexplored territory. Maybe you'll meet some old friends – as I hope you'll find some new ones. Don't forget your cat and your hat – and, with a long enough piece of string, you'll always be sure to find the way home.

River Song

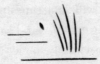

Stories are like Russian dolls: open them up, and in each one you'll find another story. This particular story was written when I was in the Congo with Médecins Sans Frontières. Why I was there in the first place is a story in itself, but while I was in Brazzaville I met a gang of small boys who had devised an ingenious (and perilous) means of earning a living. They would gather by the river under the veranda of one of the city's few surviving restaurants and, for a coin or a handful of scraps, would entertain the diners by leaping into the rapids at the river's most dangerous point and riding the current downstream. These children – none of them older than ten years old – would risk their lives dozens of times a day, often for nothing more than a chicken bone or a piece of bread. What's more, they seemed to enjoy it.

Well, *there's always the river.* That's what Maman Jeanne says, with that look old people get when they're talking about something you can't possibly understand, like how an aeroplane stays in the air, or why the Good Lord made the tsetse fly. It's her answer to everything; complaints, questions, tears. Well, there's always the river, she says. The Congo river is always there.

I should know: I've watched it all my life. I know its moods; like a fierce dog that will sometimes play, but goes for the throat if you take the game too far. I know the fishing spots and the best places to swim; the rapids and the shallows; the islets and the sands and where they shot the last hippo, years ago. To hear them talk, you'd think everyone in Brazzaville was there that day – if so, that old hippo should be right there in the Bible, next to the miracle of the *foufou* and the fishes. Still, says Maman Jeanne, fishermen and hunters are born to lie.

Maybe it's the river makes them do it.

It's true that stories collect here. Like the water hyacinth, they float downriver from the north, dividing and flowering as they go. The story of the Three Sorcerers, or the Eagle Boy, or the Devil-Fish, so huge it can snap a hippo's spine, or swallow a crocodile in a single gulp. That, at least, is true; I have a devil-fish tooth to prove it, traded (for a cigarette and half a stick of chewing gum) from a boy on one of the barges. It's longer than my finger, and I wear it round my neck on a piece of wire. Maman Jeanne says I shouldn't; there's bad magic in a devil-fish tooth, and anyway, it's not right for a ten-year-old girl to be hanging around those river barges.

If she was *my* mother, says Maman Jeanne, she would teach me to cook and sew and work my hair into little plaits and cornrows to catch myself a man. *That's the catch for you, girl,*

she says, *not some nasty old devil-fish that you couldn't eat even
if you could pull it in*. But I can look after myself, and I don't
have to do what Maman Jeanne tells me. Besides, like she
says, people may come and go, but the river is always there.

There are four of us here, work-working the rapids.
Monkey, Catfish, Hollywood Boy and me. Of course those
aren't our real names. But names are secret things, full of
power. They call me Ngok – the crocodile – because I'm such
a good swimmer. And swimming, of course, is what we do.

Right at the edge of our patch, there's a place called Les
Rapides. It's a big place, all white, with a balcony looking out
over the water. Before the war a lot of people came here, but
now it's never more than a quarter full: businessmen in their
grey square-shouldered suits, or pretty ladies with dyed hair
and flouncy dresses, soldiers, officials, even the occasional
mendele – white men here for business, I suppose – it's been
a long time since any actual tourists came here. They come
to eat, of course – *trois-pièces* with *pili-pili* and fried bananas;
baked squash with black rice and peanut sauce; crocodile
with *foufou* and beans.

It makes me dizzy even to think about so much food; and
there are tomatoes swimming in oil, and riverfish stew and
saka-saka and fresh crusty white bread and hot-fried chicken
and manioc and peas. They come to eat – of course they
do – but they also come because of the river, because of the
rapids. From here you can see right across for miles and miles,
right into Kinshasa where the fires burn across the water and
the river is a wild thing, prancing and rolling from boulder
to boulder and hurling up great gouts of spray. Not as wild

15

as Hippo Island and the giant yellowgrey jumble of broken water beyond, but wild enough, and it sounds like—

Like elephants crossing, says Maman Jeanne. Big brown elephants with feet like palm trunks. Of course I've never seen an elephant, but in the city zoo there's a skull the size of a lorry cab, all chalk and honeycomb, one splintery tusk lolling from the toothless mouth.

Like Sunday morning, says Monkey; like cathedral voices; like dancing; like drums.

Like helicopters, says Catfish, when he says anything at all. Like mortars and shells and the washboard clatter of gunfire. *Or the noise,* says Hollywood Boy, *of a radio between stations,* that eerie, dead sound of rushing and whispering, scratching and stirring.

The river has a song for everyone, says Maman Jeanne; and no song is ever the same. That's why they *really* come: not for the food, or the view or the shady veranda under the mango trees, but for the river, the sound and the swell and the surge of the river song. I know; and the others are the same. Even Catfish, who is fourteen and thinks he knows so much more than the rest of us. There's more to our business than just business.

Which is not to say we are not professionals. Some people carve wood for a living; some turn to the army; some work the markets, or the cabs, or the side of the road. We work the river. More precisely, we work the rapids.

Our rapids are a highway for all kinds of trade. Fish trappers, stonebreakers, washerwomen, thieves. I know them all: boys with nets, old men in pirogues, scavengers with poles and sacks. Downriver is the shallow place where Maman Jeanne takes her washing. It's a good swimming hole, too, for babies and women, but we don't swim there. Oh no. We swim further up, from Les Rapides to the stonebreakers' flats, and we don't let anyone else work our strip. We earned that strip, Monkey, Catfish, Hollywood Boy and me. Especially me; partly because I'm the youngest, but mostly because I'm a girl. And, as Maman Jeanne says, girls don't dare, girls don't bare, and most of all, girls never, *ever* ride the rapids.

There are three corridors dividing the rapids on our side of the river. One – we call it the Slide – is close to the bank, sweeping and doglegging breathlessly between the rocks. The second – the Swallow – is much further out, and to reach it you have to swim outwards in a wide curve, skirting a sinkhole and a bad drop over some big boulders. You have to be strong – most of all you have to be quick, because no one can swim *against* the current; all you can hope for is to use the current to swing you far enough out to reach the safety of the corridor. But if you miss by even an arm's length, then the current whips you – with a *shake-shake-snap* like a dog with a rat – right into the sinkhole. If you're lucky and it spits you out again, the ride ends with a quick scuttle down a bumpy little rockslide and no harm done – except maybe for a skinned backside and the sting of laughter from the riverbank. It happens sometimes, though never to me. And sometimes – well. Better not to think of that. *The good God harvests his crop*, says Maman Jeanne, *and all your tears will never bring back a single seed of it.*

The third ride is almost a legend. Far, far beyond the others

– perhaps three times the distance between the Swallow and the bank – it can only be reached from the Swallow itself. Halfway down to the stonebreakers' flats, the current divides over a big pink rock, which we call the Turtle. The Turtle's shell is round, and on one side there's a good smooth ride into the mainstream. On the other, there are underwater rocks – ankle-biters, we call them – but if you're fast – and lucky – I reckon you could break away from the Swallow and ride the river's great round shoulder into the Deep.

I've never done it, though I've charted its path, using river junk and clumps of hyacinth, and I'm almost sure I could. No one else has, as far as I know; Monkey says there are crocodiles, but he's just scared. With his crooked leg he doesn't swim as well as the rest of us, and never even rides the Swallow. But he has a rubber ring from a truck tyre, and fits it just as neat as a bird on a nest, so Catfish lets him come. I don't think that's fair – if it had been me, you bet he wouldn't have allowed it – but Catfish is the General, and we have to do what he says. I don't always like that – it's especially hard being a Lieutenant when even Monkey's a Colonel – but Catfish is pretty fair in most other things, and besides, who else would have let a girl join in the first place?

And so, every day between nine and five, we meet up under the balcony at Les Rapides, and we practise our moves. Easy ones, to warm up, with Monkey on his rubber ring and the rest of us bobbing along, yelling. Then comes the trick-tricky stuff – high dives, star-jumps, crocodile, with all of us in a long unbroken chain. We stop mid-morning for a rest. A snack, too, if we can get it; perhaps a dough ball or a slice of cold manioc scrounged from Maman Jeanne. Sometimes there are small green mangoes on the trees over the veranda, and we throw sticks at them until one falls down. After twelve, though, the company starts to arrive, and we have to be good, or risk losing our business.

Like I said, we work the river. More precisely, we work the *people*: and if you ask me, anyone who can afford to spend a couple of thousand CFRs on a meal is fair game. It isn't begging – we'd never beg – but we can't stop them watching us, can we? And if sometimes they drop a coin or two, or a chicken bone, or a piece of bread, then where's the harm in that? Maman Jeanne doesn't like it, but she turns a blind eye. It's a wage like any other, after all, and it's more fun than breaking rocks.

I was born somewhere upriver. That was before the war – I can't remember the name of the place, or anything much about it, except that there was a house with palm thatch, and chickens running around it, and my mother used to carry me in a sling on her back, and there was a smell – not city smells but a forest smell – of wet mud and trees and rushes and steam from the manioc pots. Maybe that's why I ended up on Hippo Island; it's a fair long walk into town each day, but it feels good to be out of the city at night and to hear the river song as I go to sleep, with its choir of frogs and peepers.

No one else goes there much, except the fishermen. It's supposed to be bad magic. Papa Plaisance says it's the spirit of that last hippo, waiting for his chance to be avenged. Maman Jeanne says it's because things happened there during the fighting. She won't say much, but I can tell they

19

were bad, because normally Maman Jeanne can talk the legs off a centipede. Still, that was a long, long time ago, three years at least, and the island is a good quiet place now. But most people keep away, and there are stories of ghosts and sorcerers. I've never seen any. Papa Plaisance hasn't, either, and he comes every day in his pirogue. I have seen some pretty good catfish, though; and I'm glad the others stay away. Besides, I like being on my own.

Maman Jeanne has a shack near the other bank. She lives there with Maman Kim, her daughter, and Petite Blanche, her granddaughter. Maman Kim's husband used to live here, but doesn't any more. There's a story behind it, but that's *man–woman bizness*, as Maman Jeanne says, and doesn't interest me much. Papa Plaisance has a shack, too, with a vegetable patch and a workshop under the big mango tree. Papa Plaisance is Catfish's uncle. He makes pirogues, or used to, before the war came, beautiful slim pirogues that sliced through the water without a sound. He's the one who taught me how to ride the current and how to paddle from the stern to keep the little boat from tipping over. He goes out a long way, right into the rapids, and sets his traps among the ankle-biters. Sometimes I have to help him; but it's dull work compared with riding the rapids, and he never pays me anyway, so I sneak past him when I can, and make my way alone upriver.

Today I got to Les Rapides early, an hour after daybreak. The others weren't there yet, and I sat on the bank and waited, chewing on a piece of bitter bamboo shoot and watching the river for devil-fish. There was no one else around, except for an old man with a pirogue, and a few birds flying low over the brown water. I'd been there for an hour before Monkey turned up with his rubber ring, and by then I'd already gathered that something was wrong. I'd have known it even without the way Monkey looked at me, all sideways and sly-fashion, with that little smile that means bad news for someone not him. He's always been jealous of me, I know. Perhaps because I'm a better swimmer; perhaps because my legs are long and straight, while he has to walk short and twisty-style on his crooked foot.

'Where the others, Monkey?' I said.

'Coming soon,' he told me. 'Papa Plaisance call us round. Give us dough balls for breakfast.'

Well, *that* was a surprise, for a start. Old Papa never gives out food for free. I wondered what he wanted, and why he'd asked my friends to eat, but let me go to Les Rapides alone.

'Papa say you wasting time,' said Monkey, bringing out the remains of his dough ball and beginning to eat it. 'He says there's money to make on the river.'

'What, fishing with *him*? I leave that to the ones who don't swim so well.'

Monkey's eyes narrowed. 'Well,' he said, 'Papa say he don't want you hanging around here any more. He tell Catfish. You work for him now. No more Rapids.'

I could hardly believe it. 'Papa Plaisance, he's not my family,' I said. 'He has no right to decide what I do. Just because Catfish's uncle says so, doesn't mean I have to do his work for free.'

'*He* tell Catfish,' repeated Monkey stubbornly. '*I* tell *you*.'

'But *this* is my business,' I said, hearing the silly little shake in my voice.

'Not any more,' said Monkey. 'The Rapids belong to the Catfish gang.'

There was a silence as I let that flow past me. Monkey ate his dough ball, watching me with that look in his eyes, expecting me to cry, perhaps, I don't know. Anyway, I didn't give him that satisfaction. 'You just the errand boy,' I told him haughty. 'Where's the General?'

He gave a shrug in the direction of the stonebreakers. 'Don't go there, Ngok,' he warned as I began to climb down towards the path. 'You not welcome.'

'You want to stop me?' I shot over my shoulder.

Monkey shrugged again, and followed me at a distance, limping. 'You'll see,' was all he said, and even then I pretended not to hear him.

I found the others down by the rockbreakers. Catfish wouldn't look at me, and Hollywood Boy was playing jump-stone across the swim-hole and pretending cool. 'Monkey tells me you don't want me on the Rapids any more,' I said, attacking straight away, before Catfish could find his voice.

Catfish said nothing, just picked at his feet and wouldn't look.

'Cat got your tongue?' I said.

Catfish muttered something about not wanting to hang with little girls.

'The Rapids are mine as much as yours,' I said, hearing that sound in my voice again, halfway between tears and devil-fish rage. 'You can't stop me if I want to be here.'

But he could, and he knew it. Three against one; besides, on land they were bigger and older and stronger than me, even coward Monkey with the bent foot. Still, I didn't care. Let them try, if they were men enough. I fingered my devil-fish tooth on its wire and prayed; *devil-fish, send me your spirit to make me strong.*

'Go home,' said Catfish.

'You want to stop me? You just try.' And then a sudden inspiration halted me, fresh and strong as a voice from God. God or devil-fish, anyway, I couldn't tell, but it was so clear that it took my breath, and then I started laughing, gaspy-style, till the boys must have thought I was crazy.

'Why you laughing, Ngok?' said Hollywood Boy, looking a little uncomfortable now. He should be; I'd seen him try the Swallow just last week, and he took it wide, bumped over the Turtle and ended up on his face in a mudhole. Catfish is better; but Monkey never tries the long rides, and I knew I could beat any of them – maybe even Catfish – on a good day, and with the devil-fish tooth to bring me luck.

'You want the Rapids for yourself?' I said, still laughing. 'We'll make a deal, boy. We see who's the best. We let the river decide.'

That made them stare. Monkey looked scared; Hollywood Boy laughed. Only Catfish was quiet, serious. 'What you mean?' he said at last.

'I mean a challenge,' I said. 'The Catfish gang against the Ngok gang. Winner takes the Rapids. Loser goes back to Papa Plaisance.'

Monkey sniggered. 'You got to be crazy,' he said.

'Crazy perhaps, but I can swim like a crocodile.'

Catfish frowned. He doesn't say much, and when he does, people listen. He was the General, after all, and he knew that a good General can never turn down a challenge. Do that once, and people start to think you're afraid. Twice, and nobody obeys orders any more. Three times, and you're a dead man.

'What kind of a challenge?'

'The big one,' I said at once. 'The Deep.'

There was a long silence. Then Catfish nodded once. 'OK,' he said, and without looking back at me, he stood up and began to walk upriver towards Les Rapides.

Reaching the swimming place, I thought the Deep looked darker and more distant than ever before. The river was already swollen from last week's rain; patches of water hyacinth, some as large as boats, rushed by on the sour-smell water. In a month the long rains will come; then the Rapids will be too dangerous to ride, even for a good swimmer. During the rainy months even crocodiles die in the tumbling rapids. Now was too soon for that time, though not too far away either, and I was beginning to feel a little nervous as we reached our strip – no customers eating there now, not yet, but a waiter laying out tables under the big mango tree, and the smell of roasting something drifting down from the open kitchen.

'You sure?' said Catfish, looking at me. His face was calm, but I thought he was sweating; maybe the heat, or maybe something else, too. Monkey stood at his side with the rubber ring under his arm, his eyes round open with all the whites showing.

'You scared?' I said.

Catfish shrugged, as if to suggest that the Deep was just another long ride to him and not the biggest, furthest and most dangerous section of the near Rapids.

'OK then.' We looked at each other.

'You first.'

'No, you.'

His face was like wood, stiff and brown and expressionless. 'OK then. We go together.'

'No, man,' said Hollywood Boy in dismay. 'That's too risky!' In a way, he was right; those long rides were safer when taken alone, for the distance has to be calculated absolutely precisely, and even an inch to the wrong side can mean a lethal sweep into a sinkhole's gullet, or a battering run over the ankle-biters. Two swimmers together will clump, like weed islands, breaking the current and risking disaster.

'All right,' I said. 'Both together.'

Even on a day with nothing to prove, we practise before we try the big runs. A couple of runs down the Slide, perhaps; a crocodile or two, some jumps, and then we are ready to try the Swallow. Today, there was none of that childishness. Monkey sat on the bank and watched, his legs tucked into his rubber ring; Hollywood Boy sat hunched under the arch of Les Rapides, and Catfish and I observed the river, occasionally throwing in objects – a plastic bottle, a piece of wood – to gauge the speed and the course of the distant Deep.

Neither of us wanted a practice run. It would have shown weakness, somehow; though I knew it made our chances of success so much smaller. By rights we should have done the Swallow a dozen times or so before we even attempted the Deep – but only the heat of my anger was keeping me there in the first place, and I didn't want the river to put a damp on that before I was ready.

Twenty minutes, and I could feel it beginning to ebb. Catfish was still watching, testing wind speed and water, occasionally glancing quick-quick at me to see if I'd lost my nerve. I prayed again to the devil-fish god – *speed, courage, luck* – and shot Catfish a big, bright smile. I don't know whether it fooled him; either way I wasn't waiting any longer, and I stood up, tucked my skirt around my legs and tied it in place and said, 'Ready?'

'You crazy, man,' said Monkey with gloomy satisfaction. 'If the river don't get you, the crocodiles will.'

'Crocodiles don't like fast water,' I said, looking beyond him towards the far corridor. You could hardly see it now for reflections: a bare strip, smoother than the rest, simmering gold in the distant haze. It was pretty, I thought; pretty like the back of a shining snake. And like the snake, it had a bite.

'Still ready?' He was counting against it; I could see it in his eyes.

'As ever,' I said, and both together we stepped back to give ourselves maximum run. One-two-three steps, hands almost touching, and we were at the edge; a fourth and I flung myself far out into the air, riding far beyond the Slide, landing feet first with a *plunk* of air on to the tail of the Swallow.

I sank, went under; felt the tow of the river, far greater

26

beneath than on the surface, and pulled my feet up fast. Catfish was somewhere very close, I knew; but I couldn't afford to look for him just then. With all my strength I stretched out, leaning forward, kicking my feet, reaching for the current like a lifeline. Downriver the Turtle shrugged its giant pink shoulder out of the water and I struck out for the Swallow, knowing that if I reached the Turtle from the wrong side I would miss the opening, and be dragged into a mess of sinks and ankle-biters – that is, if the river didn't crush me like a rotten egg.

Behind and to the left of me, further into the corridor, I could sense Catfish striking and panting. He was strong, but he was heavy, too; I raised my feet from out of the drag-water and kicked along ahead, light as a lily. Neither of us spoke; there was water in my nose and mouth; water in my eyes and all I could think of was the corridor that drew me, spinning and gasping, closer to the Turtle and the sink on either side.

Bump-bump-bump. A little bump-slide, a string of round rocks scattered under the surface like the bones in a skinny man's spine. I rode them, losing speed and breath, and then the Turtle was already on me, its smooth sweep of Swallow ride on the bank side, its rough tangle of uncharted territory on the other. I took a deep breath. Braced – and kicked out at the Turtle just as the river swelled me over the top, pushing out with my long strong legs and boosting myself into the unknown. The current was stronger here than ever before, sucking at my legs in hot–cold bursts, and there were stones here, stones and rocks I did not recognize, striking my feet and legs and skinning my left shin from instep to knee.

Ankle-biters. I'd expected no less; but these were whole-body ankle-biters, reaching up out of the depths like the teeth of the river. I tucked my legs up, kicking, and still they bit; behind me, Catfish cried out, but I could not see why. And still the Deep seemed twice as far, twice as fast as ever before, like some road in a story about castles that move and countries that vanish overnight only to reappear somewhere else, on the other side of the world, perhaps, under a magic cloud-carpet of snow.

Once more I prayed to the devil-fish tooth – *bring me far, bring me fast* – and boosted myself as hard as I could away from the rocky strip. Beside and behind me, I saw Catfish do the same; but as I shot forward I saw him slip – slide away towards a crookleg gully that swept back into the Swallow – while I sailed ahead of him, quick and straight as one of Papa Plaisance's pirogues, over the danger zone and into fast, smooth water.

The Deep! I could see it now, and in my path; the curve of my course would lead me straight towards it now, using the very speed of the river to fling me across, as a boy may use a purse-sling to throw a stone. I opened my mouth in a blaze of triumph – *Wheee!* – then I sat on the river, hugging my knees the way Monkey does when he rides his rubber ring, and let the river take me, far out and far away, into the corridor.

It felt like flying. Flying and falling and dreaming all in one; with the heavy water riding black on yellow-brown beneath me, and small pieces of river debris stinging and lashing against my burning skin. But it was a wonder; for a moment there I was not simply *in* the river; I *was* the river;

28

I sang its song; and the river sang back to me in its many voices, and if I'd wanted to, I believe I could have swum all the way over to Kinshasa and nothing – not even crocodiles – could have touched me.

And then I looked back. I shouldn't have done it. I was almost there, my fingers combing the skirts of the Deep. But I looked round, perhaps to check if Catfish had seen my triumph, and the joy fell away from me in a sudden cold.

Catfish had slipped, as I'd first thought, into the crookleg gully that led back to the Swallow. If he'd stuck to that run, he would have been all right; it was a straight, smooth channel that bypassed the Turtle and brought the swimmer back into the long, clean corridor towards the swimming hole. But Catfish hadn't stuck to the run. Instead he had tried to boost himself back; a desperate, impossible move against the current. The river had stopped him; first tumbling him on to his back, then dragging him back towards the Turtle, the rocks and the black sink between. Too late, Catfish had understood his mistake; I could see him clinging, all dark head and skinny arms, round an exposed spike of river rock as over him the water heaved and hurled, bucking like some bareback creature that does not want to be ridden. I saw all this in an instant: the angry river; Catfish clinging on for his life; the gullet of darkness below. With a little more speed, he could have made it past the sink; but he had lost his momentum and his nerve. Now he clung, slip-slipping on the greasy stone, and wailed soundlessly over the howl of the river song.

Before me, the Deep was an arm's length away. Its song

too was deafening – *come to me, Ngok* – but there too was my friend, and though it tore me inside to abandon the dare, I knew I could not leave him to be swallowed by the sink.

I pushed away, back into the rocks. For a second, the Deep clung to me, singing its song; then it spat me out as hard as a child spitting out a pawpaw seed, and I shot away, skimming the rocks with my knees, towards the Swallow. It was risky, I knew. I would have to follow Catfish most precisely, and without losing momentum, grab him from where he clung without letting the sink inhale us both. A second's miscalculation and we would go under, never to surface. An inch to either side, and I'd miss him altogether. I prayed to the devil-fish one last time – *oh please, devil-fish, may my aim be true* – and taking a deep breath, sitting squarely on the wave and with my lungs filled to bursting, I skidded down the final run at top speed towards Catfish.

He must have seen what I was trying to do. He grabbed my hand and dropped his grasp from the rock, and I let my speed take us both, like bottles on the water, shooting right over the nasty sink-hole and into the harrow of ankle-biters.

'Hold on, Catfish!' I could hardly hear myself over the river song. But his hand was in mine and I held tight, both of us yelling as the rocks bit into our legs and feet. The river was laughing now, I could hear it; a low chuckle of rocks and pebbles, like drums around a campfire. And the Swallow was smoothing out again; slowing, easing out towards the swimming hole. The stones fell away under our feet; Catfish dropped my hand and began to swim, slow and limping-style, towards the shallows.

The others were waiting there for us, unsure of what they had seen.

'What happen, man?' said Monkey impatiently, as Catfish and I lay out on the dry stones of the rockbreakers' flats and examined the cuts and scrapes on our legs.

I looked at Catfish. He didn't look back. His face looked more wooden than ever, except for a big scrape over one eye that had probably come from his hitting that pointy rock.

'Did you reach the Deep, Ngok?' said Hollywood Boy, his voice quivering with excitement. 'I thought I saw you, maybe, but you were too far for me to be sure—'

This was the time to speak, I thought. To reveal how I'd touched the Deep – actually *touched* it with the tips of my fingers, like a mythical fish no one ever catches except in dreams. If I told them, then I'd be General. Catfish would go home to Papa Plaisance. Les Rapides would belong to me.

Catfish still wasn't looking at me. His face looked closed, like a rock.

'Well?' said Monkey. 'Did you win?'

There was a long silence. Then I shook my head. 'Nah,' I said. 'I nearly did, but the Swallow pulled me in. Call it a draw, man. Nobody won.'

Hollywood Boy looked disappointed. 'Hey, Ngok,' he said. 'You lost your magic tooth.'

I reached for it then, but I already knew it was gone. Maybe the river took it back; or maybe it was the spirit of the devil-fish, taking what was due.

*

We still work the river, the four of us: Catfish, Monkey, Hollywood Boy and I. There was a little tension with Papa Plaisance at first, but Maman Jeanne unexpectedly took my side – unlikely, I'd have thought, but it seems Papa was in her bad books over some unpaid work.

The river is ours again, for the moment – at least that strip of it that runs from Les Rapides to the stonebreakers' flats – and we work it every day, though no one has ever attempted the Deep since then. Maybe we will again, some day. Catfish is still the General, though he doesn't give orders in quite the way he once used to, and I've seen a gleam in Hollywood Boy's eye that tells me there may one day be another challenge. Not from me, though. Not again. Foolish to imagine I might ever have been a General – it's bad enough trying to keep up with the boys – though I can see it in their eyes sometimes: that awe, that knowledge of something dared, some secret glimpsed, some glory almost won. One day, perhaps, I'll find it again.

Meanwhile there's always the river, as Maman Jeanne says, with its sleepy silences and its terrible rage and its song that keeps on going, and going, and going, carrying spells and dreams and stories with it all the way into the belly of Africa and out again into the open, undiscovered sea.

Faith and Hope Fly South

In Jigs & Reels, I included a story called 'Faith and Hope Go Shopping', the tale of two indomitable old ladies living in a retirement home. I grew very fond of those two old ladies, and from the amount of correspondence I received about them, so did many of my readers. Since then, I have revisited them several times, and probably will again.

How nice of you to take the trouble. It isn't everyone who would give up their time to listen to two old biddies with nothing much to do with themselves but talk. Still, there's always *something* going on, here at the Meadowbank Retirement Home; some domestic drama, some everyday farce. I tell you, some days the Meadowbank Home is just like the West End, as I often tell my son, Tom, when he calls on his weekly dash to somewhere else, bearing petrol-station flowers (usually chrysanths, which last a long time, more's the pity), and stirring tales of the World Outside.

Well, no, not really – I made that last bit up. Tom's

conversation tends to be rather like his flowers: sensible, unimaginative and bland. But he *does* come, bless him, which is more than you could say for most of them, with their soap-opera lives and their executive posts and their touching belief that life stops at sixty (or should), with all of those unsightly, worrying creases neatly tucked away. Hope and I know better.

You know Hope, of course. Being blind, I think she appreciates your visits even more than I do; they *try* to find things to entertain us, but when you've been a professor at Cambridge, with theatres and cocktail parties and May Balls and Christmas concerts at King's, you never *really* learn to appreciate those Tuesday night bingo games. On the other hand, you do learn to appreciate small pleasures (small pleasures being by far the commonest) because, as some French friend of Hope's used to say, one can imagine even Sisyphus happy. (Sisyphus, in case you don't know, was the fellow doomed by the gods to roll a rock up a hill *forever*.) I'm not an intellectual, like Hope, but I think I see what he means. He's saying there's nothing you can't get used to – given time.

Of course in a place like this, there are always your malcontents. There's Polish John, whose name no one can ever pronounce, who never has a good word to say to any of us. Or Mr Braun, who has quite a sense of humour in spite of being a German, but who gets very depressed when they show war films on TV. Or Mrs Swathen, whom everybody envies because her son and his family take her out every single week, who has grandchildren who visit her and a sweet-faced daughter-in-law who brings her presents; but Mrs Swathen gripes and moans continually because she is bored, and the children don't come often enough, and her bowels are bad, and the food is dreadful, and no one knows what she has to suffer.

Mrs Swathen is the only person (except for Lorraine, the new nurse) who has ever made Hope lose her temper. Still, we manage, Hope and I. Like Sara in *A Little Princess* (a book Hope loved as a child and I re-read to her just last month, as soon as we finished *Lolita*), we try not to let the Mrs Swathens of this world poison our lives. We take our pleasures where we can. We try to *behave* like princesses, even if we are not.

Of course, there are exceptions. This week, for example, this August 10th, on the occasion of the Meadowbank Home's annual day trip to the sea. Every year in August we go, all of us packed into a fat orange coach with blankets and picnics and flasks of milky tea and the Meadowbank nurses – cheery or harassed, according to type – on what Hope calls the Incontinence Express to Blackpool.

I've always liked Blackpool. We used to go there every year, you know, when Tom was little, and I remember watching him playing in the rock pools while Peter lay asleep on the warm grey sand and the waves sighed in and out on the shingle. In those days it was *our* place; we had our regular guesthouse, where everyone remembered us, and Mrs Neames made bacon and eggs for breakfast and always cooed over how much Tom had grown. We had our regular tea-shop, too, where we went for hot chocolate after we'd gone swimming in the cold sea, and our chip shop, the Happy Haddock, where we always went for lunch. Perhaps that's why I still love it now: the long beach; the parade of shops; the pier; the waterfront where the big waves crash over the road at high tide. Hope loves it by default; you'd think Blackpool would be a bit of a climbdown for her, after holidays on the Riviera, but Hope would never say so, and looks forward to our trips, I think, with as much enthusiasm and excitement as I do myself – which made it all the harder to take when Lorraine told us that this year we couldn't go.

Lorraine is our newest nurse, a poison blonde with pencilled lips and a smell of Silk Cut and Juicy Fruit gum. She replaces Kelly, who was dim but innocuous, and she is a great favourite of Maureen, the General Manager. Lorraine, too, has her favourites, among whom Hope and I do not count, and when Maureen is away (which is about once a week) she holds court in the Residents' Lounge, drinking tea, eating Digestive biscuits and stirring up unrest. Mrs Swathen, a great admirer of hers, says that Lorraine is the only really *sensible* person at the Meadowbank Home, although Hope and I have noticed that their conversation revolves principally around Mrs Swathen's undeserving son, and how much he is to inherit when Mrs Swathen dies. Far too much, or so I understand – with the result that, after only a couple of months here, Lorraine has already managed to convince Mrs Swathen that she is badly neglected.

'Ambulance-chaser,' says Hope in disgust. You get them from time to time in places like this; insinuating girls like

Lorraine, flattering the malcontents, spreading their poison. And poison is addictive; in time people come to *depend* on that poison, as they do on those poisonous reality shows Lorraine enjoys so much. Little pleasures fade, and one comes to realize that there are greater pleasures to be had in self-pity, and complaint, and viciousness towards one's fellow residents. That's Lorraine; and although Maureen is no Samaritan, with her Father-Christmas jollity and vacuum-salesman's smile, she is infinitely better than Lorraine, who thinks that Hope and I are too clever by half, and who tries in her underhand way to rob us of every small pleasure we still have left.

Our trip to Blackpool, for instance.

Let me explain. A few months ago, Hope and I escaped from the Home – a day trip to London, that's all, but to the Meadowbank staff it might as well have been a jailbreak. That was just before Maureen's time – Lorraine's too – but I can tell that the thought of such a breakout appals her. Lorraine is equally appalled – for a different reason – and often speaks to us in the syrupy tones of a cross nursery-teacher, explaining how *naughty* it was of us to run away, how *worried* everyone was on our behalf, and how it serves us right that we missed the chance to sign up for the Blackpool trip this August, and must now stay behind with Chris, the orderly, and Sad Harry, the emergency nurse.

Sign up, my foot. We never *used* to have to sign up for our day trips. With Maureen in charge, however, things have changed; Health and Safety have got involved; there is insurance to consider, permission slips to sign and a whole administrative procedure to put into place before even the shortest excursion can be considered.

'I'm sorry, girls, but you had your chance,' said Lorraine virtuously. 'Rules are rules, and *surely* you don't expect Maureen to make an *exception* for you.'

I have to say I don't much like the idea of Tom having to sign a slip – it reminds me so much of the times when he used to bring those forms home from grammar school, wanting permission to go on trips to France, or even skiing in Italy; trips we could barely afford but which we paid for anyway because Tom was a good boy, Tom was going to do well, and Peter and I didn't want to show him up in front of his friends. Now, of course, Tom holidays all over the place – New York, Florida, Sydney, Tenerife – though he has yet to invite *me* on any of his trips. He never had much imagination, you know. He never imagines, poor boy, that I might dream of hurtling down the *piste noire* at Val d'Isère, or being serenaded in Venice, or lounging in a hammock in Hawaii with a Mai Tai in each hand. I suppose he still thinks Blackpool's all I've ever wanted.

As for Hope – well, Hope rarely lets her feelings show. *I* see them, because I know Hope better than anyone, but I doubt Lorraine got much satisfaction.

'Blackpool?' she said in her snootiest, most dismissive Cambridge voice. 'Not really my cup of tea, Lorraine. We had a villa, you know, in Eze-sur-Mer, on the French Riviera. We went there, the three of us, twice a year, all the time Priss was growing up. It was quiet in those days – not as overrun with film people and celebrities as it is now – but we used to pop down to Cannes from time to time, if there was a party we *really* wanted to go to. Most of the time, though, we stayed by the pool, or went sailing in Xavier's yacht – he was a friend of Cary Grant's, you know, and on *several* occasions Cary and I—'

By then, though, I was laughing so much that I almost spilt my tea. 'It's all right,' I said, taking Hope's arm. 'She's gone.'

'Good,' said Hope. 'I hate showing off, but sometimes—'

Lorraine was watching us from the far side of the Residents' Lounge. Her face was a study in pique. 'Sometimes it's worth it,' I said, still grinning. 'If only to see that woman's face.'

Hope, who couldn't see it, smiled. 'No Blackpool, then,' she said, pouring tea expertly into one of the Meadowbank cups. 'Still, there's next year, God willing. Pass me a Digestive, Faith, if you would.'

Next year, next year. That's all well and good when you're twenty-five, but at our age, *next year* isn't something that all of us can count on. Hope and I are still all right, not like Mrs McAllister, who hardly knows what day it is, or Mr Bannerman, whose lungs are so riddled that he has to have a machine at night to help him breathe – and who *still* smokes like a chimney, foul-mouthed old tosspot that he is, because, in his own words, *who the hell wants to live forever?*

Besides, I happen to know how much those occasional day trips mean to Hope. Oh I enjoy them, of course, even though most of the things I remember so well have gone. The Happy Haddock is an Irish pub nowadays, and the guesthouses have all been knocked down to make way for that new housing estate. Hope, on the other hand, does not have to bear with these small disappointments. She can still smell the Blackpool sea, that peculiarly *British* seaside smell of tidal mud and petrol, fried fish and suntan oil and candy-floss and salt. She likes the sound of the waves, the long crash-hiss of the water on the pebbly shore, the cries of the children testing the water with their toes. She likes the feel of the sand beneath her feet – in my wheelchair I can't guide her on the soft sand, but Chris always takes her down to the beach – and that half-yielding crunch of shingle before the beach gives way to pebbles. She enjoys the picnic we share – always in the same place, a part of the beach that slopes down a cobbly ramp to give wheelchair access to those of us who need it – the thermos of tea, the two neat quarter-sandwiches (always the same, barring allergies: one tuna, one egg) and the single pink fairy cake, nine-tenths sugar with a bright red synthetic half-cherry on top, like the ones we used to have for our birthdays when we were girls. She likes to pick up shells on the tideline – big, thick, English shells, flaky and barnacled on the outside, pearly-smooth inside – and line her pockets with worn, round stones.

What she doesn't see, I can always describe to her, although in many ways Hope notices far more than I do myself. It isn't a sixth sense, or anything like that; it's simply that she always makes the most of what she has.

'It'll be fine,' she told me, when I complained once again about being left out. 'We'll manage. Remember Sara—'

Remember Sara. Easily said. But it's the unfairness of it that kept me awake at night; the petty unfairness of it all. *Rules are rules*, Lorraine had said, but we both knew why we were being denied the treat, like children caught smoking behind the sheds. It's about *power*, like all bullying, and Lorraine, like all bullies, was both weak and addicted to the weakness of others. Of course we knew better than to show her our disappointment. Cheery Chris saw it – and was angry on our behalf, though there was nothing he could do to help. We never even complained to Maureen – though personally I doubted it would have any effect. Instead we talked about the Riviera, and the scent of thyme rolling off the hills, and the Mediterranean in shades of miraculous blue, and barbecued mackerel and cocktails by the pool, and girls in isty-bitsy polka-dot bikinis lounging on the decks of yachts with sails like the wings of impossible birds.

Only Chris knew the truth. Cheery Chris with his one earring and messy hair drawn back in a ponytail. He isn't actually a nurse at all – although he does a nurse's job on less than half the pay – but he's our favourite, the only one who really talks to us like fellow human beings.

'Bad luck, Butch,' was all he said when he heard the news, but there was more real sympathy in the way he said it than in all of Lorraine's syrupy little lectures. 'Looks like you're stuck with me, then,' he said, grinning. 'Seems like I'm not wanted, either.'

That made me smile too. Lorraine doesn't like Chris, whom all the residents like even though he isn't a proper nurse, who calls me Butch and Hope Sundance, and who shows none of the proper respect and deference to his superiors that you might expect from someone in his position.

41

'We'll have an old sing-song, just the three of us, eh?'

Chris often sings to us when the boss is out of earshot: rock ballads, tunes from the musicals and old vaudeville songs he learned from his Gran. He has quite a nice voice and he knows all the old hits, and he has been known to waltz me about in my wheelchair so that I feel quite dizzy with laughter; although in all his silly nonsense I have never caught a glimpse of the kind of condescension you see in people like Maureen or Lorraine.

'Thank you, Christopher, that would be lovely,' said Hope with a smile, and Chris went away feeling he'd cheered us up a little. I knew better, though. Hope would never say it, but I knew her disappointment. It wasn't the Incontinence Express and the flasks of lukewarm tea; it wasn't the single fairy cake; it wasn't the feel of sand between her bare toes or the scent of salt coming off the water. It wasn't even the hurt of being talked down to as if we were children; or the knowledge that we were being left out. It was the illusion of freedom; the promise of parole; the air; the sound of young people going about their business on an ordinary summer's day. Meadowbank air has a certain smell: of floral air freshener, school cabbage and the bland, powdery smell that comes off old people living in close proximity to one other. Hope wears Chanel Number Five every day because that way, she says, she can at least avoid *smelling* like an old woman. I know exactly how she feels.

And so when the day came it was with a secret sense of desolation that we watched them go, although we would rather have died than show it. One by one, the residents shook out their summer coats (Meadowbank chic dictates that coats, hats, scarves and, sometimes, gloves *must* be worn on even the hottest day) and collected bags, hankies, umbrellas, dentures and a variety of other items indispensable for a day at the sea.

Mrs Swathen gave me a look as she picked up her handbag. 'They're saying it's twenty-five degrees by the coast today,' she said. 'Just like the Med today, they're saying.'

'How nice,' said Hope. 'But Faith and I don't like it when it's too hot. I think we'll just stay in and watch TV.'

Mrs Swathen, who would normally have spent all afternoon watching *Jerry Springer* and getting more and more indignant about it, ground her teeth. 'Please yourselves,' she said, and stalked off towards the coach.

Polish John watched her go. 'Don't listen to her,' he said. 'It will rain again. I know it will rain. It always rains when we go to the sea. I myself do not enjoy the sea, but anything is better than another day in this Auschwitz, no?'

Mr Braun, who was passing, turned round at that. He is a small, neat, bald man who walks with a stick and likes to bait Polish John. 'You ignorant,' he said fiercely. 'Don't you know my father *died* at Auschwitz?'

Well, that fairly stumped Polish John. It was the first we'd heard of it, too, and we all stared at Mr Braun, wondering if he'd suddenly gone strange, like Mrs McAllister.

Mr Braun nodded. 'Yes,' he said. 'He got drunk one night and fell out of the guard tower.' And then he was off, leaving Hope and me laughing fit to burst and Polish John frothing (not for the first time) with indignation in his wake.

'Well, if that's the level of camaraderie we can expect on this trip,' I said, 'then I for one can bear to give it a miss.'

'I agree,' said Hope. 'Imagine being stuck in a coach for two hours with those two – and Maureen – and Lorraine – and Mrs Swathen. I'm beginning to believe Sartre was right when he said, *Hell is other people.*'

Sometimes Hope forgets that I'm not familiar with these French colleagues of hers. Still, that was a good one. But as the party got ready to leave at last, I felt that sense of desolation return. The orange coach opened its doors and the staff nurses got on board, little Helen, cross Claire, then Lorraine, looking pleased with herself (as well she might), and finally fat Maureen, swollen with jollity, baying, 'Isn't this *fun*! Isn't this *fun*!' as she shooed the last of the residents inside. At the back window, Mrs McAllister, small, shrivelled and bright-eyed, was piping; '*Goodbye! Goodbye!*' in her thin, excited voice. I suppose she thought she was going home again. Mrs McAllister always thinks she's going home. Perhaps that was why she seemed to be wearing *all* of her wardrobe that day – I could see at least three coats, a tartan, a brown and a light blue summer raincoat, pockets bulging with extra pairs of shoes. That made me laugh; but as the coach finally pulled out of the drive, making the gravel *hishhh* underfoot like breakers on shingle, I felt tears come to my eyes, and I knew Hope was feeling just the same.

'Remember Sara,' I muttered, but this time I knew that *A Little Princess* wasn't going to help. A cup of tea might not help either, but I poured one anyway, from the urn on the sideboard, and wheeled my chair to the bay so that I could look out of the window.

It was going to be a long day.

My tea tasted of fish. It often does when it has stood for too long, and I put it aside. Hope came to sit next to me, using the ramps to feel her way forward, and she sat there quietly for a while, drinking the fishy tea and feeling the morning sun on her face.

'Well, Faith. At least we're alone,' she said at last.

That was true; the Meadowbank Home doesn't have a hospital wing, and anyone needing day-to-day medical help has to go to All Saints' down the road. I went there once when I had my bout of bronchitis, and Mr Bannerman goes there every week for his check-ups. But today even Mr Bannerman had gone to the sea, and we were alone with Denise, the receptionist, Sad Harry, the emergency nurse, and Chris, who had been given so many jobs to do in Maureen's absence (washing windows, changing light bulbs, hoeing flower beds) that I doubted if we'd see him at all.

For most of the morning I was proved right. Tea came and went; then lunch (cottage pie), which we picked at without much appetite. Time passes at a different rate here, but even so it seemed unbearably slow. Usually there's a film on TV in the afternoon, but that day there wasn't; just a dull procession of people like Mrs Swathen complaining about their relatives. Hope tried her best, but by two o'clock her conversation had dried up altogether and we just sat there like bookends, wishing it was over, waiting for the sound of the coach on the gravel. Even then, I knew, it *wouldn't* be over. Even then we would have to bear with their talk of what they had seen, what they had done. Days out are rare at Meadowbank; this one might give them six months' worth of gossip, six months of *do-you-remember-that-time-in-Blackpool*, so that I felt almost sick at the thought of it. Hope felt it too; in fact Hope feels it all the time to some extent – after all, she has to deal with a fair amount of that kind of thing, those thoughtless, well-meaning *if-only-you-could-have-seen-it* comments that only serve to remind her that she is blind.

I looked at her then, and saw the expression on her face. At first I thought she'd been crying; but Hope never cries. I did, though. I made no sound, but Hope took my hand anyway, and I thought maybe I'd been wrong about that sixth sense. We sat there for a long time – until I couldn't hold it any longer and had to call Sad Harry to take me to the bathroom.

I got back to the Residents' Lounge to find Chris waiting for me. 'Hey, Butch,' he said, grinning, and all at once I felt much better. There's something about Chris that does that; a kind of nonsense that pulls you along like a crazy dance. When I was a girl I used to ride the waltzers at the fair, spinning round and round in a two-seater chair shaped like a giant teacup and laughing breathlessly all the time. Chris makes me feel like that sometimes. I suppose it's because he's young – although Tom *never* made me feel like that, not even when he was twenty.

'Have you finished your work?' I asked, knowing that Chris works very hard, but hoping that he might spare us a few minutes, just this once.

'I'm all yours, sweetheart,' he said, grinning, and spun me round in my wheelchair, causing Harry to protest. 'In fact, I brought you a few things.' He waved Harry away with an airy hand. 'Secret things, Harry, so scat.'

Sad Harry huffed and rolled his eyes. He's not a bad fellow – not so cheery as Chris, but not half as bad as Lorraine – and I saw his grin as he closed the door.

'Secret things?' said Hope with a smile.

'You betcha. Cop a look at these, for a start.' And he dropped a pile of glossy magazine brochures into my lap. The Algarve, the West Indies, the Riviera, the Cook Islands all spilled out across my knees; lagoons, Easter-lily beaches, yachts, spas, wooden platters of tropical fruits piled high with pineapples, coconuts, mango, papaya.

When it comes to reading, Hope likes books and I have always had a soft spot for magazines. The glossier the better; couture and garden parties, city breaks and designer shoes. I gave a little squeak as I saw the brochures, and Chris laughed.

'That's not all,' he said. 'Close your eyes.'

'What?'

'Close your eyes. Both of you. And *don't* open them until I say so.'

So we did, feeling like children, but in a good way this time. For several minutes Chris moved around us, and I could hear him picking things up and putting things down. A match flared; there came a chink of glass; then a rustle of paper, then a number of clicks and rattles that I did not recognize. Finally I felt him pulling my chair backwards into the window bay; a second later there came the sound of him dragging Hope's armchair alongside. Warmth on my hair; soft air from the open window; outside, a distant drone of bees.

'OK, ladies,' said Chris. 'Off we go.'

We were sitting in the bay with our backs to the window. Late-afternoon sunlight illuminated the room, making the Residents' Lounge into a magic-lantern show. I turned my head and saw that Chris had hung several of the crystal pendants from the hall chandelier in the bay, so that prisms of coloured light danced across the flock wallpaper. Several posters had been tacked to the walls (quite contravening Meadowbank regulations): white houses under a purple sky; islands seen from the air like flamenco dancers shaking their skirts; bare-chested, beautiful young men standing hip-deep among green vines. I laughed aloud at the sheer absurdity; and saw that he had lit four glass-covered candles on the sideboard (another Meadowbank rule broken). On them I could read a foreign word – Diptyque – that I did not recognize. From them a faint scent diffused.

'It's thyme, isn't it?' said Hope beside me. 'Wild purple thyme, that used to grow above our house in Eze. Our summers were filled with it. Oh Christopher, where did you find it?'

Chris grinned. 'I thought we might fly down to the coast this afternoon. Italy's too hot in August, and the Riviera's really so busy nowadays. Provence? Too British. Florida? Too American. Thought instead we could try that big dune at Arcachon, with the long white drop towards the Atlantic, or sit in the shade of the pine woods listening to the crickets and in the background, the sea. Can you hear the sea?'

Now I *could* hear it; the soft *hissh* of water with a throatful of stones. Behind it, a burr of crickets; above me, the wind.

Hypnosis? Not quite; now I could see the Residents' Lounge tape recorder running; from the four big speakers came the sounds. Chris grinned again. 'Like it?'

I nodded, unable to speak.

'There's lavender, too,' said Hope dreamily. 'Blue lavender, that we used to sew into our pillows. And grass – cut grass – and figs ripening—'

More of those candles, I thought; but Hope's sense of smell is better than mine, and I could barely make them out. I could hear the sea, though, and the sound of the pines, and the *scree* of birds in a sky as hot and blue as any in those brochures.

Now Chris was on his knees in front of us. He took off Hope's shoes, then mine – Meadowbank slip-ons in sensible brown – and flung them (rules, rules!) across the room. Then, turning, he came back with a square basin, water slopping messily over the curved edges, and placed it at Hope's feet. 'I'm afraid the Atlantic's a little cold, even at this time of year,' he warned, and looking down I saw that the basin was filled with water and stones, the flat round pebbles you find on a beach. Hope's bare old feet plunged into the water, and her face lit with sudden joy.

'Oh!' Suddenly she sounded fifteen again, breathless, flushed.

Chris was grinning fit to split. 'Don't worry, Butch old love,' he told me, turning again. 'I haven't forgotten you.'

The second basin was filled with sand; soft, dry, powdery sand that tickled my toes and made small crunching noises in my insteps. Deliciously I dug my feet in – I can move them a little, though I haven't done any dancing in a long while – and thought back to when I was five, and Blackpool beach was twenty miles long, and the candy-floss like summer clouds.

'After that lunch I don't expect you're hungry any more,' went on Chris, 'but I thought I'd try you on this, just in case.' And from some magical place at the back of the Residents' Lounge he brought out a tray. 'Not quite champagne and caviar, not on my budget, but I did my best.'

And so he had: there were canapés of olive and cream cheese and pimiento and thin-sliced salmon; there was choc-olate cake and mango sorbet and strawberries and cream. There were iced whisky sours (*definitely* against the rules) and yellow lemonade; best of all there was no tuna, no egg and no pink fairy cake.

I hadn't thought I was at all hungry, but Hope and I finished the lot, to the final cracker. Then we paddled again, and then Chris opened the lounge piano that no one but he ever seems to play and we sang all our old favourites, like 'An Eighteen-Stone Champion' and 'You Know Last Night'; and then Chris and Hope did Edith Piaf with 'Non, Je Ne Regrette Rien', and then we were very tired and somewhere along the line we both fell asleep, Hope and I, and awoke to find the empty tray gone, and the water, sand and pebbles gone, and the posters removed from the walls and the danglers back on the chandelier.

Only the tape was still playing (he must have turned it

over while we slept). But although the candles were gone, we could still smell them, grass and fig and lavender and thyme, quite covering up that Meadowbank smell, and when I popped back to my room I found the brochures there, stacked tidily behind a row of books, with a note from Chris lying on top.

Welcome back, it said.

I returned to the Lounge just in time to hear the coach pulling into the driveway. Hope heard it too, and neatly removed the tape from the machine before putting it into the pocket of her dress. Neither of us spoke, though we held hands and smiled to ourselves as we waited for our friends to return: Polish John and Mrs McAllister and Mr Bannerman and Mr Braun and poor Mrs Swathen, who had, she said, lost her lace handkerchief on the beach, had sand in her shoes and had *surely* caught heatstroke from that horrid sun, it was a dis*grace*, no one *knew* how much she suffered and if she had only *known*—

No one noticed, among that disorder, that we, too, had sand in our shoes. No one saw us pick at our 'celebration dinner' (rissoles) – unless it was Sad Harry, who never talks much anyway – and no one seemed to care when we went to bed early, Hope to smell the candles that Chris had slipped into her bedside drawer, and I to read my brochures and dream of orange groves and strawberry daiquiris and plane rides and yachts. Next week we might try Greece, I think. Or the Bahamas; Australia; Paris; New York. If Tom can do it, so can we – besides, as Hope always says, travel broadens the mind.

There's No Such Place as Bedford Falls

When I was a small child I believed implicitly in the magic of Christmas. Now, try as I may, I seldom see anything but tawdry commercialism, false hopes and increasing disillusionment. I wrote this story to combat that feeling. I'm not sure it quite worked out that way.

It's six in the morning, and Santa's on the blink. Good job I checked; can't have a malfunctioning Santa on the front lawn, today of all days. Lowers the tone, you know – and the neighbours are a snotty bunch, always complaining about one thing or another. Last week it was the penguins. Three of them, cheery little fellows, the latest addition to the Wall of Lights at the front of the house; one wearing a Santa hat, the other two carrying ice skates, all three wired to play 'Winter Wonderland' and twinkle the whole night through.

They'd been up for less than a day when Mr Bradshaw complained.

'Listen, mate. We can live with the fairy lights, and

52

the dancing snowflakes, and the Christmas trees, and the inflatable snowman, and the magic grotto, and the Three Wise Men and even the flashing Santa and his twelve reindeer, but that's it. The bloody penguins have got to go.'

Talk about overreaction. I mean, what harm is there in my putting up a few Christmas lights at this time of year? I'm not asking anyone *else* to do it. I'm not offended when the neighbours don't return my cards. To be honest, I'm not expecting peace or goodwill from any of them, but you'd think they could just leave me to enjoy the spirit of the season in my own personal way. But no. There's always something. If it isn't the penguins, it's the sleigh bells keeping the neighbours awake. Or some estate agent trying to blame me for the drop in house prices. Or someone complaining about the daily deliveries. Or the postman giving me funny looks as he comes up the drive. Or the local yobs belting out 'Silent Night' at one in the morning and leaving empty beer cans outside the door. Only the other day in the supermarket, a lad yelled, 'Where's yer reindeer, Santa?' over the aisle, and the girl at the checkout (a new girl, a blonde) sniggered in a most unprofessional way.

That's why I try to get all my groceries delivered nowadays. It's quite easy; I phone in the order every Monday at nine, and two hours later the van comes round with the week's goods. 1 medium turkey, frozen. 5 lbs King Edward's potatoes. 1 lb Brussels sprouts. 1 lb carrots. 1 packet sage and onion stuffing. 1 packet Bisto gravy. 7 chipolata sausages. 7 rashers streaky bacon. 1 luxury Christmas pudding. 1 packet luxury mince pies. 1 packet Bird's custard. 1 bottle sweet sherry. 1

jar Branston's pickle. 1 medium Warburton's loaf. 1 small box Milk Tray chocolates. And last but not least, 1 packet economy crackers, the red and green kind, with party hats and clean jokes.

I love Christmas. I really do. I love writing Christmas cards and wrapping presents. I love the Queen's Speech and the Phil Spector Christmas album. I love my tree, with its tinsel and its little foil-wrapped chocolates. I love my Wall of Lights. I love the artificial snow on the mantelpiece and the wreath of plastic holly on the door. As for the food – well, I still don't know which I love the most: Christmas dinner with all the trimmings, or cold turkey and pickle sandwiches and the late film – *White Christmas* or *It's a Wonderful Life* – with the fire on and my stocking up by the chimney, the single chocolate, glass of sherry and the giddy, breathless feeling that tonight, of all the magical nights of the year, anything – just *anything* – could happen.

White Christmas . . . Doesn't happen very often, I'm afraid. Most of the time I have to make do with artificial snow, cotton wool, and that spray-on stuff you get in cans. Still, it doesn't beat the real thing: the silence of it; the feeling that everything has been miraculously renewed. *Let it snow, let it snow, let it snow.* Not much chance of that, not with all that global warming you hear about, but we can only hope.

Phyllis gave up two years ago. She left between Morecambe and Wise and the Queen's Speech (1977, one of many, video-ed and kept for the occasion), without even staying to open her present. Her note was typically confused; couldn't bear it any longer; thought we'd travel now we'd retired; wanted a change; would write when she was settled. And so she does, once a year; a long and dutiful letter (but never a Christmas card), wishing me well.

She never did get into the spirit of things the way I do.

Oh I wish it could be Christmas every day –

Imagine that. If every day was Christmas Day – every day a new start, a new celebration. *Chestnuts roasting on an open fire* (though I make do with Living Flame); and *I Saw Mommy Kissing Santa Claus.*

In fact, I'm slightly worried someone might have interfered with Santa. Someone with a grudge perhaps, or just kids out to cause a nuisance. Still, it could be the fuse, or even a dead bulb – we go through rather a lot of them, and although I do turn off the illuminations during the daylight hours (I'm on a pension, you know, and I have the electricity bill to think of) I know I'm putting more pressure on the Wall of Lights than it was ever really designed to take. Still, I wouldn't change it. Not for Mr Bradshaw, not for the Residents' Association, not for all the tea in China.

Wonderful Life. To date, I've watched that film 354 times. 1946, Frank Capra, with James Stewart and Henry Travers. Made when I was six years old, in a world where men wore hats and controlled the family's finances, rosy-faced children went ice-skating on the village pond, and neighbours were real neighbours and not stuck-up yuppie homeowners looking to increase the value of their house.

Bedford Falls, they called the town. For years I thought it was a real place. For years I wanted to live there – even applied to emigrate once, hoping to find it waiting for me, knee-deep in snow and Yuletide spirit. Now they tell me there's no such place. But I proved them wrong, renamed my house, and now I live in Bedford Falls Cottage, Festive Road, Malbry, and it's Christmas whenever I say it is.

Of course, everyone else thinks I'm crazy. I don't care; I'm no crazier than that bloke at the chippy who thinks he's Elvis, or that fellow Smith down the road who's a druid or something, or Mrs Golightly, walking around Tesco's car park at three in the morning, or Al and Christine, trying to lose five stone each in time for New Year. Why *should* Christmas come only once a year? And why shouldn't I celebrate *what* I like, *when* I like, any time I want to?

I'm not saying it's always easy. It's hard to be different – Jimmy Stewart knew that in *Wonderful Life* – harder still to give up what you want for what you know to be the right thing to do. But Jimmy Stewart had integrity. What he did *changed* people. Made a difference. And that's what I'm trying to do, in my way. To change things. To light up the sky. To bring wonder back into the faces of the children who slouch down the street with fags hanging out of their mouths. Christmas is supposed to be a time of miracles, isn't it? Magic and mystery and tiny tots with eyes all aglow? I do believe in miracles, you know. You have to – don't you? – when there's nothing else left.

But it's hard to have faith, day in, day out, when no one else believes and everyone thinks you're a bit of a joke. I had that TV news programme round last year, in December, trying to find out why I do what I do. I thought they were nice; the lady interviewer was pretty and kind; the cameramen ate mince pies and drank tea and laughed at my jokes. But they ran the piece in August, during the silly season; it made the papers – *Time-Warp Santa Prays for Snow* – and for a while people came from all over the country to look at my Wall of Lights and laugh at the mad old bastard who thinks it's Christmas every day.

For a while it was rather fun. Children came to talk to me; some even sent me Christmas cards. And then it stopped. Word got round in the wrong quarters; vandals broke into my garden and smashed my illuminations; some paper even started a rumour that I was some kind of pervert, luring little kids into my house under false pretences. A new headline – *Sinister Santa* – and after that the children ran away, or sprayed slogans on my garden wall. Four months on, and they still do.

I fixed Santa. Turned out to be a loose connection after all, and not deliberate vandalism. I suppose that should make me feel better, but it doesn't somehow. It's still dark at six a.m., and I give the Wall of Lights a final burst, just to see it in action before the sun comes up. Funny, but it doesn't *feel* like Christmas Day. For once, the calendar says it is; for once I am in step with the rest of the world. *Even a broken watch is right twice a day*, as Phyllis used to say, and that's how I feel this Christmas morning. Like a broken watch, all face and no ticker.

Most days at six I make myself a cup of tea, have a small breakfast of toast and marmalade, then peel the sprouts, carrots and potatoes and get the turkey in the oven ready for lunch. But today of all days, I don't feel like it. Television?

There's *A Christmas Carol* (the classic 1938 version, with Reginald Owen) – on one of the cable channels, and today of all days I won't need my videos. But I've seen it 104 times already (and I've watched the 1951 remake with Alastair Sim 57 times), with *White Christmas* coming a close second (301 times, and counting) to *It's a Wonderful Life*. They're all on today, on various channels, but strangely, today, I don't feel like watching any of them. I try the radio. Christmas music on all stations. I have a library of Christmas tapes, from the King's College choristers' eerie rendition of 'Silent Night' to Mike Batt's 'A Wombling Merry Christmas'. I know them all; but today I can't concentrate. The music makes my head spin; the cheery voices of the DJs fill my heart with a terrible silence.

Let it snow, let it snow, let it snow.

I look, but there's nothing out there. Just a great sweeping blue-black sky with no stars. All around me, houses are beginning to light up. The Bradshaws' children, five and seven, have been up for hours. I've seen the movement at their bedroom window, their smudgy faces peering out at the dancing penguins on my roof.

Those bloody penguins. Singing 'Winter Wonderland' night and day. How can I stand it? Mr Bradshaw was right, they *were* a mistake – and in a swift movement I get up, though I still have a good two hours before dawn, and switch off the Wall of Lights.

The sudden darkness is quite a shock; usually, with the curtains open, there's enough light from outside to illuminate my entire living room. Now there's nothing but the glow from the small artificial tree by the TV, and the fairy lights on the mantelpiece. Just out of curiosity, I switch those off too. The darkness is soothing. I imagine just not doing Christmas this year: no pudding; no pies, no Queen's Speech, *Wonderful Life*, creamed potatoes and Bisto gravy. No turkey sandwiches and video-ed *Morecambe and Wise*; no presents; no tinsel; just peace and goodwill.

For a moment the thought holds me, magical. To give in; to be free; to read – a thriller, perhaps, or a historical romance – over a simple lunch of cheese and crackers. Perhaps I could even call on Phyllis. She doesn't live far – just a bus ride away, down the Meadowbank Road – and for a second I see myself actually *doing* it, buying the ticket, walking down the gravel drive, knocking on the door (perhaps there will be a garland of holly pinned to the knocker), saying, 'Good morning, Phyllis' (though perhaps not 'Merry Christmas'), seeing her smile, smelling her scent of rose and laundry. Just that. No lights, no miracles. No angel to point the way. No Bedford Falls.

You could do it, you know. It's easily done. The voice sounds a little like that of Alastair Sim in the 1951 version of *A Christmas Carol*. A clipped, authoritative voice, not easily dismissed. *You could just stop. Today. This minute. Now.*

Could I? The thought brings me indescribable relief. Relief, and with it, a terrible, inarticulate fear. Stop? Just *stop*? But what would I *do*?

Once more, I see myself walking down the gravel drive to Phyl's house. I imagine the sound the gravel makes, that frosty crunch. There will be a pot of lavender by the door, and a row of winter pansies lining the path. She has a smile of exceptional sweetness, especially when taken by surprise, and a habit of tucking her unruly hair behind her ears. Perhaps there will be a pot of tea on the hob, and a box of biscuits by her chair. She enjoys looking at travel brochures; perhaps this time I will join her, and we can spend Christmas in Portugal, or Italy, or Spain. It's really much too cold for us in England at this time of year. We could do with a change.

I can almost see it; almost hear it now, like music in my mind. A new life; a new hope; a place beyond Bedford Falls and its eternal, ersatz snow. For a second, delirious, I am out of my chair; my hand on the door; my coat and hat left hanging on the hook, as if the moment of turning to pick them up might be the final, fatal moment in which Bedford Falls drags me back—

And then, suddenly, unexpectedly, the doorbell rings.

Today? At six? Unheard of. It's not the postman (no post on Christmas Day). And it's surely not the Bradshaws complaining about the lights. Who then? A visitor? A joker? In haste, I yank the door open. An icy breeze drifts into the room, scented like Christmas – cloves, apple, pine and brandy – but there's no one at the door. The gate is closed; the street deserted. And yet the bell rang.

Every time you hear a bell ring—

I know that voice. It's the voice of Henry Travers in *Wonderful Life*: kind, warm and impossible to resist. And yet it sounds like *my* voice too; so close that an observer might struggle to tell us apart. How can I think my work is done? How can I even consider abandoning my post on this, of all days? There are presents to be wrapped, the voice protests. Sprouts to be cleaned, carols to be sung, potatoes to be roasted, stuffing to be rolled into walnut-sized balls and laid in a baking tray with sausages and bacon strips; giblets to be removed from the defrosted turkey; the pudding to be placed in a ceramic basin and steamed. If these duties are not performed, what terrible floodgates might then be opened? What stars might go out, what gospels founder, what salvation be squandered?

I see now that there can be no leaving. I am a broken clock, frozen forever at an impossible hour. Let others move on, if they must, if they can. For myself, I have duties to carry out. Sacrifices to make. Stockings to fill. Warnings to deliver. Lives to touch. Like it or not, I am the Ghost of Christmas Present, and I have a job to do.

Very slowly I turn away from the door. A flick of the switch, and the Wall of Lights shines forth again. On the mantelpiece, fairy lights twinkle. That scent of pine, strangely nostalgic, that must have wafted in through a crack in the door. And now, looking up, from a violet sky slowly brightening towards dawn, I think I can just see the first small flakes of snow.

Would You Like to Reconnect?

To me, the internet seems the natural place for a certain kind of ghost story. The late-night glow of the laptop screen; voices from another world. Writing Blueeyedboy – which, arguably, is in itself a kind of ghost story – I found myself becoming increasingly fascinated by our growing dependence on the virtual world; the relationships we build there; the communities we create; the connections we make with people we may never meet in real life. This world can be a feast of friends, or the loneliest place on the planet. It's all a matter of perspective.

No one really dies online. It's a truth I'm only just starting to learn. What seems wholly ephemeral is stored away forever here, hidden perhaps, but recoverable for those who really want to find these little slices of the past, these flashes from the archives of oblivion.

I first joined Twitter two years ago as a means of keeping in touch with my son. That was Charlie; nineteen years old; away at university. We'd always been close, and I'd always known his absence would leave a hole, but not the size or depth of it; the hours spent waiting for him to call, that perpetual sense of anxiety. Not that there was anything to fear; but to be without him, alone in this house, was worse than I'd expected.

It's a big house; perhaps too big for just a mother and her son. Four acres of garden; a paddock; a wood; a river running through it. But Charlie managed to fill it somehow; to make it come alive, to explode, to buzz with restless energy. Now it was almost unbearable. Not empty, no; but peopled with ghosts: Charlie, at five, in his treehouse; with a jar of tadpoles; Charlie, playing his guitar; or staging performances of *We Will Rock You* using an old wooden puppet theatre and a CD copy of *Queen's Greatest Hits*. I hadn't realized until then how much space a boy could occupy, or how much silence his absence would bring; a silence that presses on the house like a sudden increase in gravity.

But then my son introduced me to the world of social media: Facebook, YouTube, and most importantly, Twitter, which I had at first dismissed as the most trivial of all, but which, I now realized, was to become a lifeline. To have my son at my fingertips; to know what was happening in his world; to connect whenever I wanted – these things were far from trivial, and in spite of my technophobia, I embraced it for his sake.

My online name was @MTnestgirl, a play on his love of musical theatre as well as my maternal role. Charlie's name was @Llamadude, a name I found ridiculous, but somehow oddly like him.

'I'll always stay in touch,' he said. 'Wherever I am, I promise I will.'

And he did: from university; from internet cafés around the world; from his phone; his BlackBerry; from concerts and campsites and festivals. It isn't always easy to find a good wireless connection, but Charlie kept his promise, and always tweeted every day. A moment is all it takes; a hundred and forty characters, or the time that it takes to click on a link or send a picture from your phone—

And suddenly, I was not alone; I was *there*, with Charlie and his friends. I went to their lectures, watched their films, listened to their music. Charlie used Twitter to connect with a wide variety of people: some friends of his in real life; some stage performers he'd never met; actors; singers; writers; technicians. These virtual friends became mine as well. I visited their websites and blogs; watched clips of their concerts; shared in their lives. Through a glass, darkly, I watched my son and all his interactions. I couldn't be with him in the flesh, but I was in everything he did; a loving presence; a watchful eye; a ghost in the machine.

News breaks fastest on Twitter. Hearts can be broken as quickly. A winter's morning, an icy road, an oncoming truck, and my son on his bike, the bike I'd bought him a year ago, for his eighteenth birthday—

A hundred and forty characters is more than enough to end the world. First came the scatter of messages all across my timeline and his – OMG, *it is true about @Llamadude? What's the news? Does anyone know? Has anyone heard from @MTnestgirl?*

And then, almost instantaneously, repeated over and over: *Oh, fuck.*

Death should be silent, I told myself. Death should be a black hole. But the news of Charlie's death was propelled by Twitter's morphic resonance, that mystic and mysterious force that holds flocks of birds together, shaping them into a widening gyre of screeching semi-consciousness—

They say that birds are messengers between the waking world and the next. That morning they were out in force, those virtual harbingers of death, tweeting madly and help-lessly, the sound of their wings like a wall of white noise.

Before Charlie's death I'd had only about a dozen follow-ers. Now, total strangers were following me. Hundreds of them. What did they want? To offer sympathy, to gloat, to share in a real-life tragedy?

I told myself I should go offline. My timeline was almost unbearable. The terrible news of Charlie's death had taken only minutes to spread. Thousands of Twitter users reached out. Strangers sent their condolences; singers and actors my son had followed posted words of sympathy. It was more than I could bear, and yet I couldn't turn away.

I remember Charlie once telling me about Schrödinger's Cat, a creature both alive and dead; poised between realities. On Twitter, Charlie was *alive*; I could still read his status and know that barely an hour ago he'd been excited about a performance of *Les Misérables* he'd been planning to see in London; that he'd had a bacon sandwich for breakfast, that he'd changed his current avatar to a picture I'd taken years ago – Charlie at twelve, by the seaside, standing triumphantly astride a monumental sandcastle, while the incoming tide hurled white-topped waves at the parapet and the seagulls swooped—

Meanwhile, in that *other* world, I went through the motions of being alive. But everything now seemed to me like a series of sepia photographs. Making arrangements; the funeral; Magritte men and women, like black birds flocking around a hole in the ground. I flew back to Twitter with a sense of mingled anguish and relief – relief at leaving that dead world, anguish at having to watch Charlie's status receding from *24 hours ago* to a series of ever more distant dates.

I considered deleting his account. But I would have needed his password for that. It was equally true of *all* his accounts; his Facebook page was still open, his wall covered in messages. His YouTube channel was still alive with videos of Charlie; and when I logged into Twitter again, the first thing I saw was a recommendation, listing *@Llamadude* among the people I might like to follow.

Even worse were the e-mails. Automatically generated, they arrived in my inbox at intervals: *An account you have been following (@Llamadude) has not posted in 14 days. Would you like to reconnect?*

At first, I deleted the e-mails. I tried to disable the messages. But Charlie had set up my account, and I didn't know how to alter it.

Would you like to reconnect?

I thought about closing my account. But Twitter, for me, had become much more than just a means of staying in touch. It was here I felt closest to Charlie. Here, among his virtual friends. People here still mentioned him; when they did, his name would appear on my timeline. Sometimes, whole conversations would be tagged with Charlie's name; and it was easy to picture him there, listening, taking part. It was their way of keeping him alive, I suppose; of making sure we remembered him.

'You ought to go out more,' my mother said. 'It isn't healthy, moping around the way you do. And spending hours on that Twitter isn't going to bring our Charlie back—'

Well, of course it wasn't, Ma. But—

The Egyptians had their pyramids. The Victorians, their marble. And Charlie had Twitter; unhealthy, perhaps, but *here* was where my son lived on; cached, encrypted, stored away. I found myself including him in everything I tweeted. My comments filled up his timeline. The day of his last post receded. Some people talk to their loved ones standing by the graveside; I talked to Charlie from my room, with a cup of tea and a biscuit. I told him how I spent my days; I talked about the garden. I quoted lyrics from musicals. I re-tweeted posts I knew he would like. Steadily, my followers increased. I now had over two thousand.

Only those automated e-mails reminded me of that other world: *An account you have been following (@Llamadude) has not posted in 40 days. Would you like to reconnect?*

This time, I clicked the option: *Yes.*

And then, one day, in my mailbox, there came a notification:

@Llamadude has replied to your tweet.

Of course, it was impossible. It must be a mistake, I thought. No one else used Charlie's account. My son had been meticulous about online security; his passwords carefully chosen to defy any attempt at hacking. I logged on to my Twitter account and rapidly scrolled down my Mentions page.

There! There it was. From @*Llamadude*. That little trigram of symbols – semi-colon, dash, closing bracket – one of the many devices known to the online community as *emoticons*. In this case, a wink, with a little smile, beside my dead son's avatar.

;-)

For a long time I just stared at it. That cluster of punctuation points. Of course, I *knew* it wasn't my son; but part of me didn't believe it. Tests on Twitter users have proved that we experience the same surge of endorphins when looking at a friend's avatar as when we see them in the flesh – and this was Charlie, smiling at me, somehow, from beyond the grave—

Someone must have hacked the account. Either that, or one of Charlie's friends had somehow got hold of his password. Anxiously I awaited the inevitable wave of junk mail that would follow if his Twitter account had been hacked; or worse, the drunken ramblings of some flatmate assuming his identity. But nothing happened. Just that smile—

;-)

No one else seemed to have noticed. Most of Charlie's friends had moved on. My followers, too, were drifting away, their attention claimed by riots and wars. I told my mother, who urged me to seek some kind of bereavement therapy.

But something had changed inside me. My mother would never have understood. The message from my son's account had changed the texture of my grief. Something I'd believed was lost had slowly emerged from the darkness—

It's not always easy to stay in touch. The internet, for all its complexity, is still a work-in-progress. In the remotest parts of the world, you can still wait for minutes – even hours – to make that vital connection.

The thought was almost too absurd for me to put it into words. And yet, as I sat at my desk at night staring at the computer screen, there was something compelling about the idea. Charlie had promised to stay in touch. He'd just taken longer to get online.

An account you have been following (@Llamadude) has not posted in 90 days. Would you like to reconnect?

I waited for confirmation. It came at last, in the form of a link, a complicated chain of code that had been abbreviated to fit Twitter's 140-character requirement.

@Llamadude has sent you a link.

I clicked on the link. The screen went blank. For a moment I thought: *it's a virus*. Then an hourglass icon appeared, and I realized that I was waiting for a picture to load. It took a few minutes; then, reading the script at the top of the screen, I saw that the link had taken me to a page from GoogleEarth. Taken from the air, I could see a house; some trees; a little stream—

That's my house, I realized.

My house, captured on a day when the trees were beginning to turn; my car parked outside; and there, on the ground at the edge of the lawn, something bright that caught the sun—

It was Charlie's bike, I knew. The one he'd been riding the day he died. And now I also knew exactly when this picture had been taken: September 2009, just before he'd started college. A helicopter had flown overhead – you could just see part of its shadow in the photograph as they'd taken the picture, and Charlie and I had been sitting there in the shade of the big trees. If you could look through the canopy, you'd even be able to see us there, tiny, hopeful figures, frozen in eternity.

I found myself beginning to shake. Why had he sent me this picture? No message had come with the link, not even an emoticon. What was he trying to tell me? That nothing need be lost for good? That somehow, I could reach him?

I stayed at my computer all night. I was afraid that if I logged off, or navigated away from the page, I would never find it again. I slept a little in my chair, ate a sandwich, checked my mail, opened a window to Twitter. I found that I could do this without losing my link to Charlie. I stayed at my desk all day, all night, waiting for instructions. Outside, the days and nights flashed by like windows on a passing train.

My mother called a few days ago. I heard her knocking at the door. I didn't answer; I don't like to leave my computer unattended. Eventually, she went away. She still sometimes tries to phone me, but I never answer.

A hundred days since Charlie's death. Most of my followers are gone. I don't really care about that any more, as long as I still have Charlie. I'm starting to feel slightly faint whenever I stand up from my desk. Maybe I'm not eating enough. I don't seem to have any appetite. But looking at Charlie's picture helps; the one of our house seen from above, like an angel's-eye view of a loved one—

And if I really concentrate, I can sometimes believe the picture has changed; a blur in the far left corner, a flash of colour through the trees. And wasn't Charlie's bicycle lying flat at the side of the lawn, when now it's standing against the wall? Wasn't it? I'm sure it was.

An account you have been following (@Llamadude) has not posted in 120 days. Would you like to reconnect?

;-)

Rainy Days and Mondays

Some people are particularly sensitive to atmospheric conditions. I happen to be one of them. On sunny, bright days, I am filled with creative energy; on dull, grey, rainy days I can barely type a sentence. I combat this seasonal lethargy by filling my workspace with lamps and bright colours; even so, rainy days continue to get me down.

You'd think you'd need to apply to be a raingod. That when someone was dishing out the heavenly attributes, they might just have stopped to think for a moment about what it might mean to the recipient – to be rained on, day in, day out, winter and summer, morning and night. Though to be fair, it isn't just rain; all kinds of precipitation apply, including snow, sleet, mizzle, drizzle, sudden downpours, Scotch mist, London fog, April showers, lightning storms, hail, tropical monsoons and of course plain old rain: light, moderate, heavy, and all other possible variants thereof.

But *someone* has to do it; and for the past five thousand or so years in this place, that someone has been me.

Of course I have Aspects all over the planet. In the rainforests of South America I still exist as Chac, of the Mayans, or Tlaloc, the Aztec god, spouse of Chalchiuhtlicue of the Jade Skirt; in parts of Africa I walk as Hevioso, keeper of the celestial draught; in Australia as Bara, the monsoon deity, forever at war with Mamariga, the dry wind. I have seen dragons in China, *kami* in Japan; as Yu Chi, the Master of Rains, I defeated Huang Di in the time of the Yellow Emperor. I was Taranis the Thunderer; Enlil, the Barley-Sprouter; Triton, the Calmer of Storms. I was revered; loved; worshipped; blessed; cursed; entreated and invoked.

Nowadays, I just do my best to keep dry.

You know, it's tough being a raingod past his prime. In the old days, rain *mattered*; a winter storm brought fear and awe; a summer shower was cause for celebration. Nowadays the weather forecasters have it all stitched up. Nowadays you just watch the people go by with their raincoats on and their umbrellas unfurled and you think: why bother?

Of course, I couldn't have chosen a worse location to settle down. Manhattan, New York; where nobody notices *anything*; where the sidewalks are slick with takeaway grease and the elements are just another part of the city's big twenty-four-hour light show. And yet they are *aware* of me – on some subconscious level, I sense it – depressed and sour-faced as they are, turning up their collars at my approach, glancing at the sky with bewildered expressions as the month's average rainfall doubles, trebles, in a single day.

I've been here twelve months. That's twice as long as I

usually stay in any one place. But New York suits me; I like the way the neon shines through the wet windowpanes of my little fourth-floor two-room flat; I like the hot, sour smell of summer rain on dusty pavements; the crack of electricity over the tall buildings; the crystal-powder snow.

My present name is Arthur Pluviôse. *Sounds kinda French*, my landlord says, with a trace of disapproval. I tell him (quite truthfully) that I have never been to France (although I've heard that another of my Aspects still lives in Paris – as a cabaret dancer, it so happens, specializing in wet T-shirts and working under the sobriquet Reine Beaux). I myself have no particular occupation. I'm still living off the earnings from my former job as aide to a quack rainmaker from the Southern states, who, after a lifetime of fraudulent claims, finally went mad in the summer of last year, after a visit to the little farming town of Deuteronomy, Kansas, resulted in a freak six months' worth of uninterrupted rain.

I still think back to Deuteronomy with some nostalgia. That was the last of the great freak rainstorms, corn washed clean away, clouds louring overhead, thunder rolling like a wagon train across the sky. A man could be proud of that kind of work; making a difference; wide open spaces; walking the land like he owned it instead of the other way around.

This city's different, though. At first I didn't see it – just another forest of city block trees, all glass and concrete dark in the rain, neon stuttering over dripping storefronts, and people in black overcoats, heads down, eyes lowered, the occasional pinwheel umbrella shape tumbling gaily down

74

the street – oh yes, I thought; I'd seen all this before. London; Moscow; Rome; all cities are the same under the rain. All people, too.

And then I met her. The girl. You know who I mean. I'd seen her from my window a couple of times; you can't miss her, she stands out in a crowd. Hair to her waist; eyes like the sea; even in the rain she was wearing a yellow dress.

This time she'd stopped to shelter in the lobby. My lobby. Happenstance, you see. I happened to be on my way down; I happened to see her; she was soaked to the skin and crying bitterly. I led her into my bare little room with the rain-grey curtains and the cloud-grey carpet, gave her one of my sweaters to wear and made her a cup of lemon tea.

'Damn rain,' she said.

I gave her a towel to dry her hair. She was a true blonde; hair like the sun as it first opens its eye from behind a storm-cloud. She had some kind of a foreign name – Swedish or something – though her friends called her Sunny, and there were little daisies embroidered on the hem of her yellow dress – or maybe they were real daisies, I don't know – and she was wearing summer sandals made of green string, and I fell in love with her right there and then, slam, bang, without any warning, like a hailstorm out of the blue.

'Damn rain.'

'I know,' I said. 'You should have taken an umbrella.'

'I don't have one,' said Sunny.

'Help yourself,' I told her, opening a cupboard door and showing her the contents.

For a while she studied them, blue eyes widening.

Well, I guess I do have rather a lot of umbrellas. Black umbrellas with teak handles; silk umbrellas with ivory handles; sensible blue foldable umbrellas that fit in a pocket; frivolous fruity red umbrellas; children's umbrellas with stand-up frog eyes; transparent umbrellas like jellyfish hoods; umbrellas emblazoned with works of art (Monet's water lilies, Lowry's little men, Modigliani's sleepy sloe-eyed beauties); psychedelic English golfing umbrellas; American college umbrellas in fraternity colours; chic French umbrellas with the caption *Merde, il pleut!*

She looked at them for a long time. 'I guess you must really like umbrellas,' she said, wiping her eyes.

'I'm a collector,' I said. 'Go on, choose one.'

'I wouldn't like to spoil your collection.'

'I don't mind. I'd be happy.' Outside it was raining harder than ever. 'Please,' I said. 'I think it's going to be a wet summer.'

She chose one then: a sky-blue umbrella with a slim silver-gilt handle and a pattern of daisies. It suited her, and I said so, aware that something quite unprecedented was happening to me. Alarm bells were ringing in my mind, but I could hardly hear them for the angel voices that seemed to follow her around wherever she went.

'Thank you,' said Sunny, and then she was crying again, her face in her hands like a little girl, the umbrella held up against her chest. 'I'm sorry,' she said, hiccupping a little. 'It's just the rain. I can't bear it. Like in the song, you know? *Rainy days and Mondays*. It's so cold. And it gets so *dark*—' She broke off and gave me a forced smile. 'I'm sorry,' she said again, 'I know it's stupid, but I just hate it. Does that sound crazy?'

I swallowed my pride. Even a rain god has it, you know, and I have to say I'd considered that rainstorm one of my finest. 'Of course not,' I said, taking her hand. 'You've probably got that – what do you call it? – that SAD thing – Seasonal Affective Disorder. Right?'

'I guess.' She smiled again, and it was like daybreak. Birds sang, flowers flowered, assorted wildlife gambolled joyously through the springtime forests. Oh, I had it, all right. I had it *bad*.

'Look,' I said. 'The rain's stopped.'

It gave me heartburn to do it, but it was worth it just for the expression on her face. I wiggled my big toe, and the clouds opened, just a little. In a wheatfield in Kansas, workers were astonished to see fat clumps of snow drifting from a hitherto cloudless sky.

Over our heads, a single feather of sunlight fluttered down.

'Look, a rainbow,' said Sunny.

'Hm. Whaddya know.' I once had an Aspect – as Ngalyod, the Rainbow Serpent – that could conjure up a highway right across the worlds into the Kingdom of the Dead. I lifted my little finger. In Kinshasa the rainy season arrived nearly three months early. In Manhattan the rainbow brightened, the rainbow doubled, and suddenly half of the city was alight in a sevenfold blaze of colour.

'Wow,' said Sunny.

'Couldn't have had the rainbow if we hadn't had the rain.'

She looked at me with those amazing eyes. 'Can we go out in it?'

'Sure, if you like.'

I chose an umbrella – brown, with a pattern of concentric circles – and together – she with her own umbrella of blue skies and daisies – we went out once more into the street. The sun glittered on the flat blue puddles as she stamped and splashed them with her sandalled feet. Light rain fell, but with a cheery sound, like small hands clapping. Stormclouds gathered, sensing my approach, but I dispersed them as best I could with a discreet wave of the hand. In Okinawa, Japan, a freak hailstorm blitzed a shopping mall, causing fourteen million dollars' worth of damage.

Around us, rainbows dervish-danced.

'This is crazy,' said Sunny, laughing. 'I've never seen anything like this before.'

Smiling, I nodded. I doubt anyone else in New York had, either.

There must be Aspects of us in every single part of the world. Old gods, lost gods, half-forgotten mortal gods, eking out a living in cabarets and travelling sideshows where once we had kingdoms of our own. It's easy to forget oneself; to work in terms of human lifespan, moving regularly, finding ways to camouflage the skills we may have retained – the occasional healing, that unexpected flash of divine inspiration, the stormclouds gathering out of a blue August sky to settle sullenly on the parching land.

I wondered if she knew – whether she suspected, even in dreams – what she really was. Fragments of Aspect, scattered and sown over an ever-expanding world. Atum hatching from the solar egg; Theia, consort of Hyperion; Amaterasu in Japan; Tezcatlipoca in Mexico; or just Sól, the Bright One; sweet, simple Sunny with her daisy umbrella under the shining rain.

On the whole, I thought she didn't know. She was too much a creature of the moment; in tears one second and laughing in delight the next. She was one of a kind – unique. Oh, I'd met *gods* before – Aspects – Incarnations. You sometimes do in my business, though most of them are broken-down old things, always moaning about their glory days and the lack of proper temples, and how worshippers aren't what they used to be.

Sunny wasn't like that. Even in New York, where nobody notices anything, people noticed *her*. Just in passing, from the corner of their eye, but they noticed her; faces brightened, bent backs straightened as if by magic; traffic cops with faces like dough relaxed imperceptibly as she went by; and very often people just stopped and looked up, or smelt the wind, or smiled suddenly without knowing why.

And what about me? Tell you the truth, it was killing me to keep up the pretence. My gut ached; my head was splitting; my fingers and toes were all in knots from wiggling and twitching the clouds away. All around the world *things* were happening beyond my control: a shower of fish in Mexico City; a mini-hurricane in Ealing, London; twelve centimetres of rainfall in less than ten minutes over a French village on the river Baïse. And there were live frogs in the rain. Green ones.

But Sunny was happy, and that's what mattered. All around her rainbows danced; the rain sang; the sun shone from its bracket of purple cloud. It was killing me; and yet I wished it could last for ever, sun and rain walking hand in hand along a busy street in Manhattan, New York.

She was wet, so I bought her some rubber boots – yellow, with ducks – to splash with in the puddles, and a blue raincoat with buttons shaped like little flowers. We ate ice cream under the shelter of her daisy umbrella, and talked – she of a childhood in sunny Sweden or wherever it was she imagined she'd lived, I of my adventures in Deuteronomy, Kansas. And all the time the rainbows danced, and people walked past with vague and bewildered expressions of delight and sometimes commented on the unusual weather, or, most often, said nothing at all.

I held out for a long, long time. For her sake I did, but even I couldn't keep it up forever. My head was throbbing; my fingers itching to let the clouds do their worst. And at last they did; they obscured the sun, the rainbows died, the clapping hands became great hammering bolts of rain on the daisy umbrella, and just like that, her smile went in.

'Arthur? Please? I have to go.'

I looked at her. Tell the truth, I hadn't stopped looking at her. 'Rainy days, right?'

'Sorry.'

'That's OK. It's not your fault.'

'But I want you to know I had a real good time.' She smiled once, the shy smile of a little girl thanking a grown-up for the nice party. She turned – then she darted back towards me and dropped a kiss on my cheek. 'Can we do this again?' she said. 'Some time when it isn't raining?'

'Sure we can,' I lied. 'Anytime.'

Of course I knew even then that it was impossible. Even in my rosy haze I was already making plans to move out, to pack my bags and flee the city, perhaps even the continent itself. As it happened, I didn't have to go that far. I simply moved out of my little flat, taking my umbrella collection with me. I ended up in a room in Brooklyn, where for some reason it now rains far more often than it ever did in Manhattan.

It wasn't that I didn't want to see her again – gods alive, I wanted it more than anything – but there was the business of our opposing Aspects to consider, and the repercussions that our meeting might have on the world. Hurricanes, twisters, tidal waves – even the truest romantic knows you can't build a love affair on nothing but rainbows.

And so I let her go, and watched her all the long way down the street, yellow dress and daisy umbrella and all, and as she reached the end of the road I distinctly saw a wand of sunlight pierce the clouds and land directly onto the small bright figure walking out of my life forever.

'I love you,' I told her, as I stood there in the rain. Water ran down my face in cold little rivulets. My headache was gone, but there was a new pain in my heart that hadn't been there a moment before.

Like I said, it was going to be a wet summer.

Dryad

Love comes to us from the strangest of places. This odd little tale may well be the only inter-species non-mammalian love story ever written.

In a quiet little corner of the Botanical Gardens, between a stand of old trees and a thick holly hedge, there is a small green metal bench. Almost invisible against the greenery, few people use it, for it catches no sun and offers only a partial view of the lawns. A plaque in the centre reads: *In Memory of Josephine Morgan Clarke, 1912–1989.* I should know – I put it there – and yet I hardly knew her, hardly noticed her, except for that one rainy Spring day when our paths crossed and we almost became friends.

I was twenty-five, pregnant and on the brink of divorce. Five years earlier, life had seemed an endless passage of open doors; now I could hear them clanging shut, one by one: marriage; job; dreams. My one pleasure was the Botanical Gardens, with its mossy paths, its tangled walkways, its quiet avenues of oaks and lindens. It became my refuge, and when David was at work (which was almost all the time) I walked there, enjoying the scent of cut grass and the play of light through the tree branches. It was surprisingly quiet; I noticed few other visitors, and was glad of it. There was one exception, however: an elderly lady in a dark coat who always sat on the same bench under the trees, sketching. In rainy weather, she brought an umbrella; on sunny days, a hat. That was Josephine Clarke; and twenty-five years later, with one daughter married and the other still at school, I have never forgotten her, or the story she told me of her first and only love.

It had been a bad morning. David had left on a quarrel (again), drinking his coffee without a word before leaving for the office in the rain. I was tired and lumpish in my pregnancy clothes; the kitchen needed cleaning; there was nothing on TV and everything in the world seemed to have gone yellow around the edges, like the pages of a newspaper that has been read and re-read until there's nothing new left inside. By midday I'd had enough; the rain had stopped, and I set off for the Gardens; but I'd hardly gone in through the big wrought-iron gate when it began again – great billowing sheets of it – so that I ran for the shelter of the nearest tree, under which Mrs Clarke was already sitting.

We sat on the bench side by side, she calmly busy with her sketchbook, I watching the tiresome rain with the slight embarrassment that enforced proximity to a stranger often brings. I could not help but glance at the sketchbook – furtively, like reading someone else's newspaper on the Tube

– and I saw that the page was covered with studies of trees. One tree, in fact, as I looked more closely; *our* tree – a beech – its young leaves shivering in the rain. She had drawn it in soft, chalky green pencil, and her hand was sure and delicate, managing to convey the texture of the bark as well as the strength of the tall, straight trunk and the movement of the leaves. She caught me looking, and I apologized.

'That's all right, dear,' said Mrs Clarke. 'You take a look, if you'd like to.' And she handed me the book.

Politely, I took it. I didn't really want to; I wanted to be alone; I wanted the rain to stop; I didn't want a conversation with an old lady about her drawings. And yet they were wonderful drawings – even I could see that, and I'm no expert – graceful, textured, economical. She had devoted one page to leaves; one to bark; one to the tender cleft where branch meets trunk and the grain of the bark coarsens before smoothing out again as the limb performs its graceful arabesque into the leaf canopy. There were winter branches; summer foliage; shoots and roots and wind-shaken leaves. There must have been fifty pages of studies; all beautiful, and all, I saw, of the same tree.

I looked up to see her watching me. She had very bright eyes, bright and brown and curious; and there was a curious smile on her small, vivid face as she took back her sketch-book and said: 'Piece of work, isn't he?'

It took me some moments to understand that she was referring to the tree. 'I've always had a soft spot for the beeches,' continued Mrs Clarke, 'ever since I was a little girl. Not all trees are so friendly; and some of them – the oaks and the cedars especially – can be quite antagonistic to human beings. It's not really their fault; after all, if you'd been persecuted for as long as they have, I imagine you'd be entitled to feel some racial hostility, wouldn't you?' And she smiled at me, poor old dear, and I looked nervously at the rain and wondered whether I should risk making a dash for the bus shelter. But she seemed quite harmless, so I smiled back and nodded, hoping that was enough.

'That's why I don't like *this* kind of thing,' said Mrs Clarke, indicating the bench on which we were sitting. 'This wooden bench under this living tree – all our history of chopping and burning. My husband was a carpenter. He never did understand about trees. To him, it was all about product – floorboards and furniture. They don't *feel*, he used to say. I mean, how could anyone live with stupidity like that?' She laughed and ran her fingertips tenderly along the edge of her sketchbook. 'Of course I was young; in those days a girl left home; got married; had children; it was expected. If you didn't, there was something wrong with you. And that's how I found myself up the duff at twenty-two, married – to Stan Clarke, of all people – and living in a two-up, two-down off the Station Road and wondering, is this it? Is this *all*?'

That was when I should have left. To hell with politeness; to hell with the rain. But she was telling my story as well as her own, and I could feel the echo down the lonely passages of my heart. I nodded without knowing it, and her bright brown eyes flicked to mine with sympathy and unexpected humour. 'Well, we all find our little comforts where we can,' she said, shrugging. 'Stan didn't know it, and what you don't know doesn't hurt, right? But Stanley never had much of an imagination. Besides, you'd never have thought it to look at me. I kept house; I worked hard; I raised my boy – and nobody guessed about my fella next door, and the hours we spent together.'

She looked at me again, and her vivid face broke into a smile of a thousand wrinkles. 'Oh yes, I had my fella,' she said. 'And he was everything a man should be. Tall; silent; certain; strong. Sexy – and how! Sometimes when he was naked I could hardly bear to look at him, he was so beautiful. The only thing was – he wasn't a man at all.'

Mrs Clarke sighed, and ran her hands once more across the pages of her sketchbook. 'By rights,' she went on, 'he wasn't even a *he*. Trees have no gender – not in English, anyway – but they do have *identity*. Oaks are masculine, with their deep roots and resentful natures. Birches are flighty and feminine; so are hawthorns and cherry trees. But my fella was a beech, a copper beech; red-headed in autumn, veering to the most astonishing shades of purple-green in spring. His skin was pale and smooth; his limbs a dancer's; his body straight and slim and powerful. Dull weather made him sombre, but in sunlight he shone like a Tiffany lampshade, all harlequin bronze and sun-dappled rose, and if you stood underneath his branches you could hear the ocean in the leaves. He stood at the bottom of our little bit of garden, so that he was the last thing I saw when I went to bed, and the first thing I saw when I got up in the morning; and on some days I swear the only reason I got up at all was the knowledge that he'd be there waiting for me, outlined and strutting against the peacock sky.

'Year by year, I learned his ways. Trees live slowly, and long. A year of mine was only a day to him; and I taught myself to be patient, to converse over months rather than minutes, years rather than days. I'd always been good at drawing – although Stan said it was a waste of time – and now I drew the beech (or *The Beech*, as he had become to me) again and again, winter into summer and back again, with a lover's devotion to detail. Gradually I became obsessed – with his form; his intoxicating beauty; the long and complex language of leaf and shoot. In summer he spoke to me with his branches; in winter I whispered my secrets to his sleeping roots.

'You know, trees are the most restful and contemplative of living things. We ourselves were never meant to live at this frantic speed; scurrying about in endless pursuit of the next thing, and the next; running like laboratory rats down a series of mazes towards the inevitable; snapping up our bitter treats as we go. The trees are different. Among trees I find that my breathing slows; I am conscious of my heart beating; of the world around me moving in harmony; of oceans that I have never seen; never will see. The Beech was never anxious; never in a rage, never too busy to watch or listen. Others might be petty; deceitful; cruel, unfair – but not The Beech. The Beech was always there, always himself. And as the years passed and I began to depend more and more on the calm serenity his presence gave me, I became increasingly repelled by the sweaty pink lab rats with their nasty ways, and I was drawn, slowly and inevitably, to the trees.

'Even so, it took me a long time to understand the intensity of those feelings. In those days it was hard enough to admit to loving a black man – or worse still, a woman – but this aberration of mine – there wasn't even anything about it in the Bible, which suggested to me that perhaps I was unique in my perversity, and that even Deuteronomy had overlooked the possibility of non-mammalian, inter-species romance.

'And so for more than ten years I pretended to myself that it wasn't love. But as time passed my obsession grew; I spent most of my time outdoors, sketching; my boy Daniel took his first steps in the shadow of The Beech; and on warm summer nights I would creep outside, barefoot and in my nightdress, while upstairs Stan snored fit to wake the dead, and I would put my arms around the hard, living body of my beloved and hold him close beneath the cavorting stars.

'It wasn't always easy, keeping it secret. Stan wasn't what you'd call imaginative, but he was suspicious, and he must have sensed some kind of deception. He had never really liked my drawing, and now he seemed almost resentful of my little hobby, as if he saw something in my studies of trees that made him uncomfortable. The years had not improved Stan. He had been a shy young man in the days of our courtship; not bright; and awkward in the manner of one who has always been happiest working with his hands. Now he was sour – old before his time. It was only in his workshop that he really came to life. He was an excellent craftsman, and he was generous with his work, but my years alongside The

Beech had given me a different perspective on carpentry, and I accepted Stan's offerings – fruitwood bowls, coffee tables, little cabinets, all highly polished and beautifully made – with concealed impatience and growing distaste.

'And now, worse still, he was talking about moving house; of getting a nice little semi, he said, with a garden, not just a big old tree and a patch of lawn. We could afford it; there'd be space for Dan to play; and though I shook my head and refused to discuss it, it was then that the first brochures began to appear around the house, silently, like spring crocuses, promising en-suite bathrooms and inglenook fireplaces and integral garages and gas-fired central heating. I had to admit, it sounded quite nice. But to leave The Beech was unthinkable. I had become dependent on him. I knew him; and I had come to believe that he knew me, needed and cared for me in a way as yet unknown among his proud and ancient kind.

'Perhaps it was my anxiety that gave me away. Perhaps I underestimated Stan, who had always been so practical, and who always snored so loudly as I crept out into the garden. All I know is that one night when I returned, exhilarated by the dark and the stars and the wind in the branches, my hair wild and my feet scuffed with green moss, he was waiting.

'"You've got a fella, haven't you?"

'I made no attempt to deny it; in fact, it was almost a relief to admit it to myself. To those of our generation, divorce was a shameful thing; an admission of failure. There would be a court case; Stanley would fight; Daniel would be dragged into the mess and all our friends would take Stanley's side and speculate vainly on the identity of my mysterious lover. And yet I faced it; accepted it; and in my heart a bird was singing so hard that it was all I could do not to burst out laughing.

'"You have, haven't you?" Stan's face looked like a rotten apple; his eyes shone through with pinhead intensity. "Who is it?"

'"You'll never know."

'I spent the rest of the night under The Beech, wrapped in a blanket. It was windy, but not cold; and when I awoke the wind had dropped and I was lying under a glorious drift of purple-green foliage. When I returned to the house, I found that Stan had gone, taking his woodworking tools and a case of his clothes with him. By the end of the week, Daniel had joined him; a boy of twelve needs his father, and besides, Dan had always been more Stanley's boy than my own. All the same, I was happy. I saw no one, but I was not lonely. Instead I felt curiously free. With Stan and Daniel gone I sensed much more than I had previously and I spent much of my time under The Beech, listening to the sounds of movement in the earth and of grass popping and of slow roots growing, inch by inch, under the dark soil.

'For the first time I was aware of everything; of birds high in the branches; of insects tunnelling under the bark; of water half a mile underground. I slept there every night. I forgot to eat. I even stopped drawing. Instead I lay for days and nights under the royal canopy of The Beech, and there were times when I was sure I could have grown roots of my own, sinking softly and sweetly into the ground, leaving no trace of myself. It was blissful. Time had no meaning; I forgot the language of haste and flesh. Twice, a neighbour called to me over the fence; but her voice was shrill and unpleasant, and I ignored her. It rained, but I didn't feel cold; instead I turned my face towards the rain and let it fall gently into my open mouth. It was all the sustenance I needed. As the days passed I understood that at last I was joining him, like the two lovers in the old myth – Baucis and Philemon, I think it was – who were turned into trees so that they would never be apart. I was supremely happy; I pulled the earth over me like a quilt and sank my fingers into the ground. It would be soon, I knew; already my limbs had taken root; even when I tried to move them, I could not. The cries from over the fence were barely audible now; I turned my face into the soil like a sleepy child into a pillow; and all around me was the sound of The Beech; soothing; loving; calling.

'But something was wrong; something disturbed us; we sensed it in our roots. A shrill voice, too high for us to hear; a movement, too fast for us to follow. The rats were back; the horrid pink rats; and as we slept and dreamed our cool, slow dreams, they rushed and scurried about us, squeaking and gnawing and harrying and pawing. I tried to protest, but I had lost my tongue. I was uprooted; their faces loomed above me and as *we* became *I* once again, I heard their voices – and that of The Beech, raised for the first time in sorrow and loss – drowning out the sound of the world below.

'*Oh my dear my sweet my*

'Call the ambulance she's

'Oh my love

'I awoke in a bed of clean white sheets to the realization that time had recommenced. Stan, I was told, had sat by my bed for fourteen nights; the nurses were filled with praise for his doglike devotion. It had been close, they said. I had been lucky. Pneumonia had set in; I was malnourished and dehydrated; a few more hours and they might have lost me. Stan, they said, had gone back to the house, but he returned quickly enough, and though I tried not to hear him, I soon found that I had lost the knack.

'"I'm sorry, love," he told me. "I should have recognized the signs." Apparently it all fitted: the neurotic behaviour; the sexual disgust; the desire for solitude; the obsessive-compulsive studies of trees. A breakdown, that was all; and I would get better very soon, he promised, with good old Stan to look after me. That silly quarrel was all in the past; there never had been a fella; and very soon I'd be right as rain. And there was good news: he'd found a buyer for the house. First-time buyer; no chain; and before I knew it we'd be living in that little semi we'd always wanted, with a nice bit of garden and no bloody trees.

'I struggled to speak and found that I could not. Stan took my hand and held it.

'"Don't worry, love. It's all arranged. They're very nice people; they'll take good care of the house. Course, that big old tree'll have to go—"

'My mouth worked.

'"Course it will, love. It can't stay there; it blocks the light.

92

Besides, I don't want to risk that sale. You go to sleep now, and don't you fret. I'm looking after you now."

'I never did go back to the house. I don't think I could have borne it, knowing what I knew. I never saw the little semi, either; instead I moved out as soon as I could to a rented flat near the Botanical Gardens. Even so, Stan didn't give up. For almost a year he and Daniel called on me every Sunday. But there was nothing to say. They had saved my life, but I had left the best part of myself under The Beech, and there could be no going back to my old life, even if I had wanted to. Then one day, nearly twelve months after my release from hospital, he brought me a present wrapped in crêpe paper. "Open it," he said. "I made it for you."

'It was a wooden dish about two feet across. Roughly heart-shaped, it was made from a perfect cross-section of tree trunk, with concentric circles shimmering through the wood.

'"Thought you'd like it as a reminder," said Stan. "Seeing as you were always so fond of it, and all."

'Wordlessly, I touched the edge of the dish. It was smooth and cool and flawlessly polished. With the tip of my finger I found the place at the heart of the tree, and it might have been my imagination, but for a second I seemed to feel a shiver of response, as if I had touched some dying nerve.

'"It's beautiful," I said, and I meant it.

'"Thanks, love," said Stan.'

I keep the dish on my dining-room table. She left it to me, you know; along with her sketchbooks and her drawings of trees. She didn't have anyone else, poor old dear; Stan had been dead for ten years and she'd been living in a retirement home since then. The Willows, it was called. I tried to find Daniel, but there was no contact address. The lady at The Willows thinks he might be living in New Zealand, but no one knows for sure.

In a quiet little corner of the Botanical Gardens, between a stand of old trees and a thick holly hedge, there is a small green metal bench. Almost invisible against the greenery, few people use it, except for me. They're all too busy with their own concerns to stop and talk; besides, I don't need them any more. After all, I have the trees.

Harry Stone and the 24-Hour Church of Elvis

Sometimes someone hands me a story, often without knowing it. This one came to me from a T-shirt, sent to me by an American fan, with the logo: 24-hour Church of Elvis. Apparently this is a genuine church, with many sincere worshippers. Nowadays I guess we find our religion wherever we can. I transferred the church to a Yorkshire town, reduced its congregation to one, but the principle remains the same.

What would Elvis have done?

That's a question that's often helped me through hard times; difficult choices; moral dilemmas. Sitting on a crowded train, people standing; woman gets on, might be pregnant, might not – hard to tell under the acres of pinafore – sandwiched between a kid in a Burberry baseball cap and an old lady with some Tesco's bags. Me, I've got my guitar case, I'm knackered from last night's show at the Lord Nelson and I ask myself: *What would Elvis have done?*

Well, apart from the fact that he wouldn't have been on

the train to Huddersfield in the first place, it's pretty obvious. So I get up, don't I, with a smile and a suave gesture (only slightly marred by the guitar case bashing into the grab-rail). The kid behind me sniggers; the old lady with the shopping gives me a dirty look, like it should have been her; and the maybe-pregnant woman plops down without a word of thanks and opens a bag of smoky bacon crisps. Ignorant cow.

I was telling all this to Lil, half an hour later, in the Cape Cod chippy. Fishcake Lil, my number-one biggest fan (and agent in the field); sees everything, knows everything that's going on from Malbry to the village, which is a serious bonus to someone in my line of work.

'What a shame, love. I'll put you some more scraps in, shall I?'

Elvis would – I decided against. 'Better not. Gotta be fit in this business, Lil.'

Lil nodded. She's a big girl, with a smooth, powdered face and long brown hair. Works at the chippy four days a week, and does Tarot readings down the pub on Thursday nights under the name Lady Lilith. So she understands showbiz, which is a relief, because, let's face it, most people have no idea of the strains and demands involved in being a top Elvis act.

'Good gig last night?'

'The best.' Actually it was a bit rough; there's a new crowd at the Lord Nelson, and you can see they're not used to class. One of them – a tall skinny bloke in a torn-off T-shirt that made him look a bit like Bruce Springsteen – kept shouting: *Stand up!* and making comments like: *This un's only half! Does that mean we get half us money back?* I had a go at Bernie (he's the compère, goes under the stage name of Mike Stand) for not building me up enough during his intro. I know I'm on the short side, I told him, but the King himself wasn't *that* tall, it's the camerawork that does it, and besides, it's all a question of attitude. At which Mike said he was pretty bloody sure that Elvis had never got down off stage in the middle of a number and twatted a member of the audience just for saying *I'll have half.*

Fair's fair. I overreacted. Still, you'd think that six months of incident-free performances would have counted for something.

'To be honest, Lily,' I told her, splashing vinegar on my chips, 'I've been thinking of moving on. There's other places than the Lord Nelson, you know. The Rat, for instance.'

That was the Ratcliff Arms, the roughest pub in Malbry. I'd played there once, years ago, fifty quid a night and all of it danger money.

Lily's face fell. 'He's not sacked you?'

'Course not.' I gave her my 'Jailhouse Rock' look over my turned-up collar. 'I just wanted something a bit nearer home.' I lowered my voice. 'For *professional* purposes.'

Her eyes widened. 'You mean—?'

'Uh-huh.' Lily knows better than to mention it openly in the shop, with people coming in and out all the time, but she's the only person (apart from my clients, of course) who knows my secret. By day (and on Wednesday evenings) all Huddersfield knows me as Jim Santana, Top Elvis Act (pubs, weddings and private parties considered); but by night I walk the city streets as Harry Stone, lone gumshoe and private investigator, scourge of the criminal classes and one-man crusader against vice in all its forms. If you have a problem – and *if* you can find me (try the Thomson local or that little noticeboard in Malbry Post Office) – then I will solve it. Remember the Raj Fruit & Vegetable grocery job? That was one of mine. Mr Raj thought he could get away with buying raisins at the wholesaler's at fifty pence a pound, then soaking them, repackaging them and selling them at one-twenty for a small punnet under the label 'Jumbo ready-to-eat Raisins'.

But he hadn't counted on Harry Stone. I reported him to the Weights and Measures, who sent a strongly worded letter by return of post. Sorted. He won't be trying *that* scam again in a hurry, I can tell you.

Then there was Darren Bray, of Bray's lumber yard, with that van with the out-of-date tax disc parked on the road. And that John Whitehouse, claiming his dead Dad's DSS benefits while his Mum built that extension to their garage without informing the Planning Department. And Mrs Rawlinson in the snack bar down by the Methodist Church, labelling her cheese and pickle sandwiches *Suitable for Vegetarians* when she knows full well that neither the cheese nor the margarine had been approved by the proper authorities. *That* was an Advertising Standards job, and it took me a week of sitting there with my digital mini-camera waiting for deliveries and drinking Mrs Rawlinson's milky tea. But I got there in the end. I always do. For the community. For myself. And for Elvis.

Having said that, the pay isn't always that good. Most of my income still comes from my act, but every good investigator needs a cover, and mine's as good as they come. In my line of work, I get around; I get to know people, and, of course, I have my informants.

Lily, for example. Fishcake Lil to most (Lady Lilith on Thursday nights, and by appointment). She glanced quickly over her shoulder to check that no one could overhear, then whispered: 'Who is it?'

'Brendan Mackie. Football coach for Malbry Miners.'

Lil had a think. 'Big bloke. Bit of a temper. Likes a drink. Always has haddock, chips, two scallops, battered sausage – always makes the same joke about the sausage (*not as big as some, love, but then it's got a lot to live up to*); wife sometimes comes in with him. Gail. Stripy blonde; perma-tan; bit tarty; brother works at B&Q; Diet Coke; never wants batter on her fish.'

'Perfect.' I told you she was good. I looked around, but the shop was empty, and the only person I could see outside was Mr Menezies eating his chips by the bus stop with his hearing aid turned off to save the battery. 'Between you and me, Lil, *she's* the target.'

'What, Gail?'

I nodded. 'Had a word with Brendan the other night. After-the-match gig at the Golden Cock. We got talking, as you do. He thinks she might be playing away.'

'He *hired* you?' said Lily.

'Uh-huh.' Well, nearly. What he'd actually said was: *I'd give a lot to know what she gets up to when I'm at footie*, but an investigator has to read between the lines if he isn't to blow his cover. I reckoned I could charge him a tenner a day, plus expenses, if I got a result. It wasn't much, I know, and I was dying to get my teeth into a *real* crime and not just a marital, but I figured that if Brendan Mackie *did* find out that his wife was cheating on him, I'd be at the head of the queue to solve the murder.

Brendan Mackie. Lily was right. I can just about make it to five-five, if you count the quiff and the cowboy boots, and he towered over me even though he was sitting down and I wasn't. He was pleased with the act, though; told me he hadn't laughed so much since Granny got her tit caught in the mangle, and bought me a drink.

'So. D'you enjoy it then, this Elvis lark?'

'Uh-huh.'

'Z'it pay much?'

'It's all right.' I sensed from the start that he wouldn't understand the subtleties; the costumes; the lights; the exhilarating glamour and freedom and thrill of life on the road.

'Is Jim Santana your real name, or is it, like, a *noom-de-ploom?*'

'It's my real name,' I told him. 'I changed it by deed poll in 1977.'

'Crucial.' He swigged his lager for a moment, while I did the same to my rum and Coke. 'I suppose it's all got to be genuine, like, for your act. Like them trannies you get in Amsterdam. Twenty-four-seven, eh? I mean, there's no one going to take it seriously if you're a regular bloke all day and at night you're Elvis.'

'Uh-huh-huh.'

'That slays me, it really does.'

We talked awhile. I was halfway through the set, two

costume changes in and two more to go. I do all the hits: 'Love Me Tender'; 'Jailhouse Rock'; 'King of the Road'. People love it, specially the older ones; it reminds them of the time when they were rebels. Nowadays it's hard to find anything worth rebelling against. It's all been done. Nothing's new; and however bright you burn – your Kurt Cobains and your Jim Morrisons – you're all going to end up in the same old hotel room at the last, doped and desperate. Except for Elvis.

I've got a shrine to him in my living room, you know; with photographs and album covers and figurines. Lily calls it the 24-hour Church of Elvis. Not that I think he's God, or anything like that; but he's my inspiration. My idol. My muse.

I tried to say as much to Brendan Mackie, but I could tell it wasn't getting through. Waste of time, really. The more he drank, the more he wanted to talk about his wife. And so I let him; and I watched the case unfold.

Consider the suspect. Gail Mackie. Thirty-two. Married nine years, no kids, no job. Bored witless – I would be, if I was married to Brendan – nothing to do all day but take baths and have my nails done and go to the Body in Question for Pilates and lunch. *Was* she cheating? It sounded likely. Everything fitted: the furtive manner, the unanswered mobile, the evenings out, the late-night showers as Brendan lay in bed. A doting husband, he'd never confronted her. Gail had a temper, so Lily said, and I guessed that Brendan would accept nothing less than photographic proof. Finally, I thought, a job worthy of Harry Stone.

'When do we start?' said Lily, her eyes brightening.

That *we*. Her and me. If only I could. But it's a proud and

lonely thing to be a professional gumshoe and Elvis imper-
sonator, and if my enemies ever found out about Lily and
me—

'I can't afford a partner, Lil,' I said, not for the first time.
'Work in the shadows. In and out—' I demonstrated, using
my chip-fork as a weapon. 'You'd only slow me down if it
came to a fight, and if ever anything happened to you—'

'Oh, Jim,' said Lil softly. 'I wish you'd let me help.'

I gave her my 'Love Me Tender' look. 'Sweetheart,' I said.
'You've done enough.'

Well, that was the first stage done and dealt with. Now to
confirm the client's suspicions, obtain photographic proof of
his wife's infidelity and, finally, cash in on a job well done.
I reckoned it might take me a week or so – say, ten days,
plus expenses, we might be talking about a hundred and fifty
quid or thereabouts: not bad at all, and a lot easier than the
Lord Nelson on a Saturday night.

My first job was to locate the target. Easy enough, that,
I thought; as it happened, there was a match that day, so I
just turned up outside the house with my mini-camera and
waited. It was cold for September; I wore my mac belted
tightly with the collar turned up and walked around a bit
to keep warm. Gail finally came out at three o'clock, ten
minutes after Brendan left the house, carrying her gym bag
and swinging her ponytail like a schoolgirl.

Bugger. She was taking the car. A little Fiesta. That
stumped me a bit – I don't actually own a car at present (the
last one got written off during problems associated with a

previous case), and I had to do some quick thinking. Had to abandon the idea of leaping into a cab and driving after her – no cabs on Meadowbank Road – and although the number 10 bus was just coming round the bend at the time, I knew I couldn't count on the driver to accept my authority to commandeer his vehicle. In the end I had to sprint back down to the Cape Cod and borrow Lily's Micra, by which time Gail was long gone and the trail was growing cold.

I played a hunch, though, and followed her to the Body in Question, the local gym, where I managed to get in a couple of candid snaps just as Gail was coming out of the ladies' changing rooms. After that I went into the sports shop alongside, invested in a pair of swimming shorts (six quid, plus the swimming cap), and parked myself in the spa pool next to the glass-fronted Pilates studio, where I was able to watch the target's every move in comfort and security.

I'll give her this: she's an athletic girl. An hour's Pilates, followed by half an hour on the rowing machine, half an hour's swimming, half an hour's Step class, a shower, and then – bingo! – a tall skinny decaff latte in the gymnasium juice bar, in the company of a young man in a muscle shirt and a pair of Lycra running shorts.

I was out of the pool in a flash, showered and dressed before she could order a refill. It took a *little* longer than I'd first expected (in my haste I'd forgotten to buy a towel), but even so, I managed to find a seat not far from the couple, where I could snap a few more incriminating shots and hopefully tape their conversation using the mini digital recorder in my pocket.

I ordered a Coke. The girl at the counter gave me a funny look – well, I don't go swimming very often, my quiff gets wet – and charged me two quid. Lucky for me the case's open and closed. Two quid for a glass of Coke! Perhaps I ought to make *that* the subject of my next investigation – besides which, the Coke tasted distinctly watery. I made it last, though, all the time straining to listen to what Gail and Lycra-Boy were whispering to each other, but I'd been in the pool for much too long, there was water in my ears, and I couldn't hear a bloody word.

Perhaps that was what caused me to drop my guard. That, or someone had been stalking me – causing the hunter to become the hunted in a bizarre quirk of fate. In any case, Gail was getting suspicious; I caught her watching me a couple of times with an odd look on her face, and once Lycra-Boy turned round as well, and fixed me with a stare of such naked aggression that a lesser man might well have been intimidated.

Not me, though. Not Harry Stone. Instead I stared him out, lifted my glass and toasted him silently in watery Coke, so that Gail looked quite upset and got to her feet, and Lycra-Boy took a step towards me, then saw my steely gaze and thought better of it, turning tail and legging it through the swing doors towards the car park and Gail's Fiesta, parked (illegally, I noticed, and with a wing-mirror misaligned) in an executive slot.

I tailed them back to the Mackie residence and parked the car at the bottom of the road, opposite the Cape Cod. Lily was just closing (she does bar work at the Rat on a Saturday night), and she smiled as she saw me coming. 'All right, Jim?'

Jesus, my cover. '*Harry*,' I hissed, handing her the keys.

'Oh. Sorry, love. How'd it go?'

'Elvis himself couldn't have done a better job. Look at that now.' I glanced down the road at the Mackie house, all lit up now with the curtains drawn, and the target and the suspect alone in the sitting room, doing God knows what. 'Probable cause, they call it on TV. Means I can snoop around there as much as I like, though I do draw the line at breaking and entering.'

'Be careful, Jim.' Lily's eyes were wide. 'Don't want to get caught, do you?'

I grinned. 'You'd have to get up pretty early to catch Harry Stone with his pants down, Lil.'

For some reason, she blushed. 'I'll come with you. Keep watch, like.'

'Sorry, Lil. This is strictly a one-man job.'

Down by the Mackie place, I had another piece of luck. They'd left the curtains open a crack, and I could see straight into the living room. I reached for my camera. The room was deserted – I reckoned Gail and her fella had gone into the kitchen to make coffee – but there was a nice comfy sofa in front of the window, all lined up for a piece of illicit action, and my instincts told me that it would soon be occupied.

So I stood there for a while, watching and waiting. It was cold; it had started to rain and I could feel water trickling down the collar of my mac and into my boots. Still, it's a piss-poor PI who lets a bit of rain get him down, and besides, I was already wet from the spa pool. But I'd got a gig at seven that night – or rather, Jim Santana had – and I could tell my quiff would need some serious remedial work before I could call myself a top Elvis act again.

Still, line of duty, and all that. I must have been standing there for about fifteen minutes, getting colder and wetter. Then, bingo! The target and the suspect strolled into the living room, both carrying coffee cups, and sat down together. Not as close as I'd have liked them to, but close enough. I snapped them both through the gap in the curtains. I couldn't hear what they were saying, but Gail was laughing, and Lycra-Boy was looking down her cleavage like all his Christmases had come at once. I wondered what he'd say when Brendan Mackie caught up with him. Not a lot, most likely.

Come on, Gail. You haven't got all night. I hoped not, anyhow; I'd have to be off at seven myself, or lose the gig, and it was coming up to a quarter to already. What I really wanted was incontrovertible proof of the suspect's infidelities; something to confront Brendan with (and to earn that fee). Gail just sitting there wasn't enough; and there was no telling whether the evidence I had already gleaned would convince Brendan Mackie. I moved closer to the window, shifting the angle of the camera – and then a hand roughly the size and weight of a York ham descended on my shoulder, and a face the colour of a York ham pushed into mine, and a familiar voice rumbled up from out of the face and said: 'Bloody hell, it's Elvis.'

'Brendan!' My trained voice jumped an octave. 'Ah – how was the match?'

106

'We were robbed. Two–nil. Bloody referee.' He frowned a little, as if just beginning to take in the turned-up collar, the unfamiliar hairstyle, the digital mini-camera in my hand. 'Ay up,' he said, moving his hand to my throat. 'What's going on here?'

I began to explain. I'd hardly started, though, when Gail came running out of the house with a newspaper over her head and Lycra-Boy in tow. 'It's him!' she said shrilly. 'It's that bloody perv from the gym!'

Now was the time for some rapid thinking. 'Harry Stone,' I said, waving my card. 'Private investigator.'

'Private *what*?' said Brendan, Gail and Lycra-Boy in unison.

Gail was looking at my card.

'*Harry Stone*,' she read aloud, '*Private Investigator, all cases considered, marital disputes a speciality*. Bren?' She turned to her husband with eyes like lasers. 'What the bloody hell's going on here?'

Brendan Mackie looked shifty. His hand left my throat, and my cowboy boots went back to ground level, where they belonged.

'Anyroad, this isn't even a proper card,' continued Gail in a shrill voice. 'It's just a computer print, with the stamp drawn on in Biro.'

'He were watching us,' added Lycra-Boy, surprising me (I'd have thought he'd have legged it fast, once he saw his number was up). 'Taking pictures of our Gail and the lasses in the gym.'

'You *what*?' Ouch. This wasn't going quite the way I'd planned it. *Our Gail*. Could it be that I had overlooked some detail? Too late I remembered Lily saying something about a brother who worked at B&Q. Too late I realized that B&Q was also the Body in Question. And now, glancing back at Lycra-Boy, with his stripy blond hair and suspiciously even tan, I could see – too late – the family resemblance.

Brendan grabbed my collar again. 'You little pervert!'

Too late, I tried to pocket the camera. But Brendan was too fast for me; in a second he was going through the images on screen, his face looking more like raw ham than ever. I suppose I should have run for it. But it would have been ignoble and unworthy – of me, of Harry Stone, and, most of all, of Elvis.

So what *would* Elvis have done?

Burst into song, most likely, or sucker-punched Brendan in the mouth before he had time to react. For myself, I didn't fancy either alternative, and anyway, I bet even the King of Rock 'n' Roll might have had some difficulty getting out of *that* particular quandary, especially if he was dangling twelve inches off the ground at the end of Brendan Mackie's arm.

'It were an undercover job,' I said in a strangled voice.

'Under*wear*, more like, you perv,' said Gail.

'Look, Brendan, I don't even *fancy* your Gail—'

'What?' His face darkened. 'Are you saying my wife's ugly?'

'No! I'm sorry!'

'You will be,' said Brendan, raising his fist.

'Not me face,' I protested. 'I got a gig on tonight—'

For a second his blurry fist obscured all my vision, like some gigantic meteor about to hit the Earth. I closed my eyes, thinking *this is it, I'll never work the clubs again unless they take Elephant Man acts*, and then came a quiet and familiar voice from out of the shadows, and everything stopped.

It was Lily, of course. She must have been watching from up the road, and run across when she saw what was happening. She took Brendan firmly by the arm, and he released his grip. Like I said, she's a big girl.

'Now then,' said Lil. 'What's the matter?'

Brendan repeated the garbled tale. Gail and Lycra-Boy corroborated it. I stood by, feeling like a prat.

'And you thought he was after *Gail?*' said Lil, when he'd finished.

'Well, yeah,' said Lycra-Boy. 'I mean, who else?'

Lily just looked at him. After a moment or two, so did Gail.

'You don't mean—'

Lil nodded. 'You didn't *know?*'

They were all looking at me now. Even Brendan had a smile on his face. 'Well, come to think of it—'

'Hang on,' I said.

I was beginning to get the gist now, and I didn't like it much. 'I'm bloody straight, me. Straight as a die. Honest to God—' Then Lily gave me one of her stares, and I shut up. It wasn't easy, though; and from the looks on their faces I was sure the news would be all over the village by next week. Dammit. That really would put a crimp on my gig at the Rat – you can practically *smell* the testosterone in that place. An Elvis act – a *short* Elvis act – was hard enough – but a *queer* Elvis act would be downright suicidal.

'Bugger,' I said.

Lycra-Boy gave me a sympathetic look. "S all right, man,' he said. 'I were in denial for years before I came out.'

'Aye, he were dead shy,' said Gail. She was smiling now. Even Brendan was smiling, which was the only good news as far as I was concerned, and his face was looking more like cooked ham than raw. 'You know, there's places you can go. Clubs and that. I bet yer act'd go down a bomb at the Pink Panther. And you'd get to *meet* people' – she patted my arm – ''stead of hanging around the B 'n Q.'

Well, that was that. Words failed me. I gave Lily a reproachful glance, but she was looking the other way. She might have saved my life, I thought bitterly, but what price my self-respect?

So that was the end of the Brendan Mackie case. Well, not quite; there was an unexpected silver lining to the whole fiasco, which paid for my expenses and, to some extent, re-established my credibility. You see, Gail was right about those clubs. Top billing at the Pink Panther on a Friday night – hundred quid a gig, plus tips and drinks – and a rave review in the local press.

Jim Santana, the loudest, proudest Elvis act in the business. That's what the *Morning Post* said, and I've had it printed on my calling cards. Overnight, I've become a kind of celebrity. Suddenly everyone wants to book my act, and Bernie at the Lord Nelson's offered to reinstate me at twice my usual rate.

Still, as I told Lily the other night at the Cape Cod, this means that now I'll have to work even harder to keep Harry Stone in the shadows. 'I'm not in it for the money, Lil,' I said.

'Fame's a fickle friend, as Elvis knew, and I'll never let those bright lights seduce me. The stage may be my secret passion, but detective work's my *life*.'

Lily nodded awkwardly, without meeting my gaze. I have to say I might have been a bit harsh with her recently, what with the comments I'd been getting from Brendan Mackie and the blokes down the pub. In fact it was the first time I'd been in the Cod since the Mackie affair, and I could tell that Lily was worried that her contribution to the fiasco might have soured our special relationship. Her hands were shaking slightly as she checked the temperature of the deep-fat fryer, and there was a flush on her cheeks that was more than just the heat. Seeing that, I felt something begin to thaw inside me. I can never stay mad with Lily for long, you know, and besides, it was Friday night, and that means fish for supper.

'So what now?' she asked shyly, putting a haddock in to fry. The deep-fat fryer hissed and slurred as the fish hit the fat, and I felt my mouth begin to water. No one does fish like Lily does; and no one does chips like she does, either; skin on, hand-cut, and just the right size. Salt, vinegar, mushy peas and scraps, all wrapped in hot greasy paper and a copy of the *Daily Mail*.

It was just one small step away from perfection.

'Fishcake?' she said, looking at me.

Elvis would.

'Yeah, go on then.'

So I did.

The Ghosts of Christmas Present

The narrator of this little tale first made his appearance in 'There's No Such Place as Bedford Falls', and since then I've managed to work out some of his story. In some ways, he's a sad, deluded little man living in a dream world. But underneath, I suspect that he has more integrity than those who consider themselves entirely sane.

It's Christmas Eve on Festive Road. Fifty-five minutes to midnight and it looks as if it's going to be a white Christmas at last, even though the whiteness only amounts as yet to a few flakes of cloud-dandruff against the sallow sky. But it's enough. We ghosts have learned to use what magic we can. God knows, there's little enough left nowadays, but tonight it's here on Festive Road.

We have an hour. That's the rule. An hour of magic once a year – and only ever if it snows. Because everything changes under snow: the greasy underlay of city pavements, the roof-tops and chimneys, the parked cars, plant pots, milk bottles and parking meters all capped with foamy festive Guinness-heads of white. And now, as the first small flakes begin to settle like daisies on the lawn, you can see them – the Ghosts of Christmas – coming from out of the white-edged shadows, the darkened doorways.

There's little Miss Gale, who loved all the old films – *White Christmas* and *Wonderful Life*, but most of all *The Wizard of Oz* – looking so young in the falling snow, skipping out from under the yellow streetlights in her red-heeled Dorothy slippers. And there's old Mr Meadowes, who used to walk to the school playing fields every day with his dog; and Mr Fisher, who was going to be a writer but never found his story; and Sally Anne, who only ever wanted to be pretty and good; and Jim Santana, who loved Elvis with such a passion that he ended up alone. All ghosts now, of course – ghosts like me, like the road itself, springing into wild half-life on Christmas Eve under the snow.

I know what to do. I've been doing it since Phyllis left, so many, many years ago. I miss her still, though we never did see eye to eye on the subject of Christmas. Myself, as you know, I've always loved the festive season. Queen's Speech and mince pies. Phil Spector and *Wonderful Life*. Strings and strings of fairy lights – not just on the tree, but all over the house, the roof, the garden, like some fabulous creeper that keeps on growing.

But Phyl was different. She felt the cold. Dreamed of the sun; worried about what the neighbours might think. And so now it's just me. Me and the ghosts, and my Wall of Lights with the neon reindeer and the dancing penguins and the garlands and wreaths of every colour under and over the rainbow from here to Bedford Falls.

Here come the ghosts; and the Wall of Lights begins to sparkle. You can only go so far with matches, you know; nowadays we require something more high-tech. There's something here for everyone – and not just lights, but sprigs of holly; magic lanterns; dancing snowmen with flashing eyes. There's a big Santa Claus for little Miss Gale, and as she steps close in her red-heeled shoes he jumps out of his sleigh with a lion's-roar of laughter and a clash of bells. Sally Anne puts a shy foot forward and is suddenly clad in a gown of many colours, while Jim Santana – dapper again in his sequinned suit, with a quiff as tall and shiny as a black silk topper – holds out his hand for the first dance. There's mistletoe and mince pies and tiny cups of fruit punch; and all the time the music plays and Mr Fisher tells tales from Dickens, and the Wall of Lights pulses from orange to gold, to emerald, to blue, scattering shards of witchlight across the settling snow.

This is our moment. Under the lights, *everyone* shines; under the snow, everything is remade. It is falling faster now, and with it comes still more magic as with soft pale fingers it wraps up the past, erasing bad thoughts, bad deeds, bad memories, covering it all with a clean thick blanket of fresh white snow.

That's why they come here – they, the ghosts. For just an hour, once a year, to be absolved; to begin again; to be, as snow falls and music plays, the people they always meant to be.

Five minutes to midnight. Will she come? Every year I wait for her, and every year I add more and brighter lights to the shining Wall in the hope that *this* year, she may – my ghost of Christmases past with her sweet face and her laugh like jingle bells. But every year I wait in vain; and it seems to me that the more lights I add, and the more ghosts come to Festive Road, the less chance I have of ever finding *my* ghost, my Phyllis, whom I lost on Christmas Eve between the Queen's Speech and *Morecambe and Wise*; lost stupidly, to an early stroke, and who has spent every Christmas since at the Meadowbank Home, staring wanly – not speaking, not hearing, not *quite* asleep, but never awake – like a princess resting under snow, like a princess from an evil fairy tale with no magic and no happy ever after.

One minute left. My ghosts sense it; and quietly begin to drift away. One by one I turn off the illuminations; Mr Fisher goes first, merging softly into the shadows; then Sally Anne, shivering as her ball dress turns back to rags. Then Miss Gale, her red shoes slipping on the icy path; then Jim, Mr Meadowes and all the rest; turning back – to tramps, pimps, whores, unwanted – as the fairy lights go out.

I leave just one as the church clock chimes the hour. I always leave the one, you know; even though the doctors have told me again and again that miracles *don't* happen, even when it snows. I think I'll sit out here for a time; the snow is unexpectedly soft, like feathers, and the single light – sky blue, the colour of hope – makes everything beautiful. Snow settles on my arms and face; swaddles me like a sleepy child; drops goodnight kisses on my eyes. And as I drift into the dark I think I can hear Phyl's voice, quite close.

Merry Christmas, she says.

And suddenly—

just for that moment—

it is.

Wildfire in Manhattan

I wrote this for Neil Gaiman's Stories *anthology. It's a kind of sequel to 'Rainy Days and Mondays', and fans of my Rune books will recognize Aspects of several familiar characters . . .*

It's not my name – well, not *quite* – but you can call me Lucky. I live right here in Manhattan, in the penthouse suite of a hotel just off Central Park. I'm a model citizen in every way: punctual, polite and orderly. I wear sharp suits. I wax my chest hair. You'd never think I was a god.

It's a truth often overlooked that old gods – like old dogs – have to die some time. It just takes longer, that's all; and in the meantime citadels may fall, empires collapse, worlds end and folk like us lie on the pile, redundant and largely forgotten.

In many ways, I've been fortunate. My element is fire, which never quite goes out of style. There are Aspects of me that still wield power – there's too much of the primitive left in you Folk for it to be otherwise, and although I don't get as

117

many sacrifices as I used to, I can still get obeisance if I want it (who doesn't?) – after dark, when the campfires are lit. And the dry lightning-strikes across the plains – yes, they're mine – and the forest fires; and the funeral pyres and the random sparks and the human torches – all mine.

But here, in New York, I'm Lukas Wilde, lead singer in the rock band Wildfire. Well, I say *band*. Our only album, *Burn It Up*, went platinum when the drummer was tragically killed on stage by a freakish blast of lightning.

Well, maybe not so freakish. Our only US tour was stalked by lightning from beginning to end; of fifty venues, thirty-one suffered a direct hit; in just nine weeks we lost three more drummers, six roadies and a truckload of gear. Even I was beginning to feel I'd taken it just a *little* too far.

Still, it was a great show.

Nowadays, I'm semi-retired. I can afford to be; as one of only two surviving band members I have a nice little income, and when I'm feeling bored I play piano in a fetish bar called the Red Room. I'm not into rubber myself (too sweaty), but you can't deny it makes a terrific insulator.

By now you may have gathered – I'm a night person. Daylight rather cramps my style; and besides, fire needs a night sky to show to best advantage. An evening in the Red Room, playing piano and eyeing the girls, then downtown for rest and recreation. *Not* a scene that my brother frequents; and so it was with some surprise that I ran smack into him that night, as I was checking out the nicely flammable back streets of the Upper East Side, humming 'Light My Fire' and contemplating a spot of arson.

I didn't say? Yes, in this present Aspect, I have a brother. Brendan. A twin. We're not close; Wildfire and Hearth Fire have little in common, and he rather disapproves of my flamboyant lifestyle, preferring the more domestic joys of baking and grilling. Imagine that. A firegod running a restaurant – it makes me burn with shame. Still, it's his funeral. Each of us goes to hell in his own way, and besides, his flame-grilled steaks are the best in the business.

It was past midnight, I was a little light-headed from the booze – but not so drunk that you'd have noticed – and the streets were as still as they get in a city that only ever shuts one eye. A huddle of washouts sleeping in cardboard boxes under a fire escape; a cat raiding a dumpster. It was November; steam plumed from the sewer grates and the sidewalks were shiny with cold sweat.

I was just crossing the intersection of 81st and 5th, in front of the Hungarian meat market, when I saw him: a familiar figure with hair the colour of embers tucked into the collar of a long grey coat. Tall, slim and ballet-quick; you might almost have been forgiven for thinking it was me. Close scrutiny, however, reveals the truth. My eyes are red and green; his, on the other hand, are green and red. Anyway, I wouldn't be seen dead wearing those shoes.

I greeted him cheerily. 'Do I smell burning?'

He turned to me with a hunted expression. 'Shh! Listen!'

I was curious. I know there's never been much love between us, but he usually greets me, at least, before he starts with the recriminations. He called me by my true name. Put a finger to his lips, then dragged me into a side alley that stank of piss.

'Hey, Bren. What gives?' I whispered, correcting my lapels.

His only reply was a curt nod in the direction of the near-deserted alley. In the shadows, two men, boxy in their long overcoats, hats pulled down over narrow, identical faces. They stopped for a second on the kerb, checked left, checked right and crossed over with swift effortless choreography before vanishing, wolfish, into the night.

'I see.' And I did. I'd seen them before. I could feel it in my blood. In another place, in another Aspect, I knew them, and they knew me. And believe me, they were men in form alone. Beneath those cartoon-detective overcoats they were all teeth. 'What d'you think they're doing here?'

He shrugged. 'Hunting.'

'Hunting who?'

He shrugged again. He's never been a man of words, even when he wasn't a man. Me, I'm on the wordy side. I find it helps.

'So you've seen them here before?'

'I was following them when you came along. I doubled back – I didn't want to lead them home.'

Well, I could understand that. 'What are they?' I said. 'Aspects of what? I haven't seen anything like this since Ragnarók, but as I recall—'

'Shh—'

I was getting kinda sick of being shoved and shushed. He's the elder twin, you know, and sometimes he takes liberties. I was about to give him a heated reply when I heard a sound

120

coming from near by, and something swam into rapid view. It took me a while to figure it out; derelicts are hard to see in this city, and he'd been hiding in a cardboard box under a fire escape, but now he shifted quick enough, his old overcoat flapping like wings around his bony ankles.

I knew him, in passing. Old man Moony, here as an Aspect of Mani, the Moon, but mad as a coot, poor old sod (it often happens when they've been at the juice, and the mead of poetry is a heady brew). Still, he could run, and was running now, but as Bren and I stepped out of his way, the two guys in their long overcoats came to intercept him at the mouth of the alley.

Closer this time – I could smell them. A rank and feral smell, half rotted. Well, you know what they say. You can't teach a carnivore oral hygiene.

At my side I could feel my brother trembling. Or was it me? I wasn't sure. I was scared, I knew that – though there was still enough alcohol carousing in my veins to make me feel slightly removed from it all. In any case I stayed put, tucked into the shadows, not quite daring to move. The two guys stood there at the mouth of the alley, and Moony stopped, wavering now between fight and flight. And—

Fight it was. OK, I thought. Even a rat will turn when cornered. That didn't mean I had to get involved. I could smell him too, the underpinning stench of him, like booze and dirt and that stinky sickly poet-smell. He was scared, I knew that. But he was also a god – albeit a beat-up Aspect of one – and that meant he'd *fight* like a god, and even an old alky god like Moony has his tricks.

Those two guys might yet have a shock coming.

For a moment they held their positions, two overcoats and a mad poet in a dark triangle under the single streetlight. Then they moved – the guys with that slick, fluid motion I'd seen before, Moony with a lurch and a yell and a flash from his fingertips. He'd cast *Týr* – a powerful rune – and I saw it flicker through the dark air like a shard of steel, hurtling towards the two not-quite-men. They dodged – no pas de deux could have had more grace – parting, then coming together again as the missile passed, moving in a tight axe-head formation towards the old god.

But throwing *Týr* had thrown Moony. It takes strength to cast the runes of the Elder Script, and most of his glam was already gone. He opened his mouth – to speak a cantrip, I thought – but before he could, the overcoats moved in with that spooky superhuman speed and I could smell their rankness once more, but so much stronger, like the inside of a badger's sett. They closed in, unbuttoning their coats as they ran – but *were* they running? Instead they seemed to *glide*, like boats, unfurling their long coats like sails to hide and envelop the beleaguered moongod.

He began to chant – the mead of poetry, you know – and for a second the drunken voice cracked and changed, becoming that of Mani in his full Aspect. A sudden radiance shone forth – the predators gave a single growl, baring their teeth – and for a moment I heard the chariot chant of the mad moongod, in a language you could never learn, but of which a single word could drive a mortal crazy with rapture, bring down the stars, strike a man dead – or raise him back to life again.

He chanted, and for a beat the hunters paused – and was that a single trace of a tear gleaming in the shadow of a black fedora? – and Mani sang a glamour of love and death, and of the beauty that is desolation and of the brief firefly that lights up the darkness – for a wing's beat, for a breath – before it gutters, burns and dies.

But the chant did not halt them for more than a second. Tears or not, these guys were *hungry*. They glided forward, hands outstretched, and now I could see *inside* their unbuttoned coats, and for a moment I was sure there was no body beneath their clothes, no fur or scale, no flesh or bone. There was just *the shadow*; the blackness of Chaos; a blackness beyond colour or even its absence; a hole in the world, all-devouring, all-hungry.

Brendan took a single step, and I caught him by the arm and held him back. It was too late anyway; old Moony was already done for. He went down – not with a crash but with an eerie sigh, as if he'd been punctured – and the creatures that now no longer even *looked* like men were on him like hyenas, fangs gleaming, static hissing in the folds of their garments.

There was nothing human in the way they moved. Nothing superfluous. They hoovered him up from blood to brain – every glamour, every spark, every piece of kith and kindling – and what they left looked less like a man than a cardboard cutout of a man left lying in the dirt of the alleyway.

Then they were gone, buttoning up their overcoats over the terrible absence beneath.

A silence. Brendan was crying. He always was the sensitive one. I wiped something (sweat, I think) from my face and waited for my breathing to return to normal.

'That was nasty,' I said at last. 'Haven't seen anything quite like that since the end of the world.'

'Did you hear him?' said Brendan.

'I heard. Who would have thought the old man had so much glam in him?'

My brother said nothing, but hid his eyes.

I suddenly realized I was hungry, and thought for a moment of suggesting a pizza, but decided against it. Bren was so touchy nowadays, he might have taken offence.

'Well, I'll see you later, I guess—' and I sloped off rather unsteadily, wondering why brothers are always so damned hard, and wishing I'd been able to ask him home.

I wasn't to know, but I wish I had – I'd never see that Aspect of him again.

I slept till late the next day. Awoke with a headache and a familiar post-cocktail nauseous feeling, then remembered – the way you remember doing something to your back when you were in the gym, but didn't realize how bad it was going to be until you'd slept on it – and sat bolt upright.

The guys, I thought. *Those two guys.*

I must have been drunker than I'd thought last night, because this morning the memory of them froze me to the core. Delayed shock; I know it well, and to combat its effects I called Room Service and ordered the works. Over coffee, bacon, pancakes and rivers of maple syrup, I worked on my recovery, and though I did pretty well, given the circumstances, I found I couldn't quite get the death of old Moony out of my mind, or the slick way the two overcoats had crawled over him, gobbling up his glam before buttoning up and back to business. Poetry in motion.

I pondered on my lucky escape – well, I guessed that if they hadn't sniffed out Moony first, then it would have been Yours Truly and Brother Bren for a double serving of Dish of the Day – but my heart was far from light as it occurred to me that if these guys were really after our kind, this was at best a reprieve, not a pardon, and that sooner or later those overcoats would be sharpening their teeth at my door.

So I finished breakfast and called Bren. But all I got was his answering machine, so I looked up the number of his restaurant and dialled it. The line was dead.

I would have tried his mobile, but, like I said, we're not close. I didn't know it, or the name of his girl, or even the number of his house. Too late now, right? Just goes to show. *Carpe diem*, and all that. And so I showered and dressed and went off in haste under gathering clouds to the Flying Pizza, Bren's place of work (but what a dumb name!), in the hope of getting some sense out of my twin.

It was there that I realized something was amiss. Ten blocks away I knew it already, and the sirens and the engines and the shouting and the smoke were just con-firmation. There was something ominous about those gathering thunderclouds, and the way they sat like a

Russian hat all spiky with needles of lightning above the scene of devastation. My heart sank lower the closer I got. Something was amiss, all right.

Looking around to ensure that I was unobserved, I cast the visionary rune *Bjarkán* with my left hand, and squinted through its spyglass shape. Smoke I saw; and lightning from the ground; my brother's face looking pale and strained; then fire; darkness; then, as I'd feared, the Shadow – and its minions, the wolves, the shadow hunters, boxed into their heavy overcoats.

Those guys, I thought, and cursed. *Again.*

And now I knew where I'd known them before – and they were pretty bad in that Aspect, too, though I had more on my plate at that time than I do nowadays, and I'll admit I didn't give them my full attention. I did now, though, casting runes of concealment about me as I skirted the funnel of black smoke, the funeral pyre of my brother's restaurant – and for all I knew, of Brendan himself, who had looked pretty wasted in my vision.

I got there at last, keeping an eye out for overcoats, to find fire engines and cop cars everywhere. A line had been cordoned off at the end of the road, and there were men trying to spray water over the great fizzing spume of fire that had already dug its roots deep into the Flying Pizza.

I could have told them they were wasting their time. You can't put out the work of a firegod – even a god of hearth fire – like it was just a squib. The flames sheeted up, thirty, forty, fifty feet high, clean and yellow and shot through with glamours that would probably have looked like dancing sparks to your kind, but which, if they'd touched you, would have stripped you, flesh to bone, in one.

And Brendan? I thought. *Could he still be alive somewhere?*

Well, if he was, he must have run. There was no way anyone could have survived that blaze. And it wasn't like Bren to flee the scene. He had turned and fought; I'd seen as much in my vision, and my brother was so dead set against the use of glamours among the Folk that he wouldn't have used them if he'd had any kind of choice.

I used Ós – the rune of mystery – to scry my brother's fate. I saw their faces, thin and wolfish; saw his smile, teeth bared so that for a second in my vision he could have been me, wild and furious and filled with killing rage. He could be OK, my brother, you know; it just took more time to fire him up. I saw him draw his mindsword – flaming, it was, with an edge that shivered translucent light. A sword that could have cut through granite or silk with the same easy slice; a sword I hadn't seen since the last time the world ended, a flickering flame of a firegod's sword that just *touched* the shadow inside an unbuttoned overcoat and went out like a puff of smoke.

Then, in the dark, they were on him. Question answered. Well, at least my brother went out in style.

I wiped my face and pondered the points. Point one: I was now an only twin. Point two: unless he'd taken his assailants with him (which I doubted), by now the two coats would be on my tail. Point three—

I was just embarking on point three when a heavy hand fell onto my shoulder, another grasped my arm just above the elbow, and then both applied a painful pressure, which soon became excruciating as the joint locked and a low, familiar voice rasped in my ear.

'Lucky. I should have known you were in this somehow. This shambles has got your mark all over it.'

I yelped and tried to free my arm. But the other bastard was holding me too tight.

'Move, and I'll break it,' snarled the voice. 'Hell, perhaps I ought to break it anyway. Just for old times' sake.'

I indicated to him that I'd rather he didn't. He locked my arm a little further – I felt it begin to go and screamed – then he shoved me hard towards the alley wall. I hit it, bounced, spun round with mindsword ready half-drawn and found myself staring into a pair of eyes as grim and colourless as a rainy day. Just my luck – a friend with a grievance, which is the only kind I tend to have nowadays.

Well, I say *friend*. He's one of our kind, but you know how it is. Fire and rainstorm – we don't get along. Besides, in his present Aspect he stood taller, weighed heavier, hit harder than me. His face was a thundercloud, and any thought I had of fighting the guy evaporated like cheap perfume. I sheathed the sword and took the better part of valour.

'Hey,' I said. 'It's Our Thor.'

He sniffed. 'Try anything, and I'll douse you cold,' he said. 'I've got an army of stormclouds ready to roll. You'll be out like a light before you can blink. Want to try it?'

'Did I ever? Nice greeting, friend. It's been a long time.'

He grunted. 'Arthur's the name in this present Aspect. Arthur Pluviôse – and you're dead.' He made it sound like some weird kind of naming ceremony.

'Wrong,' I said. '*Brendan's* dead. And if you think I'd be party to the murder of my own brother—'

'Wouldn't put it past you,' Arthur said, though I could tell the news had shaken him. 'Brendan's *dead?*' he repeated.

''Fraid so.' I was touched – I'd always thought he hated us both.

'Then this wasn't you?'

'My, you're fast.'

He glowered. 'Then how?'

'How else?' I shrugged. 'The Shadow, of course. Chaos. Black Surt. Choose your own damn metaphor.'

Arthur gave a long, soft sigh. As if it had preyed on his mind for such a long time that any news – even bad news – even *terrible* news – could come as a relief. 'So it's true,' he said. 'I was beginning to think—'

'Finally—'

He ignored the gibe and turned on me once more, his rainy-day eyes gleaming. 'It's the wolves, Lucky. The wolves are on the trail again.'

I nodded. Wolves, demons, no word exists in any tongue of the Folk to describe exactly what they were. I call them *ephemera*, though I had to admit there was nothing ephemeral about their present Aspect.

'Skól and Haiti, the Sky-Hunters, servants of the Shadow, Devourers of the Sun and Moon. And of anything else that happens to be in their way, for that matter. Brendan must have tried to tackle them. He never did have any sense.'

But I could tell he was no longer listening. 'The Sun and—'

'Moon.' I gave him the abridged version of the events of last night. He listened, but I could tell he was distracted.

'So, after the Moon, the Sun. Right?'

'I guess.' I shrugged. 'That is, assuming there's an Aspect of Sól in the neighbourhood, which, if there is—'

'There is,' said Arthur grimly. 'Her name's Sunny.' And there was something about his eyes as he said it, something even more ominous than the rain-swelled clouds above us, or his hand on my shoulder, horribly pally and heavy as lead, that made me think that I was in for an even lousier day than I'd had so far.

'Sunny,' I said. 'Then she'll be next.'

'Over my dead body,' said Arthur. 'And yours,' he added, almost as an afterthought, keeping his hand hard on my shoulder and smiling that dangerous, stormy smile.

'Sure. Why not?' I humoured him. I could afford to – I'm used to running, and I knew that, at a pinch, Lukas Wilde could disappear within an hour, leaving no trace.

He knew it too. His eyes narrowed, and above us the clouds began to move softly, gathering momentum like wool on a spindle. A dimple appeared at its nadir – soon, I knew, to become a funnel of air, stitched and barbed with deadly glamours.

'Remember what they say,' said Arthur, addressing me by my true name. 'Everywhere you go, you always take the weather with you.'

'You wrong me.' I smiled, though I'd never felt less like it. 'I'll be only too happy to help your friend.'

'Good,' said Arthur. He kept that hand on my shoulder,

though, and his smile was all teeth. 'We'll keep to the shadows. No need to involve the Folk any more than we have to. Right?'

It was a dark and stormy afternoon. I had an idea that it was going to be the first of many.

Sunny lived in Hell's Kitchen, in a third-floor apartment on a little back street. Not a place I visit often, which accounts for my not having spotted her sooner. Most of our kind take the discreet approach; gods have enemies too, you know, and we find it pays to keep our glam to ourselves.

But Sunny was different. For a start, according to Arthur (what a dumb name!) she didn't know what she was any more. It happens sometimes; you just forget. You get all wrapped up in your present Aspect; you start to think you're like everyone else. Perhaps that's what kept her safe for so long; they say gods look after drunks and half-wits and little children, and Sunny certainly qualified. Transpires that my old pal Arthur had been looking after her for nearly a year without her knowing it; making sure that she got the sunshine she needed to be happy, keeping sniffers and prowlers away from her door.

Because even the Folk start getting suspicious when someone like Sunny lives near by. It wasn't just the fact that it hadn't rained in months; that sometimes all of New York City could be under cloud but for the two or three streets surrounding her block; or the funny Northern Lights that sometimes shone in the sky above her apartment. It was *her*, just *her*, with her face and her smile, turning heads wherever she went. A man – a *god* – could fall in love.

Arthur had dropped his raingod Aspect and now looked more or less like a regular citizen, but I could tell he was making a hell of an effort. From five blocks away I could see him beginning to hold it in, the way a fat man holds in his gut when a pretty girl comes into the room. Then I saw her colours – from afar, like lights in the sky – and the look on his face – that look of truculent yearning – intensified a little.

He gave me the critical once-over. 'Tone it down a bit, will you?' he said.

Well, *that* was offensive. I'd looked a lot flashier as Lukas Wilde, but looking at Arthur right then I thought it a bad time to say so. I turned down the volume on my red coat, but kept my hair as it was, hiding my mismatched eyes behind a pair of snappy shades.

'Better?'

'You'll do.'

We were standing outside the place now. A standard apartment at the back of a lot of others; black fire escape, small windows, little roof garden throwing down wisps of greenery into the guttering. But at the window there was a light, something rather like sunlight, I guess, occasionally strobing here and there – following her movements as she wandered about her flat.

Some people have no idea of how to go unnoticed. In fact, it was astonishing that the wolves hadn't seized on her before. She'd not even tried to hide her colours, which was frankly beyond unwise, I thought – hell, she hadn't even pulled the drapes.

Arthur gave me one of his looks. 'We're going to protect her, Lucky,' he said. 'And *you're* going to be nice. OK?'

I made a face. 'I'm always nice. How could you possibly doubt me?'

She invited us in straightaway. No checking of credentials; no suspicious glance from behind the open drapes. I'd had her down as pretty, but dumb; now I saw she was a genuine innocent; a little-girl-lost in the big city. Not my type, naturally, but I could see what Arthur saw in her.

She offered us a cup of ginseng tea. 'Any friend of Arthur's,' she said, and I saw his painful grimace as he tried to fit his big fingers around the little china cup, all the while holding himself in so that Sunny could have her sunshine . . .

Finally, it was too much for him. He let it out with a gasp of release, and the rain started to come down in snakes, hissing into the gutters.

Sunny looked dismayed. 'Damn *rain*!'

Arthur looked like someone had punched him hard, right in the place where thunder gods keep their ego. He gave that feeble smile again. 'It doesn't make you feel safe?' he said. 'You don't think there's a kind of poetry in the sound, like little hammers beating down onto the rooftops?'

Sunny shook her head. 'Yuck.'

I lit the fire with a discreet cantrip and a fingering of the rune *Kaen*. Little flames shot out of the grate and danced winsomely across the hearth. It was a good trick, though I say it myself – especially as it was an electric fire.

'Neat,' said Sunny, smiling again.

Arthur gave a low growl.

'So – have you seen anything strange around here lately?' Stupid damn question, I told myself. Move a sun goddess on to the third floor of a Manhattan brownstone, and you're apt to see more than the occasional pyrotechnics. 'No guys in suits?' I went on. 'Dark overcoats and fedora hats, like some-one from a bad Fifties comic strip?'

'Oh, *those* guys.' She poured more tea. 'Yeah, I saw them yesterday. They were sniffing around in the alleyway.' Sunny's blue eyes darkened a little. 'They didn't look friendly. What do they want?'

I was going to tell her about Bren, and what had happened to old man Moony, but Arthur stopped me with a glance. Sunny has that effect, you know; makes guys want to do stupid things. Stupid, noble, self-sacrificing things – and I was beginning to understand that I was going to be a part of it, whether or not I wanted to be.

'Nothing *you* need to worry about,' Arthur said with a big smile, clamping a hand on my upper arm and marching me onto the balcony. 'They're just some guys we're looking for. We'll camp out here tonight and keep an eye out for them for you. Any trouble, we'll be here. No need for you to worry. OK?'

'OK,' said Sunny.

'OK,' I said between gritted teeth (my arm felt like it had

been pounded several times with a hammer). I waited until we were alone, and Sunny had drawn the curtains, then I turned on him. 'What's the deal?' I said. 'We can't hold back ephemera. You must know that by now, right? You saw what they did to Moony and Bren. Our only chance is to outrun them, to take your lady-friend with us and to run like the blazes to another city, to another continent if we can, where the Shadow has less influence—'

Arthur looked stubborn. 'I won't run.'

'Fine. Well, it's been a blast – *Ow*! My *arm*!'

'And neither will you,' said Our Thor.

'Well, if you put it *that* way—'

I may be a trifle impetuous, but I know when to surrender to *force majeure*. Arthur had his mind set on both of us being heroes. My only remaining choice was whether to set *my* mind to helping him, thereby possibly saving both our hides, or to make a run for it as soon as the bastard's guard was down . . .

Well, I might have gone down either path, but just then I caught sight of our boys in the alleyway, sniffing and snarling like wolves in suits, and I was down to no choice at all. I drew my mindsword – he drew his. Glamours and runes distressed the night air. Not that *they* would help us, I thought; they hadn't helped my brother Bren, or the mad old moon god. And Shadow – or Chaos, if you prefer – had plenty of glamours of its own with which to strike down three renegade gods, fugitives left over from the End of the World—

'Hey! Up here!' yelled Our Thor.

Two pairs of eyes turned up towards us. A hiss, like static as the ephemera tuned in to our whereabouts. A glint of teeth as they grinned – and then they were crawling up the fire escape, all pretence of humanity gone, slick beneath those boxy black coats, nothing much in there but tooth and claw, like poetry with an appetite.

Oh, great, I thought. Way to keep a low profile, Our Thor. Was it an act of self-sacrifice, a ploy to attract their attention, or could he possibly have a plan? If he did, then it would be a first. Mindless self-sacrifice was about his level. I wouldn't have minded *that* much, but it was clear that in his boundless generosity he also meant to sacrifice *me*.

'Lucky!' It was raining again. Great ropes and coils of thunderous rain that thrashed down onto our bowed heads, all gleaming in the neon lights in shades of black and orange. From the static-ridden sky, great flakes of snow lumbered down. Well, that's what happens around a raingod under stress; but that didn't stop me getting soaked, and wishing I'd brought my umbrella. It didn't stop the ephemera, though. Even the bolts of lightning that crashed like stray missiles into the alleyway (I have skills too, and I was using them like the blazes by then) had no effect on the wolves of Chaos, whose immensely slick and somehow snakelike forms were now poised on the fire escape beneath us, ten feet away and ready to pounce.

One did – a mindbolt flew. I recognized the rune *Hagall*. One of my colleague's most powerful, and yet it passed right through the ephemera with a squeal of awesome feedback, then the creature was on us again, unbuttoning its overcoat, and now I was sure there were *stars* in there, stars and the mindless static of space—

'Look,' I said. 'What do you want? Girls, money, power, fame – I can get all those things for you, no problem. I've got influence in this world. Two handsome, single guys like yourselves – you could make a killing in showbiz—'

Perhaps not the wisest choice of words.

The first wolf leered. '*Killing*,' it said. By then I could smell it again, and I knew that words couldn't save me. First, the thing was ravenous. Second, *nothing* with that level of halitosis could possibly hope to make it in the music business. Some guys, I knew, had come pretty close. My daughter Hel, for instance, has, in spite of her – shall we say *alternative* – looks, a serious fan base in certain circles. But not these guys. I mean. *Ew.*

I flung a handful of mindrunes then. *Týr; Kaen; Hagall; Ýr* – but none of them even slowed it down. The other wolf was on to us now, and Arthur was wrestling with it, caught in the flaps of its black coat. The balcony was pulling away from the wall; sparks and shards of runelight hissed into the torrential rain.

Damn it, I thought. *I'm going to die wet.* And I flung up a shield using the rune *Sól,* and with the last, desperate surge of my glam I cast *all* the fire-runes of the First Aettir at the two creatures that once had been wolves but were now grim incarnations of revenge, because nothing escapes from Chaos, not Thunder, not Wildfire, not even the Sun—

'Are you guys OK out there?' It was Sunny, peering through a gap in the curtains. 'Do you want some more ginseng tea?'

'Ah – no, thanks,' said Arthur, now with a demon wolf in each hand and that stupid grin on his face again. 'Look, ah, Sunny, go inside. I'm kinda busy right now—'

The thing that Our Thor had been holding at bay finally escaped his grasp. It didn't go far, though; it sprang at me and knocked me backwards against the rail. The balcony gave way with a screech, and we all fell together three floors down. I hit the deck – damned hard – with the ephemera on top of me, and all the fight knocked out of me, and I knew that I was finished.

Sunny peered down from her window. 'Do you need help?' she called to me.

I could see right *into* the creature now, and it was grim – like those fairytales where the sisters get their toes chopped off and the bad guys get pecked to death by crows and even the little mermaid has to walk on razorblades for the rest of her life for daring to fall in love . . . Except that I knew Sunny had got the Disney version instead, with all the happy endings in it, and the chipmunks and rabbits and the god-damned squirrels (I hate squirrels!) singing in harmony, where even the wolves are good guys and no one ever *really* gets hurt—

I gave her a sarcastic smile. 'Yeah, wouldya?' I said.

'OK,' said Sunny, and pulled the drapes and stepped out on to the balcony.

And then something very weird happened.

I was watching her from the alleyway, my arms pinned to my sides now and the ephemera straddling me with its overcoat spread like a vulture about to spear an eyeball. The cold was so intense that I couldn't feel my hands at all, and the stench of the thing made my head swim, and the rain was pounding into my face and my glam was bleeding out so fast that I knew I had seconds, no more—

So the first thing she did was put her umbrella up.

Ignored Arthur's desperate commands – besides, he was still wrestling the second ephemera. His colours were flaring garishly; runelight whirled around them both, warring with the driving rain.

And then she smiled.

It was as if the sun had come out. Except that it was night, and the light was, like, sixty times more powerful than the brightest light you've ever known, and the alley lit up a luminous white, and I screwed my eyes shut to prevent them from being burnt there and then out of their sockets, and all these things happened at once.

First of all, the rain stopped. The pressure on my chest disappeared, and I could move my arms again. The light, which had been too intense even to see when it first shone out, diffused itself to a greenish-pink glow. Birds on the rooftops began to sing. A scent of something floral filled the air – strangest of all in that alleyway, where the smell of piss was predominant – and someone put a hand on my face and said: 'It's OK, sweetie. They've gone now.'

Well, that was it. I opened my eyes. I figured that either I'd taken more concussion than I'd thought, or there was something Our Thor hadn't told me. He was standing over me, looking self-conscious and bashful. Sunny was kneeling at my side, heedless of the alleyway dirt, and her blue dress was shining like the summer sky, and her bare feet were like little white birds, and her sugar-blonde hair fell over my face and I was glad she really wasn't my type, because that lady was nothing but trouble. And she gave me a smile like a summer's day, and Arthur's face went dangerously red, and Sunny said: 'Lucky? Are you OK?'

I rubbed my eyes. 'I think so. What happened to Skól and Haiti?'

'Those guys?' she said. 'Oh, they had to go. I sent them back into Shadow.'

Now Arthur was looking incredulous. 'How do you know about Shadow?' he said.

'Oh, Arthur, you're so *sweet*.' Sunny pirouetted to her feet and planted a kiss on Our Thor's nose. 'As if I could have lived here this long and not have known I was different—' She looked at the illuminated sky. 'Northern Lights,' she said happily. 'We ought to have them more often here. But I really do appreciate it,' she went on. 'You guys looking out for me, and everything. If things had been different, if we hadn't been made from such different elements, then maybe you and I could have – you know—'

Arthur's face went, if possible, even redder.

'So, what are you going to do now?' she said. 'I guess we're safe – for a while, at least. But Chaos knows about us now. And the Shadow never really gives up.'

I thought about it. And then an idea came to me. I said: 'Have you ever thought of a career in entertainment? I could find a job for you with the band—'

I wondered if she could sing. Most celestial spheres can, of course, and anyway, she'd light up the place just by stepping on to the stage – we'd save a fortune on pyrotechnics.

She gave that megawatt smile of hers. 'Is Arthur in the band, too?'

I looked at him. 'He could be, I guess. There's always room for a drummer.'

Come to think of it, there's a lot to be said for going on the road right now. New people, new lineup, new places to go—

'That would be nice.' Her face was wistful. His was like that of a sick puppy, and it made me even more relieved that I'd never been the romantic type. I tried to imagine the outcome: sun goddess and thunder god on stage together, every night—

I could see it now, I thought. Wildfire, on tour again. I mean, we're talking rains of fish, equatorial Northern Lights; hurricanes, eclipses, solar flares, flash floods – and lightning. Lots of lightning.

Might be a little risky, of course.

But all the same – a hell of a show.

Cookie

A couple of years ago I joined a diet club and managed to lose a lot of weight. I gained it back in stories, though; many of them about various aspects of food, and why it means so much to us. This is the tale of one woman's dark and complex relationship with baked goods. She isn't me, but I know how she feels.

The thought that she might be pregnant came to her quite suddenly, during the ad break for *CSI*. She had been eating a packet of Mr Kipling's French Fancies, starting with the pink ones (her favourites) and finishing with the brown, which she liked least because of their unappealing colour. She sometimes thought of leaving the brown ones altogether, but it seemed untidy to do so, and she always ended up eating them anyway.

Maggie liked to nibble when watching TV. It made her feel safer and more relaxed. Besides, the evenings were the only time she didn't feel guilty for eating. She always felt so self-conscious at work, with her sandwich and her muesli bar. As if the others were watching her – which, she thought, they probably were – thirteen stone, and look at her, eating carbs, for heaven's sake. And so she waited till she got home, and cooked herself a nice little meal – something simple, like pasta or rice – and poured herself a glass of wine—

But then, sometimes, it got out of hand. Things always taste better while watching TV. Especially sweet things, Maggie thought. Sweet things, white things, sugar-pink-and-yellow things. And every twenty minutes, the ad breaks were there to remind her that ice cream was good, that chocolate made you happy, and that Betty Crocker frozen cheesecakes were now on sale at Iceland.

And so Maggie ate. What else did she have? She ate Digestive biscuits, and raspberry buns, and coconut tarts, and chocolate-chip cookies and mini Swiss rolls and Rice Crispie squares and lemon meringue pie. Unlike most people, Mr Kipling and Betty Crocker could always be relied upon. They gave Maggie security, provided little islands of sweetness in a world grown increasingly sour.

But now this. This recurring thought. *What if I were pregnant?* At first she almost laughed – what a joke, the thirteen-stone Immaculate Conception – but still the thought kept coming back, like a hopeful stray that had once been fed. *What if I were pregnant?*

Certainly, she looked the part. The stomach that had once been flat was soft and round, like a half-baked loaf. Her arms, too, had softened and sagged; her thighs were pale and dimpled. Of course, the pregnancy wouldn't show. Not yet;

it was too early. Maggie knew from experience that nothing much showed till the fourth month.

Of course, she had been thinner then. Even during her pregnancy, she'd never weighed more than ten stone. She'd been anxious about the baby weight. Well, more anxious about Jack, really. Jack was Maggie's husband, and he liked to keep in shape. He ran five miles every day, made jokes about her growing bump. Except that they weren't really jokes – and Maggie knew it. Being pregnant made her crave bakery products. Iced buns; bread of all kinds; doughnuts and biscuits and flapjacks and cakes. Jack – who never ate carbs at all – tried to get her to eat raw, crunchy snacks, but her system rebelled. She just couldn't eat. An apple or a carrot stick just wasn't the same as a Krispy Kreme.

She tried to take up knitting instead, made little bonnets and sets of bootees, but that didn't stop her appetite. In fact, it only made things worse. All those balls of pastel wool in marshmallow-pink and vanilla ice cream intensified her cravings.

Jack started to avoid her. She was swelling up, of course. Not just the bump, but her face and legs. Jack didn't like curves. Maggie knew that. He liked his girls to look like boys. They worked for the same company, but Jack had an office, in which he stayed, while Maggie just had a cubicle, and so she rarely saw him at work, just as she rarely saw him at home.

It happened very gradually. At first he made it sound as if he were being considerate. *I know you're tired, Mags. Why don't you have an early night?* And she *was* tired. Desperately so. Whatever her body was going through, it seemed to need a lot of rest as well as a lot of food. And so she went to bed early, while Jack made excuses to stay up late. And straight after work, he went to the gym, while Maggie stayed in and knitted bootees, and watched *CSI* and *Fringe* and *Lost* and tried to think of babies' names, and tried not to think too much about cake.

It worked, or did for a while, at least. She even managed to lose some weight. Not enough to count, of course. Besides, by then Jack didn't care. He had his own pre-natal routine. He took it all very seriously. He ran every morning at six o'clock and worked out at the gym in the evenings. *I'll need to be fit to keep up with my son.* Once more, he made it sound like a joke, though Maggie knew it wasn't. He bought little outfits in shades of blue; little sports shirts, shorts and bootees made to look like trainers. Sometimes Maggie asked herself why Jack had wanted a child at all – he seemed to view the experience as a kind of desperate marathon. What – or who – was he running from? And why did he have to run at all?

She tried to persuade him to stay at home, but it didn't seem to do any good. *Why should I put my life on hold just because you're pregnant?* he said. *You could come to the gym with me if you really wanted to. But all you care about nowadays is baby names and baby clothes – oh, and stuffing your face, of course—*

Which was unfair, Maggie knew. She'd totally stopped eating for two. In fact, she barely ate for one, most of it rice cakes and carrot sticks. She hated those things, they made her feel sick, but she needed to get things under control. She was already fifteen pounds overweight, according to Jack's digital scale. She felt disgusting. Fat and obscene. For the first time, she began to suffer from morning sickness. That was all right at first, she thought. It took away her appetite. But even on hummus and carrot sticks, she wasn't losing any weight. And that new roll of fat under her chin seemed to be getting fuller.

So Maggie started to work out. She forced herself to go to the gym. Went on the treadmill and rowing machines, pounding red-faced and sweaty. She'd never liked working out. She'd never needed to do it before. But Jack seemed to think that it would help, and Maggie thought that they could do it together. But Jack didn't like to run alongside her. *It puts me off my rhythm*, he said. And so she watched him from afar, trying to keep pace with him, feeling tired and slightly sick and thinking of doughnuts and *CSI*—

And then she lost the baby. At twenty-one weeks (just a little too soon). *It could have happened to anyone*, the specialist told her. *It wasn't your fault*. Except that it hadn't happened to anyone. It had happened to her. And whose fault was that?

As for Jack – well, Jack just kept running. Straight out of the kitchen door one day, straight into the arms of a girl from the gym, and Maggie was left with all this useless pre-baby padding and grief, and this appetite that wouldn't let go, that nothing seemed to satisfy.

Jack thought she should go to counselling. Maggie thought Jack could go to hell. She saw him some days, in the park, running with his new girl. Jack liked lean, athletic blondes.

The latest one was called Cherry, which Maggie found hilarious. It seemed that even when it came to girlfriends, Jack favoured healthy snacking.

Which all made this growing conviction of hers – *what if I were pregnant?* – all the more difficult to swallow. To be pregnant, Maggie argued in vain, there had to be a man on the scene. Jack was gone, and the only men in her life nowadays were Mr Kipling and the heroes of the TV shows she liked to watch late into the night. And yet—

The signs were definitely there. Her belly had grown. Her breasts were swollen and tender. In the months that had followed her miscarriage, she'd always felt so empty. No matter what she ate, it seemed that nothing could fill the baby-shaped hole at the pit of her stomach. But now, there was something. A fullness, she thought. A sense of possibility. *I'm eating for two*, she told herself, in the flickering light of the TV screen, and somehow it felt almost true, even though it couldn't be. *Miracles happen. I know they do. Life sometimes gives you a second chance.*

One day, she picked up her knitting again. She found it therapeutic. She knitted a set of baby clothes in exactly the same shade of sugar-pink as the icing on a Mr Kipling's French Fancy. That gave her an appetite, which led to another set of clothes, this time in lemon-cupcake yellow, and a set of bootees in vanilla off-white. This time, there was no Jack around to curb her body's instincts. Day by day she watched her belly grow rounder, and was aware of a corresponding sense of happiness and pride. So what if she didn't have a man? This baby would be all hers. *My bun in the oven*, she thought to herself as she opened a pack of Bakewell tarts. This time around, there was no sense of guilt. After all, she was eating for two.

By the fifth month of her mysterious pregnancy, other people had started to stare. Maggie could feel the sidelong glances, the unspoken words from her colleagues at work. She had given up sandwiches and muesli bars. Now that she was eating for two, she could indulge her cravings. And so at lunchtimes, at her desk, she ate chunky Cornish pasties from Greggs, whole packs of iced buns in pink or white, and maybe even a doughnut or two, comfortingly stodgy and soft in their thick coating of caster sugar. She wondered when someone would ask her when the baby was due. But no one dared – after all, they must have known all about Jack's bit on the side. Maggie's friends in the office weren't really her friends at all, but Jack's, which meant that there was no one left to ask her the question that must have been eating them up over all these weeks – could Maggie *really* be pregnant?

But Maggie found she didn't care. Let them whisper all they liked. The fact that no one knew for sure made the baby all the more wonderful. *You're mine*, she told it tenderly. *All mine, little Cookie.*

Maggie found that bakery names were the ones that came to her most readily. Sally Lunn. Angel Cake. Quirky, but appealing. Terms of endearment were always sweet: Sugar, Cupcake, Cookie, Honey-bun, Sweetie-pie. And this time, there was no doubt in her mind that the baby would be a girl. She needed no scan to confirm it. She hadn't been to the doctor once. Why should she? She felt fine. She'd been through all that the first time. Doctors hadn't helped her then. This time, she could cope on her own.

She started feeling drowsy at work, especially after lunch. Some days she could barely keep awake. Her supervisor, Chloë, mentioned it, and finally Maggie couldn't keep the secret to herself any more. Blushing madly, she told her: 'Well, I'm doing my best, but you know, in my condition I get very tired—'

'Your condition?' Chloë said.

'Well, you know. My pregnancy.'

Chloë stared at her. 'What?' she said.

It wasn't a very flattering stare. But then, Maggie had never liked Chloë much – a skinny redhead who looked fourteen and ate nothing but low-fat yoghurts for lunch. What did she know, anyway? How could she possibly understand?

Word got around after that, of course. Her colleagues stared at her openly now as she ate lunch in her cubicle. Maggie didn't care, though; she needed to keep her strength up. And the others were simply jealous, she thought. *Jealous of you and me, Cookie.*

A week later, Jack came to see her while she was on her tea break. 'Is it true you've been saying you're pregnant?' he said. 'Chloë says you told her you were.'

Maggie shrugged. 'Well, I am,' she said.

Jack looked startled. 'Have you been seeing anyone?'

'Why should I?' said Maggie. 'I feel fine. Oh—' She paused. 'I see what you mean.'

She knew that if she'd met someone else, then Jack would have been the first to know. Jack was a genius at collecting (and disseminating) news, and although he clearly wasn't interested in getting back with Maggie, a boyfriend on her horizon would have certainly caused a ripple or two.

He looked her critically up and down. 'You look terrible,' he said.

'Really? How very like you to say that.'

At least he had the grace to blush. 'Mags, I didn't mean that. I meant you've put on a bit of weight.'

'Of course I have. I'm pregnant.'

'But you're not, Mags, are you?' he said.

Maggie shrugged. 'How would you know?' She looked at him, thinking suddenly that *he* was the one who looked terrible. His cheekbones were saggy and over-pronounced, the wrists that protruded from his shirt-cuffs unexpectedly bony. Had he lost weight, she asked herself? Was he working out too much?

'You don't look so good yourself,' she said. 'You still with Cherry, or has that fresh-fruit diet turned out not to be nutritious enough?'

'Don't try to divert, Mags.' Jack liked to think that because he'd watched *In Treatment* he knew about psychoanalysis. 'We're talking about you here. This story you've been telling people. This story about being pregnant.'

Maggie smiled. 'Why assume it isn't true?'

'Well, because – it just *isn't*,' he said, sounding like a little boy. 'Where would you get a baby from? It isn't mine, and there's no one else. So what are you going to give birth to? A family pack of Krispy Kremes?'

That should have upset her, Maggie thought. But this

pregnancy seemed to bring with it a sweet new kind of serenity. And so she simply smiled at Jack in that new, tranquil way she had, and said: 'You'll see in four months, won't you, Jack? Come on. Have a Digestive.'

After that, the news was out. Everyone had their opinion on Maggie's mysterious pregnancy. Opinions which differed only in that some believed she was crazy, and others thought she was making it up to try to get Jack's attention. Both points of view were so ridiculous that Maggie didn't even try to argue with them, but simply went on listening to that sweet, warm feeling in her belly, and feeding it with bread and cake and biscuits and pies.

Why had she ever believed that she needed a *man* to produce a child? The nursery rhyme had it right all along. *Sugar and spice and all things nice* – that's what little girls were made of, and Cookie – yes, that *was* her name – knew exactly what she needed. She became more demanding as time went on; gave Maggie a craving for sweet rice pudding; for apple pie with clotted cream; for strawberry shortcake, treacle tarts, croissants with honey and crusty French loaves.

By the seventh month, Maggie was so tired and heavy that all she really wanted was to stay at home and watch TV, coddled in a blanket, with a jug of pink lemonade on the side, or maybe a pot of hot chocolate and a plate of warm scones with apricot jam. She called in her maternity leave, and no one even questioned it. *Compassionate leave*, the letter said. Maggie couldn't be bothered to protest. They didn't believe in her Cookie? Who cared? Maggie didn't need any of them. A few people called. She knew they meant well. But Maggie didn't want their help. Nor did she want diet tips, or bereavement counselling, or relationship therapy, or any of the solutions they offered to her phantom pregnancy. Cookie wasn't a phantom, she knew. Cookie, at seven months, already had a strong enough personality to make those people feel like ghosts in comparison. Cookie was *warm*, Cookie was *sweet*, Cookie was a bundle of love – and Cookie was always hungry. And so Maggie left her job without the slightest hint of regret, and devoted her time to Cookie. The decision somehow seemed to have given her more energy. She started to do her own baking, which meant that she didn't have to go out as often. She sent for some paint from the DIY shop and finally painted the baby room – the room that she and Jack had never quite got round to preparing. She painted it in rosewater-pink, with a border of stencilled cupcakes. She made a set of curtains in the same printed cupcake design. She was just assembling the crib (blond wood, with bedding to match the curtains), keeping her strength up with the help of a pack of Wagon Wheels, when the doorbell rang.

It was Jack. This time, he looked even worse than before: unshaven, pallid and rail-thin. He was wearing his running shoes and a grey T-shirt over scruffy jeans, and he smelt of sweat, as if he'd just got back from the gym. He took one look at the baby room and sat down hard, as if he'd been pushed.

'Oh, Mags. What's going on?'

Maggie gave him a sympathetic smile. Some men took it hard, she knew; especially men like Jack. The bond between mother and child is so strong that fathers are often excluded. Still, that was hardly *her* fault – after all, Jack was the one who had written himself out of the picture. Now that she was almost due, perhaps he regretted leaving her. Too bad that Maggie didn't care. Cookie was all she needed now.

She sat down beside him on the couch. It sagged alarmingly as she did so. The baby weight had really come on over the past two or three months, but Maggie didn't feel bad at all. This time, she felt beautiful. Her skin glowed. Her hair shone. Her body expanded like warm dough. She smelt of baking, of sweetness, of yeast. She could see it in the way he looked at her, his eyes half afraid, half awed, like a child's.

'What are you doing?' he said again.

'I'm getting things ready,' Maggie said. 'It won't be long now before Cookie's here.'

'Cookie?' said Jack.

'That's her name. I never told anyone that before.' Maggie smiled again, feeling glad. He'd left her, of course, but Jack was still the man she'd loved, and it seemed only right that he should know the baby's name before it was born. She laid a protective hand over her distended belly. Inside, Cookie was fast asleep, although she would soon be hungry again. Maggie wondered whether Jack would put out his hand to feel her bump, as he had when they were together. She wondered if she wanted him to, or whether that was all in the past.

But Jack was looking agitated. His mouth pulled sharply to one side, as if he'd been running too fast. 'Maggie,' he said, looking at her. 'You have to stop this. Get some help.'

'Help with what?' Maggie said. 'I told you, I'm fine. The baby, too.'

'What baby?' said Jack. 'Whose baby is this? Where did it come from? Pizza Hut? And now you're taking maternity leave – picking out baby clothes – doing all *this* . . .' He waved a hand at the open door of the baby room with its cupcake trim. 'Maggie!' he said. 'You have to get *help*!'

'Are you volunteering?' she said, making it sound like a joke.

Jack shrugged. 'I blame myself. I shouldn't have run out like that. But losing the baby—' He looked away. 'I didn't know what to do, Mags. I acted like an idiot. I hope you know how sorry I am.'

'Sorry?' said Maggie, feeling numb.

'I shouldn't have left you. I know that now. I've told Cherry it's over. I can move back whenever you like—'

'Move *back*?' Maggie said.

He nodded. 'I'll look after you. I'll make sure you get back on your feet. I've already talked to the people at work. They'll hold your job for as long as you need. One in four people in the UK suffer from depression at some time in their lives. We'll get you some counselling, maybe some Prozac or lithium. And then we can start working out again – make you feel better about yourself. As soon as you start to lose the weight, you'll get over this – *delusion*.'

'You think I'll get over it?' Maggie said. Now, at last, she was angry. 'You think the baby's all in my mind? *Here!* Feel *this*!' She grabbed his hand and laid it on her belly. 'Can you feel her kicking, Jack?'

Jack pulled away, and muttered: 'Intestinal gas. That's all it is.'

'You think?' said Maggie.

'Oh, Maggie. I *know*.'

'All right, then. Get out.' She was shaking now. Cookie was making her hungry again. There was a cold rhubarb crumble in the fridge; with a scoop of ice cream it would be just what the doctor ordered. 'I don't have time for this right now,' she said, seeing Jack's astonished face. 'I have work to do, *proper* work, as opposed to working *out*—'

'Maggie, please. I love you,' said Jack.

He meant it, too; she could see it now. But she also knew that it was too late. Cookie was more important. And – if he really wanted her – Jack would have to make a choice.

She said: 'If you can prove that you want to be a proper father to my baby—'

'There *is* no baby!' shouted Jack. 'There never was! You made it up! You're fat because you *eat* all the time, not because you're pregnant!'

'Don't listen to him, Cookie,' she said. 'We don't need him any more.' She opened the door. 'Goodbye,' she said. 'I'm sorry it didn't work out for you.'

After that, Maggie screened her calls and put a spy-hole in the front door. She was too busy getting things ready for Cookie to deal with interference. She'd decided on a home delivery – she found it too stressful leaving the house – besides, she didn't need help, she thought. All she needed was peace and quiet.

No one saw her for weeks after that. No one answered

the phone any more; no one came to answer the door. Jack called by several times, without success, although once or twice he could have sworn he heard movement from inside the house. She'd changed the locks. He wasn't surprised. His first attempt to involve the police met with polite indifference, his second with open amusement.

Had there been a crime, sir? Did Jack have any reason to believe his ex-wife might be at risk? Had she robbed a bakery? Jack left feeling angry and humiliated – as well as increasingly anxious. Something was going on in that house. Behind those neatly drawn curtains. He started to watch the deliveries that came to the door every couple of days. Most were from various bakeries, but some were from shops supplying babycare products. Maggie never spoke to the people who made these deliveries. Instead, they left the goods on the porch, just inside the outer door. One day, watching from his car, Jack saw a large, indistinct figure wrapped in a pink dressing-gown emerge to collect a pastry-box. It moved with a curious waddling gait, then vanished into the darkened house.

Christ, he thought. *She's got so big!*

The next time, he knew what he had to do. No one else would help him. He waited until the baker's van came with the morning delivery. Then he jumped out of his own car and levelled a smile at the deliveryman.

'Thanks. I'll take it in,' he said.

The deliveryman looked uncertain.

'It's all right. It's my house,' said Jack, hefting the covered tray on to his shoulder. It smelt of bread, and the richer scent of butter pastry and slow-cooked fruit. 'My wife's pregnant,' he explained. 'She's been practically living on these things.'

'Well, OK,' said the deliveryman, and watched Jack step on to the porch. He *looked* as if he lived there, of course. Walked in as if he owned the place. And he said his wife was pregnant – well, only a pregnant woman, he thought, could want to eat so many pies.

At least, this is what the deliveryman would tell the police some time later. At the time, he simply shrugged and set off without thinking at all. And Jack, still carrying the tray, opened the door into Maggie's living room and looked inside at what was there –

He'd had visions of Maggie lying in the dark, huddled under a duvet. In fact, the room was brightly lit. A series of lamps with rose-coloured shades had been placed at intervals along the floor. Dozens of strings of fairy lights had been left to tumble over the furniture and to proliferate across the floor. Mobiles hung from the ceiling: little bells, cut-out shapes, crystals that reflected the light. And on every surface there were cakes, arranged on cake stands and doilies; little sugared fairy cakes; iced buns with cherries on top; macaroons and lemon tarts and apple pies and rich sweet rolls all stacked up in tiers to the ceiling and gleaming in the coloured light like treasure from Aladdin's cave.

To Jack it looked like a combination of Santa's Grotto and the Gingerbread House, and if there had been any doubt in his mind that his wife had run completely mad, it vanished in the face of this – this child's-eye view of fairyland.

Barbie's pleasure-dome. *Jesus wept.*

'Maggie? Are you there?' he called.

Stupid to think she'd be anywhere else. But there was no answer. The room was still, except for the twirling of paper mobiles and the tinkling of a music box, somewhere in another room.

Jack put down the bakery tray. The scent of sweet things was overwhelming. The door to the adjoining room was slightly ajar. He opened it. It was the room they'd both agreed would belong to the baby, when it was born – except that Maggie had wanted to paint it pink, whereas Jack had wanted to paint it blue, which meant that the room had stayed as white and bare as the day they'd laid their baby to rest in a box supplied by the hospital; something like a bakery box, lined in cheap white satin.

Now all that had changed, of course. Jack had noticed the last time he'd called. Now, the room was a nursery, brightly lit and painted pink; scatter-cushions on the floor, and a wooden crib in the centre, half shielded from view by curtains.

Jack took a couple of steps into the room. Maggie wasn't there. But something was playing a tinkling tune, and a lantern by the side of the crib was revolving slowly, casting little arpeggi of coloured light against the newly painted walls.

'Maggie?' He'd meant it to sound alert, in charge. But his voice in this alien room was lost, smothered beneath that sugary scent, that pastel drift of cushions and drapes. He was alone in the room, and yet he was aware of a presence, a kind of fullness in the air. It was almost as if something were there, something that was breathing.

That crib. That bloody crib, he thought. Standing there so quietly. Looking as if it belonged there, as if there could possibly be a reason for all this paraphernalia. And those curtains drawn across it, like a tent, hiding whatever was inside.

Of course, there was no baby, he thought. There couldn't be a baby. The baby had never existed outside his wife's desperate imagination. *Cookie*, she'd called it. *Kooky* was right. Whatever was in there – a teddy, a doll – was just a substitute for what she had lost, a symptom of her unreason, proof that he was right to interfere—

He would confront her, Jack told himself. He *did* still love her, after all. Once he'd forced her to face the truth, then maybe they could try again, go back to the way they'd been before. He took a step towards the crib. The scent of sweet things intensified. A sugary, floury, milky scent, like pancake batter or cookie dough. Once more he thought he heard something shift and sigh behind the patterned curtain. Was there something alive in there? A rabbit, maybe even a cat?

'Jack? What are you doing in here?'

It was Maggie. Soundless in spite of her bulk, she must have come up behind him. He turned, feeling guilty despite himself. Mumbled something about being worried about her.

'Worried?' She smiled. 'Well, as you can see, both of us are doing just fine.'

'Both of you?'

'Cookie and me.'

Now Jack could stand it no longer. He turned and stepped

up to the crib, reaching out a trembling hand to yank aside the curtain. The cupcake-printed fabric tore. A row of bells jingled merrily. Jack looked inside the crib, his mouth falling open in sudden surprise as he saw what was lying inside—

Maggie smiled. 'She's perfect,' she said. 'Isn't she, Jack?'

Jack said nothing, but stared and stared.

'I knew things would be OK if only I trusted my instincts. *Sugar and spice and all things nice. That's what little girls are made of.* Isn't that right, Cookie?' Maggie smiled. Her doughy face was radiant. She reached down into the open crib and picked up what was lying there, and Jack began to back away, away from his wife and out of the room, feeling blindly for the door, almost tripping over the strings of fairy lights that twisted like vines over the floor of the living room.

Maggie watched him go, and smiled. She thought it might take Jack some time to come to terms with fatherhood. She looked down at the baby again, and smelt that milky baby-smell. *Sugar and spice and all things nice—*

And then she kissed the thing in her arms and said:

'Hey, Cookie. Daddy's here.'

Ghosts in the Machine

I wrote this story for my daughter, a great lover of Phantom of the Opera, *who always believed that Christine Daaé ended up with the wrong man . . .*

He always takes the graveyard shift. He likes the dark and the solitude. The glow of the screen and a few LEDs are enough to mark his passing, and besides, he could do the work blindfold. He has been working here fifteen years, ever since he could patch a cable, and now he knows every inch of the place, every file in the archives. This man has nursed the studio from analog to digital. He is far more than an engineer, far more than a sound technician. To all intents and purposes, the man *is* Phantom Radio. He knows every secret, hears every word spoken on or off the airwaves. Every piece of equipment here has passed between his fingers.

But to most of the day people, he is just the man who keeps the machine alive. Some know his voice from the sound box; few have ever seen his face. At night, there's even less chance of that; the station runs on a skeleton staff, and the late shows are merely recordings, broadcast to give the illusion of life while the day people sleep at home in their beds and he can have the place to himself.

This is when he is happiest. When he can be completely alone. In the lobby, there's just one security guard; but he never pays attention to *him*, and from midnight to five in the morning, Phantom Radio whispers and hums with the seashell voices of ghosts, speaking from headphones in the dark, sending their message of fake goodwill to the sleepless and the desperate.

One such sleepless listener is sitting at her computer right now. She calls herself *Lady of Shalott*; her real name is much more prosaic. She too is nocturnal – perhaps by choice – and she likes to hear the radio – the cheery, familiar voices, the music, the songs – as they clatter and chatter and chime against the giant screen of night.

It's true that things sound different at night. Even silence has a different tone; a resonance unheard by day. Her fingers on the pad beside her move with amazing precision, summoning sounds and images. Her face – almost close enough for her forehead to touch the screen – is bathed in a subaquatic glow. She is beautiful – though she does not know it; with the pallor of one who barely goes out by day; eyes blinking with electric stars. This is her favourite radio show; pre-recorded and broadcast between midnight and three every morning. It is nothing particularly special – just three hours of oldies strung together with late-night monologue – but sometimes, for her, there is something else. Something no one else knows about. At least, she presumes that no one knows. Who else listens, anyway? It's only a local station.

She sends in a request for a track. She does this quite often, sending her choice to *requests@phantomradio.com*. Even though the show isn't live, she finds they always play her song. There must be someone, she tells herself, waiting for her e-mails. Tonight, she is feeling wistful, maybe even a little sad. What will she choose to match her mood? Something by the Carpenters, perhaps; sweet and sincere and maybe just a little hokey, like still believing in true love.

Dear Phantom,

   Are you there?

She types.

Her computer has been adapted with a vocalizer and a refreshable Braille display. Through this tactile medium she can talk with people online. See them, darkly, through the glass. Hear their voices, like echoes of life that resonate through the world of the dead.

None of it is real, of course. But the feel of the words at her fingertips, the texture of the Braille display, as familiar to her as the lines and scars on her own palm, brings with it a comfort that cannot be denied. The touchpad lets her read web pages through a series of raised pins that translate the text into a form that she can understand. She prefers it to the vocalizer; the synthetic voice is unpleasant, while the Braille display is pretty – pretty as beads, or rice in a jar, or the sound of rain on the rooftops.

Dear Phantom,

   Are you still there?

She types her message; mails it; waits – at her fingertips the web shifts and moves like a tapestry of pixels.

What am I waiting for? she thinks. *What do I think will happen?*

Sometimes she gets so tired, waiting here in front of the screen; feeling the world at her fingertips instead of confronting it face to face. She wonders what would happen if she simply turned the computer off and walked out into the world alone – and then she thinks better of it, and sighs, and returns her hand to the touchpad – that pad of raised pins that rise and fall according to the shapes on the screen, and which, with exquisite sensitivity, she interprets with her fingertips.

Are you there?

He thinks: *Yes, I'm here*.

It's something like divination; something like enchantment; and as she weaves she sings to herself, like a mermaid in a story, as if in her net she might one day catch a shimmering shoal of fallen stars.

Of course, the screen only reflects. It isn't quite reality. She knows this, and yet it is the closest she gets to the world of other people. The Lady of Shalott, she thinks; watching the world through a darkened glass; waiting for someone to pull her through; waiting for someone to see her face—

He smiles to himself as he sorts through the mail. Few people ever write in to this, the midnight-to-three o'clock show. The graveyard shift, they call it; and he is happy to work it, ghost that he is, here in the familiar dark, away from their stares and their whispers.

Most people find him difficult to look at in the daylight. It is not so much the *shape* of his face, which is eccentric, nothing more, but the birthmark that disfigures him, a slap in the face from an angry God.

Some people are better than others at hiding their reactions. Some simply smile at him fixedly, as if attempting to compensate. Others never look at him directly, perpetually fixing their gaze on a point just beyond his head. Some are exaggeratedly cheery; others will do whatever they can to avoid being anywhere near him at all.

Women and children are the worst: the children because of the fear in their eyes, the women because of their pity. Some women, he notices, seem to be curiously drawn to him – he has come to hate these especially. Middle-aged, over-weight, nurturing types, who dream of taming a monster. These are the worst of the lot, he thinks, and does what he can to drive them away, although they are tenacious as weeds, seeing in his rudeness the germ of something ripe for redemption.

The internet is his escape. No one needs to see him here. He can exist as an avatar; words on a screen; a voice in the dark. Here the world is his to explore; a world in which not only he, but *no one* has a face.

He checks the mail again. There she is. *LadyofShalott@gmail.com.* She often sends in song requests; sometimes with a little note describing what she did today; or why she chose that particular track; or simply one of her whimsical thoughts—

Dear Phantom (she always begins this way),

Have you ever wondered what happens to music when it stops? The soundwaves keep on going, of course, so I guess it never stops at all. It just keeps spooling off into space, for anyone to catch who can. Wish upon a star, they say – but can't I wish upon a song?

He never writes back. The Phantom does not indulge in personal chat. But this has never deterred her. She never seems to need a reply. In fact, her notes are longer now than they were when she started to write to him. Perhaps it is the allure of the dark; the screen of the confessional. She tells him all kinds of personal things – everything except *one* thing, in fact; the reason she's here in the first place, feeling her way into his world—

I like the songs you play (she writes). *I like the way you make them fit together, not just randomly, but in a way that tells stories. Do I ever hear your voice? Or is it just DJs recording links, while someone else makes the connections?*

It's a question no one has asked him before. The voices on the airwaves – those cheery late-night chatterers – always get plenty of mail from their fans. But she seems much more interested in what's going on *behind* the scenes. She's smart, he thinks. She knows it's a fake, cleverly rigged to make it sound like a live broadcast. Because the appeal of the graveyard show is all about the shared experience; the feeling that there's someone there, talking away into the night, sharing time, sharing thoughts—

Who'd stay up till three a.m. to listen to a recording?
She would. Of course she would.

Nowadays he has been taking more care in constructing

those late-night playlists. He knows she listens attentively, and he tries to make it a challenging game, interspersing sly references to current events, to films, to plays, even sometimes to his dreams—

Dear Phantom,

Last night I thought you were lonely. So many sad, sad songs. So many tunes in D minor. Perhaps your name begins with a D? I try to imagine what it might be. David. Dominic. That's not right. In fact, I don't think you have a name. Phantoms shouldn't have names, should they?

And Phantoms shouldn't have dreams, he thinks. Especially not dangerous dreams like this. He makes himself a cup of tea, then goes into the bathroom. Switches on the overhead light and slowly, deliberately, studies his face.

He doesn't do this often. But sometimes he must, just as sometimes in life a man has to suffer in order to grow. If she saw him now, he thinks, she would react like everyone else. She wouldn't be able to help herself; and he would see that look in her eyes, that look of half pity, half disgust, and that would be the end of it. It has happened before. It always will. And yet – and yet—

Dear Phantom,

I wish—

What does she wish? She wishes he would answer her. Better still, she wishes to hear his voice. The Braille display is always so bland, robbing words of inflection. She wishes she could know the sound of him; his dialect, the stress he puts on syllables, the texture of his words.

Dear Phantom (she says),

Do you know what I wish? I wish I could hear your voice. I'm very alert to voices. Accents, too – I can spot a fake in a crowd at two hundred paces.

A fake, he thinks. Is that what I am? A monster who believes he's a man? He wishes he could grant her wish. But that would be a mistake, he thinks. He'd never get away with it. To mess about with the broadcasts could end in his dismissal, and where would he go if he lost this job? What would he do in the human world?

I wish—

At least I can play her request, he thinks. That much *is* within my power. And yet—

I wish, he thinks. *I wish—*

The studio is empty and dark. The chair in which the DJ would sit is like a cradle of darkness. Behind it, there's a baby grand, under a canvas cover. He pulls the cover from the piano. Fingers the smooth, cool rows of keys.

Through the headphones, the seashell voice drones and hums and murmurs. It's almost two; there's nobody here; no one to report him. Who even listens in at this hour? A handful of insomniacs; a drunk; a depressive; a lonely young girl—

Dear Phantom,

Are you really there? I like to think you are, of course, but sometimes I find myself wondering. Like the music spooling off into space in the hope that someone will hear it, am I just sending out random signals without a chance of ever being heard? I know you can't answer, and maybe it's wrong of me to try to put you on the spot like this, but maybe you could just give me a sign? Anything. A dot. A dash. Or are you just like me, perhaps – a ghost in the machine?

He smiles. *A ghost in the machine.* Once more, she has seen through his disguise. This is what he has always been; nameless, faceless, voiceless—

It takes a few seconds to check the mike and to secure a channel. He waits until the end of a track. Slips on the headphones. Sits at the desk. And then he ends the broadcast and switches from Recorded to Live.

A red light blinks. He adjusts the mike. Picks up where the recording left off in the same soft and intimate voice –

This is Phantom Radio. You're listening to the graveyard show, bringing you home from midnight to three.

No one would know the difference unless they were paying attention. These voices are generic, he thinks, their tone as bland as birdsong. And yet, she will know. She is listening. Tuned in to his frequency; she will know that he is there.

And now he finds himself talking to her. Surly by nature, to his surprise he finds that he does have a voice, after all. Tonight, here in the studio, he is going to play a special request; for the first time, live and unplugged—

She hears it in the silence. Live silence and studio silence have a completely different quality, and her ears, attuned to every nuance, are quick to register the change.

Then comes his voice, and the hairs on her arms rise like the pins on the pad at her side. She readjusts the sound controls; tweaks the mid-range and the bass to give the optimum result. Digital sound is so clean, she thinks; she can hear every sound that he makes; from the creaking of his swivel chair to the way his breath catches in his throat when he pronounces certain words.

Fingers on the touchpad, she can almost see him now; seeking out the shape of his mouth, the way his face turns away from the mike whenever he glances towards the door.

The piano is slightly out of tune – others might not notice this, but she, with her eerie sense of pitch, can hear every variation. And when he sings – softly at first, but slowly gaining in confidence – she takes in every shade of sound, every modulation. Delivery; accent; mannerisms; everything is suddenly clear – and the voice itself; untrained, but rich; a woody, smoky baritone that fits perfectly with the impression she has of what his face must be like—

I wish. I wish. This is what I wish for. That this moment should never end, that it should carry beyond the stars on a single, perfect algorithm—

It lasts for less than five minutes in all. Then the recording takes over again, with its flat studio silences. He wonders what she made of it all. He wonders if she was listening. Maybe she has fallen asleep. Maybe she was never there—

He checks the mail.

Dear Phantom (she says),

Thank you.

Nothing more. He wonders why. Is it nervousness, he thinks, or has he somehow crossed a line? After all, it's easy, he thinks, to talk to someone who may not be there. But to give that person a voice – or a face – is to destroy the illusion. Perhaps she is shy of him now – or worse, perhaps she is disappointed—

He waits. She writes no more that night. The next night, his impatience is such that he can barely function. Throughout the day – and for the first time anyone can remember – Phantom Radio is plagued by technical problems. Finally, the producer comes in, and finds him asleep in the sound booth. He gives him a sympathetic talk that also serves as a warning – *get your act together, you* – but never looks him in the face.

Midnight comes. The graveyard shift. Still she has not written back. He grins bitterly at himself for expecting anything different. The fact that after all these years he is still capable of making a fool of himself gives him a perverse kind of pleasure. *As if a girl like that could ever care for someone like you*, he thinks. *Without ever having seen your face, she already knew you were a freak.*

And yet—

Throughout the show, he waits for her mail. Nothing comes, not even a song request. He is vaguely angry at himself for half expecting otherwise. She has probably moved on by now to another all-night station. Or maybe she's asleep in bed, or out with someone special.

She makes no attempt to read tonight. Her fingers are numb on the Braille pad. The screen has frozen on Phantom's homepage, but she does not try to refresh it. Instead she simply listens to the songs that he has chosen – she knows his playlists almost by heart; has even given them names in her mind. The current one is called *Blue*, and it is one of his most melancholy. One of her favourites, too, as it happens, so that she does not even suggest a song for him to play for her tonight. *All* tonight's songs are for her, and the thought is ice water and terrible heat as she listens to the lovely sounds, though none are as beguiling as his voice, the voice that has stolen into her dreams—

Could it be I have fallen in love? She asks herself the question. Can you really fall in love with just the sound of a person's voice? She moves her hand on the pad at her side and tries to conjure the shape of his face; imagines the feel of her fingertips moving over his eyelids –

Dear Phantom (she writes),

> *I love you. I think I must have loved you before, but last night, when you spoke to me—*

She sends it before she can change her mind. Halfway through a sentence, as if she expects him to finish the phrase. He has to read it several times before it really registers. The simplest words in the language, and he cannot decipher their meaning.

Dear Lady of Shalott, he begins, and then decides against it. He is not a writer, he thinks. The words will not co-operate. Instead, he changes channels again, switches the broadcast once more to Live. For a moment he has no idea what he is about to say; and then he turns to the piano, spans a chord of D minor and begins to speak, or maybe to sing—

I wish, he thinks aloud. *I wish.*

It must be something in the air. Never before in all his life has he been so articulate. Perhaps it's the night, he tells himself; or perhaps it's the thought of those soundwaves shooting off into deepest space—

Wish I may, wish I might—

On the call desk, a red light begins to blink persistently. There must be more people out there listening than he thought. Another light begins to blink. A star. A constellation. The switchboard is soon jammed with callers, red lights all across the desk. It's his job to answer the calls, but tonight the Phantom is occupied. All that can wait till tomorrow, he thinks. Tomorrow he won't *have* a job.

The thought makes his voice dry up in his throat. Phantom Radio is his life. What has he done? Has he gone mad? What demon has possessed him?

He pulls off the headphones, steps away from the mike. Switches back to the regular broadcast. Of course it's too late, he tells himself. He cannot hide what he has done. After a lifetime of hiding away, he has exposed, not his face, but his *heart* to anyone who was listening—

He checks the mail.

Dear Phantom (she writes),

> *I think it's time. Please meet me here in half an hour.*

She gives a place, a street, an address.

He types: *All right.* He presses *Send.*

And then he stands, frozen with what he has done. He puts his hands over his face – the face that makes little children cry – and stands like this for a long time; a big, awkward man with an ugly mark that looks like a splash of purple ink across his face. Behind him, on the sound desk, lights are blinking like crazy. Something – a circuit, perhaps – has failed. Phantom Radio is off the air. Not that it matters any more.

He feels his heart begin to pound.

She feels her head begin to spin.

What if she isn't there? he thinks.

What if he doesn't come? she thinks.

And he types: *There's something you need to know.*

And she types: *There's something I didn't say—*

But now the computers are down as well; the screen is blank; there's nothing to see but the cursor blinking against the blue; nothing to feel but the Braille pad frozen in its final wave.

And nobody sees her pull on her coat and pick up her white cane and open the door; and nobody sees him run outside but the doorman, half asleep at his post, while the ghosts of Phantom Radio whisper and hum from darkened rooms and the lights all over the switchboard blink out their messages in code.

Dee Eye Why

A lot of these stories are ghost stories. But ghosts, like love, like stories themselves, can come from unexpected places. The house in this tale has featured before (including in some of my novels): it isn't quite my house, but some of the ghosts belong to me.

They say the first step is acceptance. After that, letting go becomes a healing process. You have to really *feel* the pain before you can begin to move on. Well, if that was true, his suffering must have run deeper than even he had suspected. Most men, in the face of divorce, turn to their friends; or take to drink; or lick their wounds in private.

Michael Harman bought a house.

Locals called it the Mansion. It was an old, neglected house of the kind you see in those movies in which a nice, white, middle-class family moves into a Gothic Monstrosity (complete with Indian burial ground), then wonders why Bizarre Goings-on suddenly start to happen. This time, however, there was no family. There weren't even any goings-on. Perhaps that was why he bought it, he thought; that space that needed to be filled.

Everyone privately agreed that Michael had finally lost the plot. A divorce was surely costly enough without adding all *this* to the pile: this ghastly white elephant of a house in its tangled five acres of garden; its roof sagging beneath the weight of a hundred winters; its plumbing a can of lead-pipe worms; its garden – mostly woodland, but with the overgrown remains of an orchard, a Japanese mirror-pool, a walled garden, ancient pear trees *en espalier,* a rose-walk and God knows what else – in need of an army of gardeners to restore it to some semblance of order. And yet he had bought it, no one knew why; giving credence to Annie's claims that Michael had become impossible to live with; that no one knew how to deal with him; that his mood swings, his temper, his irrational behaviour had finally led her to fear for her safety and for that of the children. People who knew him doubted this. Michael had never been violent. Complicated, maybe – reserved; a man who in spite of his profession rarely betrayed his feelings; hiding his essential self even from those who loved him.

Once he had been an actor. Mostly in musical theatre; a man who had gained prominence through his powerful interpretation of certain well-known stage roles. A big and rather clumsy man with curly hair, a diffident smile and a tendency to put on weight as he entered his forties; pleasant, but unremarkable – except for his marvellous singing voice, which had earned him many devoted fans, most of them women, some of them mad. One had pursued him for almost ten years from one stage door to the next, bearing gifts; others had plagued him with letters; one had threatened to shoot his wife. All professed to love him. None of them really knew him. In fact, as time passed he grew increasingly unsure as to whether he even knew himself. Years spent living out of trunks, moving from one set of digs to the next, missing his children's first steps, their first words, their childhood. Fifteen years of Sunday roasts; Nativity plays; football matches; evenings in, all sacrificed to that dusty old god that smelt of sawdust, and greasepaint, and electronics, and sweat; the dusty old god that lived in the dark just beyond the stage lights—

And then, one day, it had fallen apart. His marvellous voice had failed him. Only once in public – fatigue, hay fever, nerves on edge – but from that moment he was afraid every time he stepped on to the stage, so that soon the fear was unbearable, and even to hear the opening chords of a song that he was about to sing made him sweat, filled his mouth with sawdust, flooded him with a panic that he could barely understand. He had left the show in mid-run, on the grounds of illness, but knowing that the dusty old god had judged him and found him wanting.

The separation had come soon afterwards. Annie had been supportive as long as he was working away; but to have him underfoot every day was more than she had bargained for. They'd had a house in Yorkshire, in which he had spent his holidays, and lived in for those few short months when he wasn't working. Now, Annie realized, it was too small for the four of them. No one knew him any more. Friends were awkward in his presence. Annie treated him like a guest. Even the children sensed that he was taking up much-needed space – and Michael had felt like a prisoner without any possible hope of reprieve . . .

And then she had left him, taking the kids and leaving him with half a life; half a bank account; half a heart.

And so, Michael Harman had bought a house. Exactly *how* that happened, he was still not certain. One moment he had been looking for a place not too far from his children – perhaps a loft conversion, or a riverside flat. Instead he had wandered into the grounds of a rambling, half-derelict house overgrown with rhododendrons gone wild, with a peeling FOR SALE sign standing among the nettles.

It should not have been love at first sight. And yet, to Michael Harman it was. Perhaps because of that garden; the silence of those overgrown paths. Perhaps because he knew even then that it was perfect for children. Perhaps even because of the sense of neglect that hung over the place like a cloud; the feeling that maybe, under it all, was something waiting to be released.

It was far from being a bargain, even in its derelict state. But a man in love sees no obstacle, and very soon the place was his. He moved in straight away, in spite of the fact that the house was barely habitable. Annie was back in the family home, and Michael was staying in digs again. The roof leaked; the walls were damp; there was barely any heating. But it was spring; the nights were warm, and surely nothing could be worse than living out of a suitcase.

They say the first step is acceptance. He spent the first

three weeks of it coming to terms with what he had bought: the Mansion; the ivy-encrusted walls; the roof of solid Yorkshire stone; four bedrooms; two bathrooms; a library; a kitchen, a pantry, a nursery, a scullery complete with butcher's block and meat-hooks on which must have hung hams, ducks, pheasants, sides of beef; an ancient wine cellar mattressed with dust; some leaded stained-glass windows. Much of the glass was damaged now, but the colours were glorious in the morning sun, casting ladders of coloured light over a parquet floor that had once been fine, but which was now scarred and battle-worn. It almost hurt to imagine now what the Mansion must once have been like: gracious in its own grounds; elegantly furnished; grand even by the standards of Malbry village, which had once boasted, locals said, more Rolls-Royces per square mile than any other town in the North.

Of course, that wasn't true any more. *Millionaires' Row*, as they called it, had mostly been converted to offices, flats and old people's homes. Only a few old houses remained intact, staunchly holding back the tide of development. Even so, it was clear to him that once the place had been beautiful. The wallpaper that peeled from the walls revealed Morris & Co. originals; one day, he stripped down a stairwell to discover a *trompe-l'oeil* mural, still in decent condition, of an Arcadian landscape beyond a painted rose trellis. The place had been uninhabited for at least eighteen months, he knew; but soon he came to realize that this was in his favour. No renovations had been made for the past five decades. The wiring might be antiquated, but so were the switches and the elaborate door-plates; the carved cedar balustrades; the stained glass; the monumental ceramic bath; the huge oak fireplaces. Some attempts had been made to modernize the kitchen; but further exploration revealed that under the Bitumastic floor lay a beautiful set of old stone flags, which, when scrubbed and treated, shone with a warm and mellow gleam.

Annie would like that, he thought. It gave him unexpected pain. Annie would also have liked the stove; the cast-iron range; the chimney; the butcher's block; the dresser and the well-worn granite surfaces. It was ironic, really. Fifteen years too late, he had found the home that she had always dreamed of.

Michael began to understand that houses, like people, need to be loved. Too long it had been neglected; and now he set himself the task of bringing the Mansion back from the dead.

Before the theatre had eaten his life, he had been the son of a builder. His father had taught him many things which now revealed their purpose; and although such things as plumbing and rewiring were still beyond his ability, he found himself applying skills he had thought long since forgotten.

At first, he worked to dull the pain. To stop himself from thinking. He worked until his hands bled; until his lungs were filled with dust; until every part of him ached; until he was so numb with fatigue that nothing mattered any more. But soon he began to feel differently. There was a pleasing simplicity in physical activity; in stripping and polishing wooden floors; in tearing off panels from old oak doors to reveal the original woodwork; in plastering and rubbing down paint; in filling and staining blistered wood. One day he even caught himself singing as he removed a damaged section of parquet veneer to reveal a beautiful pitch-pine floor—

What was happening? he thought. What had begun as a penance was becoming a kind of pleasure. His hands had toughened; they no longer bled. His body no longer hurt, but worked smoothly and efficiently. It was almost as if, in peeling back the layers of neglect from the old house, he too were sloughing off a layer of something – skin, or the past. Working alone in the empty house, he sang to himself for the joy of it; and for once, the dusty, forgotten old god went unregarded and unappeased.

Six weeks passed. Summer came. During that time, Michael barely left the house. The neighbours were discreet, he found; no one came to disturb him. Mobile reception was poor at the house, probably because of the trees, though texts still managed to get through. By text, he ordered building supplies and arranged for workmen to call round. As for his meals, there was a sandwich shop nearby, although he had little appetite. Even so, his energy continued undiminished. As he worked through the many rooms, he started to come across clues to the past: a pair of leather baby shoes hidden up a chimney; a packet of four Woodbines under a floor left there by some workman (who would no doubt have cursed his forgetfulness); pages torn from a newspaper dated 1908; names carved on the underside of a window-ledge in the schoolroom.

The more he uncovered of its previous life, the more curious he became about the house. Until fairly recently, it had belonged to a Dr Graham Peacock, and after his death it stayed empty until it was finally put on the market, along with most of its contents. A house-clearing agency had dealt with these, except for the fixtures and fittings and a number of bulky items of furniture, which had been there since the house was built. As for the house's history – Michael made enquiries and found that Dr Peacock, an elderly man, had inherited it from his long-dead parents, and that his mother, before her marriage, had been Miss Emily Lundy, the only daughter of the Mansion's original owners.

Fred Lundy had been in textiles; Lundy Mills had been well known all across the county. He'd married Frances Liversidge, the daughter of a tea merchant from Liverpool. They'd had two children, Emily and Ned, and a son, Benjamin, who had died in infancy. Michael wondered if those shoes he'd found in the nursery chimney had belonged to that long-dead little boy; whether Frances had put them there as part of some secret ritual—

He'd made no attempt to contact his wife over the past six weeks. The pain of seeing her again – and worse, of seeing their children – had kept him from even considering it. But four weeks into the separation, he found himself thinking more and more about what she would think of his new house. He saw her in the kitchen, looking at the old stone floor, admiring the work he'd done on it while the children – Holly, nine, Ben, six – raced around the garden looking for places to build dens, or explored the attics, or admired the nursery.

Finally, he invited them to see what he'd been doing. There was no question of the house being anything close to completion; but at least the roof was sound again and some of the rooms had floors. And he was *proud* of his handiwork; prouder than he'd ever been on stage, in front of an audience.

He spent the day before their arrival mowing paths through the overgrown lawn, trying to bring some order into the chaos. In doing so, he uncovered an ornamental pond and a fountain in the shape of a mermaid; his pleasure at the discovery was childlike and surprising.

Annie and the children were due at four. By five they had not arrived. There was no phone in the Mansion; Michael checked his mobile.

He found a text from Annie; heard her brittle voice in his mind.

Michael, I'm really sorry. I thought I was ready, but I'm not. The kids are doing so well now, I couldn't bear to mess that up. In a couple of weeks, maybe. Take care of yourself, A.

He deleted the message. Made some tea. Started work on the big bathroom – some of the original floor tiles were cracked, but he'd found a box of spares in the loft that he thought would cover the damage. Half an hour later he was singing to himself as he worked. The marvellous voice soared into the air like the flight of a legendary bird.

The next day, his friend Rob called by. *His* friend – well, more Annie's friend really, a neighbour who'd known them for ever. Annie was very concerned, Rob said. Annie had sent him to check things out.

Check things out. That voice again. Her bright and brittle voice in his mind. Half of him felt hope at this; if she was keeping tabs on him, then surely she wasn't indifferent? But Rob soon put him right on that. People were talking, he explained. There was bound to be curiosity. He was famous – in his way – the Press were sure to get hold of it.

'Get hold of what?' asked Michael, bemused.

Rob looked awkward. 'This house,' he said. 'This creepy obsession of yours with this house.'

Apparently the neighbours had taken more notice than he'd thought. The questions he'd asked in the village; the building supplies he had ordered; the roofer; the plumber; the electrician. All of these things had been noted. In a village, nothing goes unnoticed, and the Malbry grapevine was as vigorous as the brambles in his garden.

'Sweet Jesus,' he said. 'What obsession?'

Rob repeated what he'd heard. That Michael had gone crazy; that he was living like a recluse, working himself to a shadow. 'You've lost weight,' he pointed out.

'I needed to shed a few pounds,' he said.

'But what are you doing it *for*?' said Rob. 'There's no way you're going to live here alone. I mean, what is it, ten bedrooms? And what about when you go back to work?'

Michael shrugged. 'Who knows? Who cares?'

'Well, anyway, it's haunted,' Rob said, with the air of a man proving a point.

Michael had to laugh at that. 'Haunted by *what*?'

'All old houses are haunted,' Rob said.

The thought that Rob – who worked in advertising, owned a silver BMW and liked to play squash on Saturdays – could be superstitious made Michael laugh all the more. Some old buildings *did* have a chill – Michael hadn't worked in theatres for almost twenty years without picking up the occasional vibe – but the Mansion wasn't one of them. There were no unexpectedly cold spots; no whispering voices in the dark; not even a hint of a resident ghost. In fact, from a psychic perspective, the Mansion was a blank slate; as thin on atmosphere as the Moon.

'Look, Michael. Annie thinks that perhaps you should get therapy.'

That killed the laughter at once. *Therapy.* How typical of Annie, he thought. What did she think he was doing? *This* was his therapy, Michael said, not sessions with some half-baked kid with a degree in sociology. As for being crazy, maybe she could use some counselling herself – this talk of haunted houses was hardly a sign of rational thought—

His voice had risen as he spoke. A voice that once reached to the balcony without amplification now cut through the shadows like a scythe. Rob left soon afterwards, leaving Michael with the distinct impression that he'd somehow confirmed every one of his wife's suspicions about him.

He checked his mobile. No messages. Reception was down to a single bar. He considered walking into the village to find a clearer spot, but then decided against it. What was the point? Instead, he went to the village library and borrowed some local history books. Fred Lundy and his family had been very prominent locally. Perhaps a history of the village would reveal more about the family.

It took him three days to read the books during the breaks he took from his work. He learnt that the house had been built by Fred Lundy in 1886: that in 1910 it had been modernized (the stained glass, the murals and the landscaped garden dated back to this time); that Ned had died in 1918, just days before the end of the war, and that Emily had married late, to Mr Travers Peacock. Their son had been Graham Peacock; but the marriage had not lasted long. Travers Peacock had died abroad, and Emily had come home with her young son in '25, where she had lived until her death in summer 1964. As for Graham Peacock, according to Malbry's grapevine, he had died a bachelor, leaving his substantial fortune to some kind of charity for the blind.

So *these* were the Mansion's absent ghosts. This ordinary family. A mother, a father, a daughter, a son. Had they been happy? He imagined they had. Even when the baby died, they'd always had each other. Of course, in those days families were different. They faced obstacles together instead of running away from them. Ghosts, if they existed, he thought, were surely unhappy creatures, trying to relive scenes from a past that is unresolved or unsatisfactory.

He understood that feeling. For years he'd lived like a ghost himself; making himself invisible; speaking other people's lines; only appearing under the lights; playing his part so perfectly that in the end, he had disappeared—

Perhaps *he* was the ghost, he thought. Perhaps that was why the empty old house had welcomed him so warmly. He smiled, remembering what Rob had said. *This creepy obsession of yours with this house.* What was so creepy about wanting to make a house back into a home?

Until that moment he hadn't realized that this was precisely what he was doing. A house was not just the sum of its rooms, its ceilings, its walls, its windows. A house was the sum of the people who had lived, loved, died in it; their names scratched into the woodwork, the tracks of their feet worn into the steps. A house like the Mansion deserved respect; respect for the skill of its craftsmen, their pride and attention to detail; respect for its history and its age and all the work that had gone into its upkeep. In those days, he told himself, there would have been servants living there: a nanny for the children; a housekeeper; gardeners; a maid; a cook. Now there was only Michael left. The thought both pleased and humbled him. He found a specialist wallpaper supplier and replaced the Morris originals. He searched for the kind of furniture that the Lundys would have bought, and had it delivered piece by piece. It was expensive, but worthwhile; the wiring, plumbing and plastering had all been completed some time before, and now he could afford to pay attention to those special details – the glass, the tiles, the wall coverings – that would make all the difference.

Twelve weeks had passed since he moved in. Summer shuffled into autumn like a hand of cards. The trees began to turn; the nights, which had been mild thus far, grew cold. For the first time since he'd moved in, Michael tried the central heating. He found that it worked reasonably well; a combination of heavy schoolroom radiators and spacious fireplaces. He cleaned and re-leaded the fire grates, with the help of a book from the library on Victorian households. He found a copy of Mrs Beeton in a local antiques shop, and was surprised at how very useful he found her *Guide to Household Management*.

Venturing into the village, he found out more about the Lundys. He discovered that they had a family vault in the local cemetery: a blackened obelisk in a gravel square, surrounded by four stone posts connected by a rusty chain. Fred and Frances lay side by side with Emily and Benjamin. Ned's name was on the monument, but according to local records his remains had never been found. A space had been left for Emily's son, but Graham Peacock had not been buried in the family vault. For some reason Michael felt this was right. Peacock had not been a Lundy. He had lived in the Mansion, but had not really cared for it; and so the house had rejected him.

Michael's curiosity grew. He researched the Lundys in detail. He found that they had close links to St Mary's, the nearby parish church, and that in 1918 Fred Lundy had commissioned a small stained-glass window in memory of their dead son. A cheque in aid of the church roof ensured that Michael had access to all the local records: birth and death certificates; some correspondence between Fred Lundy and the parish priest; letters thanking Emily for a donation made to the poor. There was also a tin deposit box containing many more letters; some photographs of the family and of the house; household bills from the Mansion; a closely written notebook; postcards from all over the world addressed to Emily Peacock; detailed plans for the construction of a water garden and even some school report cards in the name of Ned Lundy, dated from 1900 to 1904. No one seemed to know or care why these papers had been kept; and a further donation to the church roof gave Michael permanent custody of the tin box and its contents.

He found it absorbing reading. Everything inside the box connected him more closely with the house and its inhabitants. He now had photographs of them all; a wedding photograph showing Fred in high collar and sideburns and Frances, looking very young, her dark hair in a braided coronet interwoven with ivy leaves. Baby pictures of Emily and Ned; flower basket; sailor suit. Pictures of them older now, in the style of Cameron. There was a family portrait too, taken in 1908; the two of them sitting side by side, with Emily standing behind them, very like her mother, in a pale dress, with loose hair, and Ned in army uniform, slightly out of focus, as if his impatience to be off had made him spoil the photograph.

Had they known? Michael asked himself. Had they somehow sensed that their circle was about to be broken? Or was it just the interminable exposure time that made their faces so solemn and fixed?

Fred had been a big man; not unlike Michael Harman himself, with dark hair that might have curled – if he had allowed it. Ned had favoured Frances; small-boned and energetic. His school reports mentioned his terrible handwriting – a criticism justified by the scrawled postcards he'd sent from France. He had been a lively, exuberant child; trees all over the garden – as well as the schoolroom mantelpiece – bore the marks of his penknife, and a number of old children's books overlooked by the house-clearing agency were marked with the same careless scrawl – *Edward Albert Lundy*.

Michael liked the sound of that. The garden would have been a haven for boys. He imagined swings; tree-houses; dens; a mongrel dog that went everywhere. Muddy football boots in the hall; the housekeeper's voice: *Master Ned! Come back right now!* Kites; jars of tadpoles; frogs. Frances trying to look annoyed, but hiding an indulgent smile. *Boys will be boys, Fred. Let him be*.

Autumn turned; the leaves fell. Michael was grateful that all his external paintwork was done. He turned his attention to the garden: cutting back the undergrowth; clearing leaves; mowing abandoned lawns that had long since turned to meadows. His agent wrote, complaining that Michael never answered his phone; he tried his mobile for the first time in a fortnight and found a dozen texts there, which he deleted unread, and returned to his work in the garden.

He found even more neglect than he had feared: walkways buried under mouldering leaves; toppled statues; roses gone wild; a Japanese-style water garden – presumably the one for which he'd seen the original plans – overgrown by ancient rhododendrons. A little wooden summerhouse stood in a tangle of briars; pushing his way inside, he found a box containing paintbrushes, dried-out watercolours and a sketch pad, ruined by damp, with a name – *Emily Geraldine Lundy* – in careful brownish print on the cover.

So, Emily liked to paint, did she? Somehow, that didn't surprise him. His own daughter, Holly, had liked it too – he'd had a picture of hers for years, pinned to his dressing-room mirror. He wondered what Holly would make of this place, and realized, with a stab of guilt, that he had barely thought of her – or of Ben, or Annie – for weeks.

How could he have forgotten so fast? No, not *forgotten*, precisely – but as he searched for the pain of his loss, he found only distant memories: his first glimpse of Annie, in the front row of some little regional theatre; his daughter's finger around his own; Ben's eyes, so blue and so trusting. But these, he saw, were now overlaid with memories that were not his own, but which stood out with a clarity that defied all comprehension. Ned in a sailor suit, climbing trees; Emily in her summerhouse, frowning in concentration over a watercolour of the Japanese garden in spring. And Frances. Lovely Frances with her loosely braided hair, still slim in spite of two children; smiling; happy; radiant; running down the avenue with an armful of roses—

A sound from behind him made him flinch. '*Frances?*'

He turned, and for a moment saw her as Orpheus saw Eurydice: pale face, dark hair, blurry with nostalgia—

Then he recognized Annie. Annie in jeans and an overcoat, hair newly cropped. He'd liked it better long, he thought – the way she'd worn it when they first met.

'Who's Frances?' Annie said.

Michael tried to explain. But already he sensed her indifference. Annie had come to deliver a speech, and she wasn't going to leave until he'd listened to it all.

In a way, it reminded him of the lecture he'd already had from Rob. She mentioned his obsession; his weight; the fact that he wasn't answering calls. Michael explained about the lack of mobile reception at the house; Annie gave him a narrow look and once more mentioned therapy.

He offered to show her around the house. Annie declined the offer. She seemed to think that to walk through the door would be to lose the upper hand; she had no interest in his work, she said, still less in his research. He asked after the children; she said that once he began to see sense, they could come to some arrangement. She left him, for the first time in weeks, feeling helpless; angry; in pain; but by the end of the afternoon he'd regained his equilibrium. A child's swing, hanging from the branch of an old laburnum tree, brought him back to reality; the chance discovery of a stone bench half hidden in a drift of leaves gave him something else to fix: and soon the memory of his wife and the cruel words she had spoken were blurred into something approaching forgetfulness.

That night he lit a bonfire in the circular firepit beyond the Japanese garden. In it, he burnt the garden waste that he had accumulated that day, as well as certain mementoes of his former life: his Olivier; some scrapbooks; the box of newspaper clippings that he had accumulated (mostly without even reading them) over the course of his career. He burnt them without a pang of regret. In fact, he felt as if the final layer of his old skin had shed itself, effortlessly, painlessly, leaving him new and whole again—

He hung pictures of his children on the nursery wall;

but they seemed out of place, somehow. Too colourful; too modern. He replaced them with his photographs of Emily and Ned Lundy: Ned at eight or nine, shock-haired, long before the Great War arrived to take him away; Emily at twelve or thirteen, artistically posed in a white dress, hair caught up with a ribbon. He found himself admiring the magic of photography; not the disposable digital kind, but the kind that had fixed these portraits of the Lundy children so beautifully out of time. What came next – her marriage, his war – none of that mattered any more. It was all forgotten now. The children need never grow up here; and Frances need never grow old or die. Her portrait was already hanging in the parlour, above the fireplace; a portrait of Frances at twenty-nine, long hair in a luxuriant knot; dark silk dress; embroidered shawl. In spite of her dress, Michael thought her face looked very modern; her eyes seemed to smile as he looked at her, and to follow him around the room.

As for Fred Lundy, somehow he felt even closer to him than to the rest of them. His presence was everywhere in the house; everywhere in the garden. Most of the letters in the deposit box had been from Fred himself; bills; instructions to workmen; letters to and from his various textile mills, as well as the local orphanage, founded and financed by the Lundys. The letters revealed Fred Lundy to be a man of some education; a generous employer; a man who showed surprising humility in spite of his status in Malbry. He took a genuine interest in the people who worked for him; worked to improve conditions for them; spoke with real passion about the terrible plight of the poor, and especially of their children—

And then there was the notebook he'd found among the papers in the box. Fred had been a lay preacher, and sometimes spoke at St Mary's, or gave little speeches during his visits to the orphanage. The notebook was filled with ideas for these, as well as what seemed to be random thoughts, scribbled down as they occurred, alongside more mundane reminders: delivery dates; personnel changes; family occasions; birthdays.

The world outside is a cruel place, Michael read as he turned a page. *The comfort of a family, of a home where he is cherished and loved, is all a man really needs in this world. With it, he is invincible. Without it, all his influence is nothing more than a fall of rain, that colours the paving stones for a while, and is gone as soon as the sun shines.*

And there, a little later:

A home is not bricks and mortar. A home is made of those things that endure when the bricks and mortar are gone.

Then, later still:

Above all, a man should live surrounded by the things he loves.

This man, he began to realize, was something of a kindred soul; a man who lived on in every brick and piece of oak in the Mansion. He hung Fred's portrait above the fireplace in the library; his favourite room, lined with leather-bound books; a place where a man could sit quietly in an armchair by a fire and breathe in the scent of leather and smoke—

Michael took to smoking a pipe. He'd never smoked

before, but now it somehow seemed very natural. The smell of pipe tobacco was as fragrant and evocative as the scent of burning leaves. He only smoked in the library. Somehow, to smoke in the kitchen, or, worse, in Frances's parlour, would have been inexcusable.

Please, Fred. Think of the children. Only in the library.

Winter came. His sideburns grew long. He ordered more books on interiors. He scoured the nearby salvage yard for original doorknobs, hinges, taps. He furnished the school-room with toys and books he found in local antiques shops. He even ordered a Christmas tree – a twelve-foot spruce that, when it arrived, grazed the parlour ceiling – and spent a happy morning decking it with pine cones and antique glass baubles. He didn't feel at all odd doing this; in fact, he found it hard to believe that his children were not outside throwing snowballs, or building a snowman, or wassailing, or picking holly to make a wreath, while his wife oversaw the baking. In fact, he could almost smell the rich scents of plum cake and butter pastry; of brandy and apples and marchpane.

He wondered if Annie would call, or if she really intended to keep the children from seeing him until he'd accepted therapy. That was ridiculous, of course. Michael could sue for access. But the truth was, he didn't like the idea of leaving his home. That world of legal representatives and banks and agents belonged to a past that he had managed to escape. The thought of entering it again seemed tiresome and unnecessary. Besides, there was still so much work to do. A house like the Mansion was never finished; every completed task revealed two more that needed attention. He did not begrudge the time spent. In fact, he was grateful for it. In his old life he had always been at the mercy of stage directors; producers; writers; critics. Here, at the Mansion, *he* was in charge. Here, he was accepted.

He'd been half expecting Annie to call. He bought Christmas gifts for the children. A doll for Holly; a kite for Ben; oranges for both of them. For Annie he bought a bangle from a local antiques shop: a bangle in white gold and sapphires, delicate as a band of lace. He wrapped the gifts and placed them underneath the Christmas tree; lit candles; waited – but for what?

Outside, snow fell. The advent calendar on the wall – a Victorian original – showed only six days to Christmas. At the hall piano, Michael sang Christmas carols; in twenty years, he'd never done that with his other family. He was slightly shocked at himself that he'd begun to think of Annie that way; but his present life was so different from the one that they had shared—

And then, on Christmas Eve, there came the sound of a car pulling up on the drive and Annie stood at the front door, staring blankly at the wreath that Michael had hung from the knocker. Holly and Ben were with her; both looking so much older now, so changed from the last time he'd seen them. Of course, it had been more than six months. And when he'd been working, there had been days when he'd looked for his children and seen nothing but snapshots out of time; Holly's hair turning brown overnight where once she had been an angelic blonde; Ben moving from wide-eyed infancy to young boyhood in one smooth, irrevocable step.

Annie was wearing a black coat that made her look older than she was. Her smile was bright as he opened the door; it slipped as she saw him.

'My God!' she said. 'What *happened* to you?'

Of course, she was overreacting. He hadn't changed *that* much, he thought. And the children – she must have primed them to look at him the way they did; as if he were a stranger.

But he *was* eager to show them the house. The fruit of all his labours. He realized that *this* was the moment for which he had been waiting; he wanted to see their faces when they saw the schoolroom; the nursery; the rocking horse on the landing; everything he had put into place ready for their arrival. The weaver-bird makes his nest in the hope of attracting a suitable partner; when the nest is completed, the female flies from one to the other, inspecting the handiwork of the prospective candidates, then makes a decision and chooses one, leaving the rest to start again, or to seek out a less discerning spouse—

'My God. The work you've put into this place. I heard it was practically derelict.' The words were encouraging enough, but Annie's voice was oddly subdued. She duly admired what he showed her. Michael grew more expansive; told her the history of the place; pointed out the detailing in the plasterwork, the cornices; listed all the jobs he'd done and everything he meant to do next. The children followed them through the house, keeping close to their mother. They seemed impressed by the nursery; but Ben was afraid of the rocking horse and the china dolls with their rows of teeth.

Holly declared it 'creepy' – a word that Rob had also used – and suddenly he understood that Annie didn't like the house any more than the children did.

'Of course I like it. It's beautiful,' she said, but her voice lacked conviction. 'It's just a little—'

'Creepy?' he said.

She shrugged. 'It's like a haunted house. Those dreadful old portraits everywhere. How can you bear to have them around?'

He realized she was talking about the photographs of the Lundys. It almost made him laugh to think that she could find them unnerving. He tried to explain, but sensed that she was conscious of the passing time. She checked her mobile repeatedly.

'There's really no reception here?'

He shook his head. 'I think it's the trees.'

She shivered. 'How can you bear it, Michael? And it's cold – so very *cold*—'

'Is it?' Michael was surprised.

'And all those funny noises—'

The sounds of an old house settling; the mellow creak of floorboards; the moaning of water in lead pipes; the *tick-tick-tick* of a grandfather clock made from an oak tree that had been young when William Shakespeare was a boy.

'I know what an old house sounds like, Michael. This is something different. I tell you, I keep hearing *voices*—'

He smiled. 'I had no idea you were so imaginative.'

She took his arm. 'Come home, Michael. The kids have missed you. I have too. Come home, and we'll try to work things out. We can make a fresh start. Just give up this place, and come back home—'

He looked at her blankly. 'This *is* my home.'

The first step is acceptance.

They left soon after; leaving their gifts unopened under the Christmas tree. Night fell. It brought more snow. Michael sat in the library and smoked. The scent of tobacco filled the air, mixed with the scents of pine needles and woodsmoke from the parlour. He poured a brandy from the decanter on the library table; then moved into the parlour, where the fire had been lit, and sat down on the sofa and waited for something to happen.

Once more, from the kitchen, came the scent of baking. It warmed his heart; it had been so long since he had eaten a home-cooked meal. He lit a branch of candles and turned off the electric light. It looked so much nicer that way; the flames striking sparks of reflected light against the Christmas baubles; the shadows warm and intimate. From the playroom he seemed to hear the voices of his children: Ned's raised in excitement; Emily's murmured warning.

The grandfather clock struck midnight.

Michael smiled. 'Merry Christmas,' he said.

And, closing his eyes for a moment, he laid his head back on the sofa cushion and listened to the sounds of the night: the tapping of branches against the panes; the crackle of logs in the fireplace; the footsteps that crept almost soundlessly across the polished parquet floor, pausing a moment by the tree; the furtive tearing of paper; the childish giggle, stifled at once—

Shh! You'll wake Papa!

Then the sense of someone beside him; sitting down on the sofa; resting her head on his shoulder and slipping her small, cool hand in his. He could smell her perfume now, like violet and sandalwood; could feel her breath against his neck like the tiniest of breezes, and through his half-closed eyelashes, was that the glint of sapphires, the tiniest crescent of white gold clasped around a slender wrist?

The first step is acceptance, they say. After that comes healing. What Michael hadn't realized was how these things mirrored one another; so that salvage could turn to salvation; that a builder might himself be rebuilt and that, in simply letting go, a man could reach further than he'd ever dreamed—

A home is not bricks and mortar. A home is made of those things that endure when the bricks and mortar are gone.

Michael opened his eyes at last.

'Hello, my darling,' he said. 'I'm home.'

Muse

For many years, my local railway station has had a café just like this one. I love it: the ancient cream cakes, crusty with age; the chipped mugs; the ominously sticky carpet; the greasy bacon sandwiches; the inexplicable surliness of the man behind the counter. It is a creative hotspot somehow; whenever I visit, I come out with an idea for a story. Now refurbishment threatens, and I sense that its days are numbered. But so far it has survived intact, like a time capsule from the Fifties. Perhaps some minor deity has the place under its protection . . .

Some people light scented candles. Some pray. Some walk the city streets at night, hoping for inspiration. With me, it's bacon sandwiches and a mug of sweet tea at the café on Platform 5 of Malbry railway station, with my laptop balanced on my knees and the sound of the trains clattering by.

Some places are just like that. Inspirational, I mean. Maybe it's something in the air, or a ley line running underneath. It doesn't look like much from outside. A faded sign that reads STATION CAFÉ, flanked with a painting of two masks, one comic, one tragic, and a musical instrument that might be a lyre. The artistic motif stops there, however. Inside, a sticky countertop; a grill; a glass case displaying a row of pastries that might have been fresh when Lloyd George was last in Downing Street. A shelf of thick ceramic mugs; a clock with a cracked face; a tea urn as big as a Dalek; a cat; a dozen small tables and wobbly chairs; a lingering reek of cigarettes.

Yes, people still smoke on Platform 5. Complaints have been made, but as far as I know, nothing as yet has been done to prevent it. The regular folk have their own café, that sells paninis and root vegetable crisps and nutritionally balanced sandwiches with the calorie content clearly marked on the wrapper. These people have little to do with the Station Café. In fact, they hardly notice it. The only people who come here now are smokers, trainspotters, the homeless, the disenfranchised – and people like myself, of course, who come here for something more than just a cup of tea and a floury bap, or a surly nod from Fat Fred, the fryer, or a place to get in out of the rain and smoke a crafty fag.

It took me some time to understand. I have a studio at home; a desk with a blotter; a telephone. In my narrow field I have achieved a certain celebrity; you've seen my books in WH Smith's; you might even recognize my face. I tell myself I don't need to write in some greasy spoon that smells of smoke and hasn't been swept since the carpet was laid. But the truth is, I do. God knows, I've tried. But this place gets under your skin, somehow. It must be something in the air.

My wife, Jennifer, thinks I'm crazy. Worse, she suspects I'm playing away. Who with, I wonder? Fat Fred, perhaps? Or Brenda Baps, who slices the bread and has to be fifty, at least, I guess, with a face like a Class 40 and an arse like a piano stool? Jennifer knows nothing about creativity. When buying books, she always looks at the author photo before she even reads the blurb. Her idea of literature is the type of novel in which middle-aged women reinvent themselves through plastic surgery, or jolly Afro-Caribbean families win over gangs of hard-bitten Cockneys with nothing but jerk chicken and a positive mental attitude. The ideal reader, in many ways. But she has no idea where it comes from – this *it* that takes hold of words on a page and brings them into sharp relief – no more idea than I have, in fact, after all these years of searching for that elusive pot of gold.

Jennifer believes in the Muse. Well, I've worked at this game for thirty years, and I've never seen hide nor hair of one. Not a swirl of drapery, not a lute string, not a phrase of celestial music. Just little glimpses on the road: a smile on the face of a stranger, a certain light in the evening sky, a dandelion growing between the cracks in a city pavement. And over the past five years there hasn't even been that. Just a desert in which words stretch out like cactus shadows towards a bleak horizon that never gets any closer.

But over the past eighteen months or so, things have changed. The desert has bloomed. Here, of all places, at the Station Café on Platform 5. I'm not the only one to have noticed it, that special gilding in the air. It draws others, too: furtive people with Moleskine notebooks and an air of vague bewilderment. Poets, mostly, I'll admit; but also the occasional novelist like myself, or some artist with his sketchbook, or some harassed writer of TV scripts, searching for perfect dialogue. They all come here, to this decrepit café that most people barely notice, and that Malbry council have been planning to close and replace with a proper waiting room, with wipe-clean chairs and neon lights and a vending machine that sells Diet Coke and Thai chilli crisp-bites.

There are too many things wrong with the old place. Things that new legislation has banned: the smoking; the dubious hygiene; the failure to provide adequate nutritional information. The absence of a wheelchair ramp; the presence of the Platform 5 cat in an area where food is served.

'It'll never happen, though,' says Fred, as he scrapes bacon bits out of the pan and adds them to my sandwich. The bacon bits are the best part, and the bacon is fried in its own grease, thereby ensuring maximum saturation of the soft white roll. The result is something that would make any nutritionist tear out their hair; yet, with the judicious addition of a dollop of brown sauce, served on a chipped and dubious plate (no Health and Safety on Platform 5), and accompanied by a large mug of strong tea, there is something magical about it, something that has fuelled the first hundred pages of a novel that, when released from its bonds, may turn out to be the best thing that this old writer has ever achieved—

Perhaps I do believe in the Muse, after all. A man who believes in the magical properties of a bacon roll can surely believe in anything. Is it the bacon? The brown sauce? The bap? Or is it Fat Fred, who, surly at first, has warmed towards me over the months, finally becoming the one to whom I turn in times of crisis?

Fat Fred knows nothing of syntax or style. But he does know plot, with the instinct of one who has watched many, many people come and go, and in the twitch of an eyebrow or the shrug of his meaty shoulders he can convey approval – or not – of the stories I casually run past him.

Then there's Brenda, whose special task it is to slice the baps for the sandwiches and whose impeccable sense of timing ensures that toast always arrives hot and luscious with half-melted butter, and which, combined with a spoonful of strawberry jam (from the container, home-made), can change the course of a cloudy day and make it feel like summertime. Her manner may seem rather sharp at first, but she can be won over quite easily with a smile and a gesture of goodwill, such as returning the tea mugs and empty plates to their place on the counter for washing-up – which task is performed by Spotty Sam, a cheery youth of seventeen whose relationship with Brenda and Fred reflects enough casual hostility to reinforce my assumption that these ill-assorted people are somehow related – although I have never dared to ask.

Eighteen months of being a regular, of arriving at eight o'clock sharp and leaving only at closing time, have earned me a certain amount of goodwill. But there is a tangible exclusion zone around these people; something more than just aloofness, or the need for privacy. It's not that they are special, in any way. In fact, they are almost caricatures: the fat man; the tram-faced woman; the boy. In all this time I have learnt almost nothing about them; where they live; their interests; what they do when they're not working here.

But today is special; one of those days when events conspire to reveal something more. The air is April in a jar; the sky, a mythical shade of spring. My new book is nearing its climax, requiring just one more ingredient before the alchemy is complete. And all the trains from Malbry are cancelled – some kind of problem on the Manchester line – which means that the Station Café is almost deserted, except for one of our regulars – a local poet (recognizable by that Moleskine notebook and the floppy hair that seems to come as standard in poetic circles) – and a couple of elderly train enthusiasts counting carriages at the end of the platform.

I take my usual seat by the door. I order tea and a bacon bap. Brenda looks tired and distracted; Fred is nowhere to be seen. The Platform 5 cat, a tabby, slinks behind the counter, where I suspect there is food, in blatant contravention of Health and Safety regulations.

Brenda makes the sandwich and brings it over to my seat. It's not quite as good as the ones Fred makes, but it's good enough all the same, hot and just lightly toasted enough to caramelize the sugary bread.

'Fred not here, Brenda?' I enquire. I always return my crockery. This, I feel, gives me the right to ask such a personal question.

Brenda gives me a measuring look. 'He'll be about here somewhere,' she says. 'Things to be getting on with, like.'

I realize that it is the first time I have been to the Station Café and Fred has not been behind the counter. *Things to be getting on with* doesn't seem sufficient reason, somehow, for such a dereliction. Sam, too, looks preoccupied, a world away from his cheery self; he lurks behind the counter, wiping a glass in a perfunctory fashion and casting occasional glances out of the window at the track with its continuing absence of passing trains.

'What's going on?' I ask him.

Sam gives me a comic look. 'Dunno.'

I lower my voice. 'Don't give me that.' The café is almost deserted. The poet with his notebook is sitting too far away to hear; besides, he is lost in his own world and will not emerge till lunchtime. 'There's something wrong. Fred isn't here. And you two look like a wet weekend. So what's the problem?'

Sam shakes his head. 'Them suits from Head Office. We got a letter. They're shutting us down.'

'The council's always saying that,' I tell him. 'We'll start a petition.' Fact is, they're *always* threatening to close down the café on Platform 5; but no one ever believes they will. The place is a part of the station. You can't imagine it not being there.

'It's not the council,' Brenda says. 'It's *our* Head Office. They're calling us home. Cutbacks, they're telling us.'

'*Your* Head Office?' I've always assumed that the Station Café stood alone. It certainly doesn't *look* like a chain – so who are the suits from Head Office?

Brenda gives a little shrug. 'I don't suppose it matters now.

You've always been a good customer.' She casts a disapproving glance at the floppy-haired poet, who will spend all morning sitting there, nursing a lukewarm cup of tea, then shoot off without a goodbye or even returning his crockery. 'If you must know,' she tells me, 'we're not really what you'd call a strictly legitimate business.'

'I'm not sure what that means,' I say.

'It means,' she tells me patiently, 'that all good things must come to an end. We've all been here on Platform 5 since practically for ever; keeping our heads down, making do, not attracting attention. We've really enjoyed working here. But now, with the recession and that, we're being pulled back to Head Office. They don't have the means to allow us to work on these personal projects any more. We have to rejoin the rest of the team, and that means closing shop, I'm afraid. By the end of the week at the latest—'

'By the end of the *week*?' I say. 'But what about my manuscript?'

I try to explain my predicament. How, for some ludicrous reason, over the course of the past eighteen months my only inspiration has been here, in the café on Platform 5; how those greasy bacon sandwiches and giant cups of builder's tea have been my only lifeline. If it closes down now, how on earth will I finish my book?

Brenda looks at Sam and sighs. 'Yes,' she says. 'Well, that's a shame.'

I try to explain my delusion in terms of simple psychology. Writers are superstitious folk, constantly under pressure; relying on personal rituals that rarely make sense to anyone else. Some can only write in a particular font, or at a particular time of day, or in a particular place—

Sam grins. 'You don't need to explain. I know exactly what you mean.'

'Really? I had no idea. What do you write?'

'Oh, no, not me. I'm more of a theatre kind of guy.'

I try to picture Sam on stage, but can't.

'That's really more Fred's cup of tea,' he says with a glance at Brenda. 'Writing, poetry, plays and that.'

'Well, that's nice,' I tell him. 'It's good to have a hobby. And what about you, Brenda?'

'I used to be a dancer.'

'Oh.' I keep my smile polite. But I can more easily picture fat, barely literate Fred as a writer, or Sam as a thespian, than Brenda Baps as a dancer.

'You shouldn't judge on appearances,' she says, as if she has read my mind. 'Inspiration comes in all shapes and sizes, as I'm sure you must already know.'

And then she goes back to the counter, where, under the guise of rearranging the cakes, she lapses into silence.

I finish my tea rather slowly. The floppy-haired poet has already gone. Brenda collects the crockery, tidies up the counter, then finally goes to the side door and flips the OPEN sign to CLOSED.

'Might as well shut early today,' she says. 'There's nobody going to come.'

'You're really going, then?'

Brenda nods. 'I'm sorry, love. It can't be helped.' Then, an idea seems to strike her. 'I suppose you could run it yourself, though. I mean, if *we* could manage the place, how hard can it be for someone like you? All you need to be able to do is fry bacon and brew tea—'

Somehow I manage not to smile. 'I don't really—'

'*And* you could keep the cat,' says Sam, his expression brightening.

I sigh. 'Much as I like cats, I don't think that solves my problem.'

'It might. You never know,' says Sam.

Which is why, ten minutes later, for reasons that I suspect will prove impossible to explain to my wife, I come home early, without having written a single word, but carrying a tabby cat, which jumps out of my arms when I arrive and heads straight for the fridge door.

Jennifer is out of the house. I pour a saucer of milk for the cat and head for my study, where I fully expect to sit in barren silence for the next three hours.

Instead, I find myself writing. The Muse, whoever she is, has clocked in. By four o'clock I have six thousand words and the final piece of my plot-puzzle. No bacon roll, no tea, no toast, but even so it keeps coming. Inspiration, when it strikes, strikes like an express train.

The cat sits purring under my chair. I almost forget it's there at all. Only at five o'clock, when my fingers are sore from typing, does it leave its place under the chair and start demanding dinner.

I give the cat a slice of ham. It purrs appreciation. It is wearing a collar, I see, with its name stencilled on to a metal tag. CALLIOPE, it says. Rather an odd name for a cat; not what I would have expected from simple people like Brenda and Fred. The name is rather familiar – I look it up on the internet.

As I thought, it's a classical name; the name of one of the Muses. The page lists all nine Muses, their names, their symbols and attributes. Three of them strike me especially, perhaps because I've seen them every day above the door of the Station Café on Platform 5: the tragic mask of Melpomene, the comic mask of Thalia, and the lyre, the symbol of Terpsichore, Muse of the dance.

Once more, I think of the Platform 5 three. Fat Fred with his air of tragedy; Sam with his cheery, comic face; Brenda, whose claim to have once been a dancer still fills me with incredulity. Of course, it's a ludicrous parallel. The Muse is just an archetype; a metaphor that represents Mankind's eternal striving. To imagine that they might be *real*, able to take on the Aspects of human beings and intervene in human affairs – well, that's just silly. Isn't it? It's the sort of thing that Jennifer might read in a book of short stories written by the kind of frivolous woman writer who happens to like that sort of thing. But I know better. I do not stoop to fanciful plot premises. I study human nature; my inspiration comes from within; from blood and sweat and hard work. This clarity is what sets me apart. I am completely self-aware.

As for the cat – frivolously named after the Muse of poetry – I don't suppose it would hurt anyone if I kept it here for a week or two. Not that I would ever believe that it's anything more than just a cat – but artists are bizarre, you know; creative; superstitious. Some light scented candles. Some pray to their ancestors. Some keep an object on their desk for luck and inspiration.

As for the Café on Platform 5 – so far, it's business as usual, though now it is run by volunteers – most of them out-of-work actors, would-be poets and other such folk with time on their hands. I still like to work here, too; I feel it keeps me grounded, somehow, more in touch with my public. I take the cat – it gets restless at home. Besides, the customers miss it.

And so the Café continues to thrive; and its customers – poets, would-be playwrights, even writers like myself, who appreciate the irony of working in simple surroundings – continue to stay in touch with their Muse over buttered toast and cups of tea and greasy bacon sandwiches.

The Game

This story came to me late one night, from that haunted warehouse of stories, the internet. I hope it's just a story. But part of me thinks perhaps it's true.

There is no fucking Level X. I know because I've played it. I've been right up to Level 1000, and I swear there's nothing but the Game in there, no secret message, no special download, no naked chicks or anything, nothing but another screen of numbers and shapes and jumbled crapola that looks like one of those old arcade games, like Space Invaders or Breakout, that style freaks buy for their converted lofts and call it Eighties Retro.

Of course you don't talk about the Game. Only losers and quitters do that. Oh, and Charlie. More of him soon. Losers talk about the Game, but they know fuck all about anything. Quitters try to pretend they got there, but you can always tell, somehow. OC – he's my best friend – says he's been past

10,000, but that's just OC mouthing off. No one spends *that* much time online.

Still, it was OC who got me playing the Game in the first place. OCD, we call him, because he can never fucking keep still. If it's not his foot going up and down, then it's his knee, or his fingers. Tap-tap-tap, like a mouse in a wheel. Still, he's a good Gamer, faster than anyone else I've seen. And he's the one who told me, way back when it all began, about this Game on the internet, this Game that everyone's playing.

It doesn't look like much at first, he tells me, *but it's addictive. It gets to you.*

It gets to you. Well, duh. No shit. There are brown circles round his eyes, like he hasn't slept for about a year. I haven't seen him at school for days. I mean, that's fucking commitment, right? Maybe he wasn't mouthing off, after all.

You got to be serious, he says, *otherwise there's no fucking point. Don't start if you're not serious.*

I told him I was.

OK, man. I'm just saying. Because there's no website for the Game, there's only these special URLs. You have to know where to find them.

Quit fucking around, I tell him. You want me to play or don't you?

Course I do, he tells me. *I'm fucking showing you, aren't I? So you start at Level 1, man, and if you get through, and if you don't quit, then you get the codes for Level 2. And 3, and 4, and so on—*

And what if you don't get through? I said.

You'll know. And he gives me this grin, like someone

214

chewing on a foil wrapper, and his eyes are half closed, but in them I can see all these little dancing lights, reflected from the computer screen. *But it only shows you the code once. And it's only good for twenty-four hours. After that the link expires. And it's no good trying again from scratch, because the Game won't let you. You gotta show commitment if you want to get there.*

So – get where, exactly?

Well, that's the interesting part, he says. *No one really knows that. No one knows how many levels there are, or if it just goes on for ever. No one knows who wrote the software. Some people reckon it's a joke. Losers or quitters, all of them. But the real players are all still here. Waiting for the big one.*

The big one, I says.

Level X. And his voice goes down to a whisper. *You'll know if you get there. Just not when. For some it's, like, Level 101, and for some it's Level 1000. I heard some guy got it at Level 12, just a newbie, and suddenly, wham! Level X. Just like that. Lucky bastard. That's what it's like. You never know. But that's the Game. That's why we play.*

It sounded kind of random to me. But I thought, why not? It's only a game.

So – what's on Level X, man?

He shrugs. *I told you. I ain't got there yet. But I will. I can tell. I can feel it. I'm close.* He grins, and his eyes light up again, bright little sparks like you get from burnt paper, dancing and flickering all the way down. *I've heard so many rumours,* he says. *Some people say it takes you to a special site. Some kind of hub for Gamers. Or a place where you can download free* porn. Or some kind of top-security site, something to do with the military. There was one guy, a Loser, who swore blind he'd found some kind of portal into another dimension or something, but it all turned out to be bullshit, and anyway, he died a week later, and his parents tried to blame the Game, but everyone knew it wasn't that, he was into all kinds of crazy shit—

You gonna show me, or what? I says.

He looks at me with those weird eyes, and he's tap-tap-tapping his foot on the floor, the way he does when he's all wired up. *You better not let me down, man. If you quit—*

I'm not gonna quit.

OK. Sit down. Just do what I do.

So he logs in. Enters this code. I put in my details, my e-mail and shit. And then, all at once, the screen comes up. No rules, no home page, no warning. I'm in the Game. I'm on Level 1.

Well, it doesn't look like much at first. No flash graphics, no artwork at all, just numbers on a black screen, like some piece of Eighties shit.

I know. It gets better. Trust me, he says.

So what do you have to do, man?

Just feel it. Move in. Take control.

And that's how I started playing the Game. Three hours later, and it felt like I'd started a minute before. OC was long gone, but at first I didn't notice. I was on my own PC at home, my folks were downstairs, doing little parent-y things. The numbers on the black screen were moving in some kind of random cascade – except that it wasn't random at all, you could see that after an hour or two. Grouping the numbers in certain ways, you could make up a picture of something else, something *behind* the numbers, like trying to tune an old TV. And although there wasn't a soundtrack or anything, I'd put in my earplugs just as an aid to concentration, and from time to time I could hear something, a whispering, or a rustling.

It was kind of original. Interesting, even though I didn't really get what to do. And then it cut off, so suddenly that I wondered if the power had gone, and I cursed for a bit and pressed Refresh, but nothing happened. I checked my PC. It was running just fine. Checked my internet access. Fine. Then I looked into my history file to see where I'd been for over three hours. But my history folder had been deleted; there was no sign of the freaking Game.

I messaged OC. He wasn't online. I tried his phone. No answer. So – how the hell was I to know whether I'd got through Level 1? I looked at my watch. It was half past twelve. I'd lost half the evening playing the Game, my homework was a dead loss, and what did I have to show for it all? It occurred to me that OC might have been trying to mess with my mind, but it didn't seem his style, somehow. So – had I won, or had I lost? Was I still in the Game, or not?

And then my inbox blipped. *Got Mail!* The sender was *admin*@something-or-other, a web address half a mile long, all made up of numbers and hashtags and stuff.

I opened it. Read:

LEVEL 1. YOU WIN. 200 KUDOS. PLAY OR QUIT?

There was a link to each option, underlined in unblinking blue.

And so I hit PLAY, and waited.

Ten seconds later, there it was: another link. A URL. I wanted to see what would happen next, so I hit the link. I was back in the Game. No homepage, no Level 2, just those numbers swimming like fish against the deep black background. Just the same as Level 1, except that it all seemed clearer, somehow; deeper, high-def, less grainy.

Makes no sense, *I* know that. But that's the way I saw it; and although I was beat, and had school the next day, I kept on playing anyway, and I swear next time I looked up, it was five in the morning and the light was poking in through the gap in the curtains, and I'd gamed away most of the damn night without even being aware of it, and my head ached like a bastard, and all I could think about, as I looked at the screen once more gone suddenly blank, was this: *Did I get through? Am I still in the Game?*

Five minutes later, an e-mail from *admin* told me that, yes, I was through to Level 3; my kudos was now at 550 and – did I want to play or quit?

Well—

No point going to school today, I told myself as I hit the link. I might as well call in a sickie, I thought; get some rest, do my homework, have a shower and a bite to eat and write the day off before it began. The decision made me feel better at once. My folks would believe me if I told them I was ill. In those days, I rarely played hookey. And so I went on to Level 3, and finished at noon, shagged out and limp, but richer by 680 kudos and all set to link with Level 4—

So that's how it began. The Game. The fucking fabulous,

pointless, addictive, soul-eating, life-sucking, beautiful Game.
Not as intense as the first time. I learned I had to pace myself.
Be a good boy during the day, then log on in the evenings.
Otherwise, my folks would have guessed that I wasn't quite
myself any more. At school or at home, I lived the Game. I ate
and drank and dreamed the Game. And when I wasn't playing
the Game, I went into websites and chatrooms and message
boards and discussion groups, trying to find out whatever I
could about who had designed and written the Game, who
was still playing, who had quit, and most especially about
Level X, which some believed was a pot of gold and others
thought was a crock of shit.

In those days, I was a believer. A born-again player of the
Game. Like OC, whom I still saw occasionally, and who
sometimes talked to me online (that is, when he wasn't playing the Game), I believed in kudos, and Level X, and the fact
that we were doing something more than just burning out
our retinas for the sake of a bunch of pixels.

Level 16, 15,000 kudos, and I was just getting started.
What's more, I'd begun to think I knew where I was going;
that somewhere in that mess of numbers and shapes there
was an answer beginning to emerge. I guess that's what we
all think – at least, until the moment it hits, the moment of
truth, you might say.

Mine was last month, when Charlie died. Some kind of a
brain incident, they said; apparently he was an undiagnosed
epileptic. He was also a classmate of mine – I said a classmate, not a friend. In fact I'd always hated him, and not just
because he was bigger than I was, or because he was good at

sports, or because he had perfect teeth, or even because he'd bullied me since both of us were still in shorts.

No, I hated Charlie because Charlie claimed to have reached Level X, and everyone believed him. Except OC and me, of course. *We* knew Charlie was full of shit. For a start, he didn't look like a hard-core Gamer. His skin was too clear, his hair was too clean, his homework results were way too good, and he had that fresh, outdoorsy glow that comes with sex, fresh fruit and sports, and being in the open air a lot.

Girls liked Charlie – and he liked them. *That* was why he played the Game. Just to pick up chicks at school. Not my idea of serious. Which was why OC and I were so supremely pissed off when we heard the rumours going round: that Charlie had scored on Level X, and that now he was selling the Game.

That's right. *Selling* it. Guys like Charlie don't give stuff away; they know how to market themselves. And last week, Charlie was selling the Game to a crowd of hopeful wannabes, spilling secrets like they were trash, totally disrespecting the ones like OC and me who kept our mouths shut and stuck to the rules, and never said zip to anyone.

Jesus. You should have heard him. The Gospel according to Charlie. Everything was out there, though more or less inaccurate; how you could move up the levels by looking behind the number screen; how you could earn kudos, and how (this was a new one to me) actually *spend* your kudos on stuff—

Spend it? How? said OC.

You have to feel it, said Charlie. *To look behind reality. To understand that all this* – he waved his hand vaguely in the air – *is really nothing but numbers and pixels stacked together to make it look as if something's there. In fact, there's nothing but space out here. No you. No me. Just space, man. Like quantum physics or something.*

At this point Charlie's bullshit got a little harder to follow. OC tried to get him to explain, but Charlie clammed up suddenly, playing coy and saying, *I gotta be careful – say too much, all kinds of bad shit could go down.*

What kind of shit? I was curious.

He grinned. His teeth were a dazzling white. *If I tell you that*, he says, *then you'd be in the shit as well. Besides, only quitters and losers blab. You want to watch what you ask for.*

The next thing I knew was OC and me, getting high in my room that night, eating chocolate-chip cookies and flipping from chatroom to bulletin board, trying to figure out ways to get back at Charlie – just for being a smug bastard, I guess, but mostly for bringing the Game into disrepute. Then we were on the Game again – we never could keep away for long – and I maxed out on Level 29 and earned another 4000 K, but this time when the inbox blipped and the message came in saying I'd come through, there was another choice to make:

LEVEL 29. YOU WIN, it said. 100,000 KUDOS. SAVE OR SPEND?

I hesitated a moment or two, fingers poised to hit the keys. The SAVE OR SPEND message started to flash.

I looked at OC, flaked out on the couch with a half-eaten cookie in his hand. 'You ever get one like this, man?'

'Wha?'

'An option to spend your kudos.'

OC sat up at that. He looked completely wasted, but any-thing new about the Game and he was on the ball at once. 'Show me,' he said, and frowned at the screen.

'So I guess old Charlie was right, after all. What do you think?'

The message was flashing insistently now.

'Hit it, man,' he said at last. 'Hit the SPEND, and see what transpires.'

'Trans-fuckin'-*what*?'

'Just hit it,' he said.

And so I did. I hit the switch. For a second or two the screen went blank, then came the message: PLAY OR QUIT?

Obviously, I hit PLAY. And then – well, I guess I zoned out for a bit. OC's dope was unusually strong, and I hadn't slept much the previous night, and when I came out of the whispery, skunky haze I found that my kudos rating was back to square one, that OC had taken off and that dawn was just a beat away. Weirder still, I'd somehow managed to go up 35 levels of the Game all in one night – which wasn't just good, it was fucking *impossible* – must be a glitch in the software, I thought, because no one's that good, I mean *no one*—

Still, I felt OK, I thought. Better than I deserved, perhaps. So I showered, got dressed, ate a massive breakfast and went off to school feeling mellow and wide awake and looking for a chance to discuss last night's Game with someone who really understood.

OC wasn't there, though. That didn't really surprise me. I guessed he was still wiped out from last night – he'd been hitting the Game harder than I had, and he never knew when to give it a break. I guess that's the OCD behaviour, but by then it was already getting so bad that sometimes he'd forget to eat – and it was starting to show, too. He had that Gamer's stoop you get, and the kind of complexion that comes from too little sunlight and too much tube. His parents didn't seem to care – or if they did they couldn't stop him. They were much older than most parents – all grey hair and Sudoku – and I guess they thought it was normal for him to spend his time the way he did. Anyway, he wasn't at school, which was how I got talking to Charlie.

I found him eating his lunch at one, all alone up in the sports grounds. Which was kind of weird, as usually in those days he'd be sitting in the JCR, surrounded by girls and wannabe Gamers, holding court and basically being awesome. Today he looked off-colour, though, as if he was coming down with flu. His hair was kind of greasy, too, and there was a patch of red across his face that might have been eczema or something.

I sat down next to him; opened my lunch. Cheese and ham on rye bread; not bad. Ma goes through these phases of healthy eating, and you never know what's going to be in there – couscous or mung beans or pasta or what; once it was fucking *falafel*—

Charlie had a French baguette. He hadn't eaten much of it. I said, 'How's the Game? You still in?'

Charlie shrugged. 'Course I am.' He didn't sound too happy, though. I tried to bring him out of it. Not because I really cared about his state of mind, but because I wanted

223

a chance to talk about what had happened that night. Not that I remembered it all; I guess the weed makes things hazy, but I did remember the whispering, and the way I'd reached in *behind* the screen – or so it felt to me at the time – like some kind of delicate instrument made up of nothing but numbers and light, and how my hand was like the bow or something, and the light was like the strings, and the music – if you could call it that – was like tuning in to some distant and strange, like, *resonance* or something—

I know. I'm beginning to sound like OC. But that was how it felt to me. Cosmic. Important. Mysterious. And Charlie knew something, too; I could tell. It was written all over his face. Maybe not a good thing. But still, important. Important to *me*.

I said: 'I thought you got to X, man. Where d'you go after Level X?'

He gave me a sour look. 'Give me a break. There is no fucking Level X.'

'So all that was bullshit?'

I'd suspected it was. Guys like Charlie are born that way, with a silver spoonful of shit in their mouths. I doubted he'd even played the Game; let alone earned kudos. But now I started to wonder again. Perhaps it was something in his face, or because he'd said the F-word. Guys like Charlie are way too clean to use the F-word. His dad's a lay preacher, his ma's a psychotherapist, *and* he gets baguettes for lunch. Probably with Gruyère or something. Bet he can pronounce it, too.

'You know what it's like,' he told me at last, looking down

at his baguette. 'People get curious, that's all. I got carried away in the moment. Emily was there, and—'

Emily. I understood. We'd all seen Charlie's girlfriend. One of those girls that get you like a fish-hook in the guts. Way, way out of my league; but somehow sweet with it, like she genuinely didn't know how the scummy half lived.

'And when someone mentioned Level X—' Charlie shrugged. 'I let it slip. So what? No harm, no foul. Anyway, there's no Level X.'

'So tell me about kudos,' I said.

He shrugged again. 'There's nothing to tell. It's just their way of keeping score.'

'What's yours?' I asked him.

He looked down at his uneaten baguette. 'I don't remember,' he said.

Well, that was a lie. When you play the Game, you *always* know your kudos score. It's like the followers on your Twitter account; you always know when you've lost one, and you always feel that little sting when one of them stops following you—

'You don't *remember*?' I told him.

'Look, leave me alone, man. I don't feel well.'

That was probably true, I thought. Old Charlie didn't look well at all. I wondered if Emily had dumped him, and whether I might be in with a chance. I knew I wasn't really, but dreaming never hurt anyone. Besides, I felt good. Maybe because of last night's Game; maybe because of the sunshine. Summer was coming in by then, and I could feel the sun on my face, like I'd spent ten years in the dark. I'd have to spend more time outside, I told myself as I left him there with his baguette. Too much Game makes Jack a dull boy, and I needed to clear my complexion.

Still, I kept on playing the Game. A couple of levels every night, just so the link wouldn't expire. I didn't want to get timed out just when I was doing so well. And I *was* doing *very* well – up to Level 100 now, and back to 1000 kudos, although since that first time I'd never again got the SAVE OR SPEND option. The Game can be kind of random that way – just like life, I guess you'd say – and I kept it under reasonable control. Partly because of my parents – they were a lot more technically savvy than OC's, and I didn't want them to start taking too much of an interest in what I was doing online. But mostly because of Emily, who turned out not only to have dumped Charlie, but to be in the market for someone like me—

I know. It sounds too good to be true. Me and Emily – so good it's almost wrong, like finding smoked salmon in my sandwiches instead of cheese and pickle. My school grades improved. I started to groom. I gave up swearing (well, almost). My complexion cleared right up. I started to run in the evenings, and soon I could do a couple of miles without even breaking sweat—

Not that I ever forgot the Game. OC was right: it's addict-ive. I told myself it was therapy; something to help me wind down after a hard day's work. Some people had music; some had TV. I had the Game. Simple as that. And if sometimes I wondered where I'd been during those whispery hours in the dark, with my face so close to the flickering screen that I felt

I could almost push myself through – into what? A cradle of pixels? A matrix of light? – I never let it get to me, but stuck to the rules, and kept in play, and never talked about the Game.

And then, Charlie died. Very suddenly. Some kind of undiagnosed condition, they said, though his mother and father blamed the Game. Turns out there was some kind of support group going, of parents whose kids had suffered what they called 'adverse reactions' – including, if you believed them, such varied symptoms as antisocial behaviour, depression, spots, loss of appetite, mood swings, secretiveness, narcissism, poor grades at school and so on.

So – welcome to Planet Teenager, huh? Except that Charlie's mother insisted that Charlie was never like that. And Charlie's mother had influence, plus Charlie's dad was a lay preacher, and so then the press got hold of it all, and there was a piece in the local rag and something else on the local news, and then the nationals got hold of it, and before anyone knew what was going on, some middle-aged officious bitch had written a piece in the *Daily Mail* blaming the Game for the *tragic death of this popular student* (funny how dead teens are always *popular students*, unless they did a Columbine, in which case they're always misfits and loners who everyone knew was going to turn bad). Go figure. Anyway, all of a sudden, the net was jammed with comments and angst. The Game was hashtagged on Twitter and everyone had an opinion, even those who'd never played. OC's parents finally twigged that their precious son was playing the Game, and took away his computer, which meant that every night he was back at my place, wanting a turn on my PC, wheedling, 'Just half an hour, man,' and generally driving me crazy.

It wasn't that I didn't want to see him or anything, but what with the Game and Emily, I just didn't have enough hours in the day, and besides, old OC was getting to be a bit of a liability, what with his twitching and his staring eyes, and let's face it, his dubious hygiene—

So anyway, I thought he must have found an alternative place to play. Maybe the games arcade, or the library, because for a few days I didn't see him at school, and I guess I forgot to call him. His parents called by mine once, asking if he was with me. I told them I hadn't seen him, but I didn't give him much thought after that. I figured he'd turn up soon enough. Besides, I had concerns of my own.

And then it happened to me again. I got the SAVE OR SPEND option. Except that this time I got a third choice: one that said GAMBLE.

I was on a roll – 300,000 kudos and up to Level 999, though still no sign of Level X. And I thought to myself as I sat by the screen, watching that cascade of numbers: What if this is all I get? Just playing the Game every night, reaching for something that never comes? What if *this* is the point of it all?

SAVE, SPEND OR GAMBLE? the screen said, and I thought: What the hell?

I pressed GAMBLE.

For a moment the screen went totally blank. Then it flickered back into life, showed me my kudos as 500,000. I waited to see what level I'd reached. The Game was slow in responding.

Finally, the main screen came back, with the PLAY OR QUIT? buttons, just like before. Except this time they didn't just say that. Now they just said DOUBLE OR QUIT?

I frowned over that one for a while. What was it supposed to mean? And then the screen began to flash, almost like it was getting impatient, and a message popped up:

TEN SECONDS.

NINE SECONDS.

And now, behind the screen, I could see numbers moving up and down; swimming in schools like tiny fish, bound by morphic resonance, occasionally breaking formation or blurting out like broken glass from a shattered windscreen—

The countdown went on.

EIGHT SECONDS.

SEVEN SECONDS.

SIX SECONDS.

FIVE SECONDS.

DOUBLE OR QUIT?

I figured my kudos was off the scale. I was in the fucking Zone. My head was filled with those numbers, my body was nothing but pixels and light; I felt like in a second I'd be able to reach through the screen and touch the face of Almighty God—

And so I typed *Double*, in a hurry.

The screen went blank again. Twenty seconds later, my inbox blipped and I got an e-mail from *admin@*. All it said was: GAME OVER.

No TRY AGAIN. No second chance. No Level X. No kudos. Game over. I was out.

I stared at the screen. 'No fucking *way*—' I remember reading in English Lit the story of this poet who'd taken acid or something and started to write this amazing poem, but some random guy had turned up at the door and stayed, like, *for ever*, and when he'd gone, there was nothing left, no poem, no soul.

Well, that's how I felt, being out of the Game. I felt like I'd seen a glimpse of God and then somebody had snatched it away. I phoned OC. No answer. I guessed he must have his plugs in, so I texted him instead.

WTF? I lost the Game!

His answer came almost immediately. *I know, man. Sorry.*

How? I said.

I'm there now. I felt it. Level 10,000 and counting.

Level 10,000? Bullshit. No one spends that much time online. Still, I guess that solved the mystery of where OC had been getting his kicks. His folks must have relented and given him his PC back.

You got to be shitting me, I said.

No shit. Amazing. Like nothing I've ever seen b4.

I'm not sure what pissed me most: that I'd lost the Game, or that OC was still in it. I even wondered if he was winding me up; but OC isn't subtle like that. *Wasn't. Isn't.* Whatever.

I had to ask him. *What's it like?*

Amazing. Wow. Amazing.

Well, OC was never going to be the most articulate of

guys, and in the heat of the Game, plus whatever he was taking, I figured that was all I'd get.

Can I come over to your place? I said.

I kind of knew it would break my heart, but I had to see it for myself. It wouldn't be the same, of course, but—

Not at my place, he said.

I was starting to ask him where he was when another text bipped into my inbox. For a moment the words on the screen swam blurrily, like something on the ocean floor.

I think this is it, man. Finally. Level X.

Bullshit! But I knew he wasn't lying. OC's never lied to me, not even when we were little kids. No time to reach him now, I thought: all I could do was stay where I was and try to make him talk to me.

Oh, man. This is awesome, he said. *4kin indescribable.*

Well, thanks, OC. The man of words. *Talk to me*, I urged him.

The pause before he answered me seemed like an eternity. Then he said: *Can't. You're not in the Game.*

What? You can't be serious! Suddenly I was so angry that I almost slung the phone against the nearest wall. I couldn't believe he was blowing me off, not after all we'd been through; not after it had been him who'd started me on the Game in the first place. All those nights I'd taken him in; all the times I'd protected him against the other kids at school who made fun of his OCD and wanted to steal his glasses—

I dialled his number. This time, he picked up. The line was freaking awful, but I could just hear OC's voice against a background of white noise, and the frantic, familiar tap-tapping of his fingernails against the desktop.

'Where the hell are you, man?' I said.

He sounded a million miles away. *Everywhere*, I thought he said. *Everywhere and nowhere. Charlie was right. It's all space. Nothing there but empty space—*

Well, of course, he was out of his head. God knows what he'd been taking. But it creeped me out to hear him like that, his voice all grainy and distant, like he was on Mars or something instead of just around the block. I strained to try and hear him, but his voice kept fading out, like there was interference.

I wish I could tell you what it's like, the dreamy, druggy voice went on. *But I guess you have to see for yourself. If a man could pass through Paradise in a dream, and have a flower presented to him as a pledge that his soul had really been there, and if he found that flower in his hand when he awoke – huh, man, what then?*

His voice was starting to zone out. 'Tell me where you are,' I said.

He gave a tiny chuckle that raised all the hairs on the back of my neck. *Gotta go. Take care*, he said—

And that was the last I heard of him. They found him two days later, in an abandoned warehouse. The coroner reckoned he'd been dead for at least a week, though the cause was inconclusive. Of course, his parents blamed the Game, but it could have been drugs or anything. The *Daily Mail* described him as a *popular, promising student*, and the school declared a holiday for those who wanted to attend the funeral, which gained him more friends and more popularity than he'd ever had in his life.

I don't play online games any more. Instead, I keep my head down. That last conversation with OC was creepy enough to put me off, but recently I've been hearing his voice in the damnedest of places. Once it was from the radio as I searched between stations. Once I was talking to Emily on the phone – the landline; I don't use my mobile so much any more – and I could have sworn I heard him then, tapping against the receiver. Once I was on my laptop, checking my Facebook messages, trying to ignore the one that keeps coming back from his account – *Would you like to reconnect?* – and I thought I heard his laughter. And then I sometimes hear his voice when I download stuff from YouTube; or mixed low in a soundtrack, or sometimes from my guitar amp, like signals from the other side—

And people keep asking about the Game. Am I still playing? Did I quit? Do I still have kudos?

Nowadays, I try not to think about those things any more. Because when I do, I find myself almost believing that maybe Life is like the Game, with nothing but empty spaces between the cradle of pixels and the grave; and that somewhere outside of space and time, there's a Player, glued to a monitor, one giant hand on the keyboard, ready to press Control/Alt/Delete on the whole damn universe—

And Level X? There's no Level X. That's just a story we tell our kids to keep them happy and playing the Game. Because if we told them the *real* truth, that there's no control, no enlightenment, no winners, no losers, no Level X, they'd all go crazy, like Charlie and me.

That's why we never mention the Game. That's why we keep pretending. And that's why the kids keep playing it – earning their kudos, counting their points, moving up the levels towards the final GAME OVER . . .

Of course, I could be totally wrong. There's no way of proving a negative. I'm out of the Game, so what do I know? Everyone gets the same chance. That's what I said to Emily the other day, when she reached Level 6. She isn't much of a player, but someone might get lucky.

So—

Are you in or are you out?

PLAY OR QUIT?

It's your choice.

Faith and Hope Get Even

The elderly are easily bullied, often neglected, sometimes by those very professionals who claim to be in charge of their welfare. We see it all too often in hospitals and care homes – old people being patronized, forgotten, denied basic care, sometimes even abused. Our society has a habit of turning away from such unpalatable realities. In this story, Faith and Hope manage to get some of their own back. If it inspires anyone else to fight back too, then all the better.

How kind of you to come and see us again. We don't get many visitors, you know – except my son, Tom, who makes regular duty calls, but never really has anything to say. You can't talk to him; all you can do is listen and nod in the right places. His job; his boss; house prices. And the weather, don't forget; in Tom's world, all old people ever want to do is talk about the weather.

I know, however, that there are things from which I ought to shelter him. The Meadowbank Retirement Home is a stage on which tragedy and farce pursue each other with Chaucerian vigour, and it takes a good sense of humour (and a strong stomach) to get by. My son, much as I love him, has neither; and so I stick to the weather. Fortunately for my sanity, I still have Hope.

Hope is my dearest friend. She was a professor of English Literature in her youth, and she still has that Cambridge manner, a certain crispness, an almost military tilt of the head, even though she has been blind for fifteen years and hasn't had a visit since the day she came in. But she does have all her marbles – more marbles, in fact, than most people were born with – and she manages, with a little help from me in my wheelchair, to maintain the dignity and humour essential for survival in a place like this.

We used to be trusties. Not so now: since last year's escapade to London the management has kept us under a supervision of near-Gestapo closeness. A receptionist guards the exit; another mans the desk in anticipation of trouble, or in case either of us attempts to exceed our five-minute weekly phone allowance.

Kelly, the blonde with the low IQ, has long since been replaced. In her place the governors have appointed a general manager to oversee the running of things: a large, capable woman called Maureen, who speaks to us with a relentless, Wagnerian jollity that fails to hide the metallic glint in her small, blue-shadowed eye.

The others defer to Maureen. There's thick Claire; chatty Denise; Sad Harry, who never smiles; trainee Helen, cheery Chris (our special friend) and the new girl, Lorraine, who smokes in the staff lounge and uses Hope's Chanel perfume when Hope is out of the room. Chris – he's the only one who really talks to us – says the change of management shouldn't affect us in any way. But he looks preoccupied; he isn't as cheery as he once was, doesn't sing to us as often as he did, and I noticed the other day that he'd even taken the gold ring out of his ear.

'Maureen didn't like it,' he said when I asked him. 'I'm already on a warning, and I really need this job.'

Well, *we* know that. You see, Chris was in trouble once, with the law, and now he has to be especially careful. Oh, nothing serious – just bad company and worse luck. A nine-month sentence for breaking and entering; then community service and a clean slate. But clean slate or not, these things have a habit of following you around. Even now, years later, he still can't get a credit card, or a loan, or even open a bank account. It's all there in his file; and people like Maureen tend to read files when they ought to be reading people.

It was Mother's Day last month. Hope always feels a bit down on Mother's Day, though she never shows it; it's just that I've known her for such a long time that I notice these things. Her daughter Priscilla lives in California, and never writes, though we do get a postcard from time to time – cheap things, badly printed, which I read to her aloud, with a little poetic licence where necessary.

I have to be careful; Hope always knows when I go too far. All the same, she has kept them all – in a shoe-box in her wardrobe – and if only Priscilla knew how much they meant to her, she might put more thought into what she writes.

Tom came, of course. His wife never does; nor do the children. I have to say I don't blame them; why should anyone want to sit in here on a lovely spring day, when they could be out and about with their families? He wanted to take me for a drive; but I didn't want to leave Hope, and I knew Maureen wouldn't allow Tom to take both of us out together. So we stayed in and ate the chocolates Tom had brought, and enjoyed the flowers – not his usual, I'm glad to say, but a very sweet-scented bunch of lily-of-the-valley, which Hope could enjoy as much as I did.

Festival days are always a bit of a chore, here at the Meadowbank Home. Too many comings and goings; too much excitement; too many thwarted hopes. The nurses are irritable, the kitchen staff edgy and overworked, trying to provide 'celebration' food on an impossible budget. Jealousies and tempers run high among the residents.

Mrs Swathen had a visit. Her family are regular visitors, and Mrs Swathen likes to preen, drawing attention to herself and announcing in a loud voice that very soon her daughter will be here to see her, with her husband, who works in accounting, and their two delightful children, Laurie and Jim. Furthermore, she adds, they will take her in their Volvo car to the garden centre, where she will have tea and scones and look at the spring plants.

She says this in the gloating voice of one who has only been a resident at the home for twelve months, and who believes that this special attention on the part of her loved ones will continue for ever. The rest of us know better; but that didn't stop us from gazing hungrily after her as she left, or feeling a stab of envy at the sight of the two rosy-faced children at the back window of the car.

Of course after that, Mrs McAllister put on her coat, scarf and gloves, picked up her handbag and went to the lobby to wait. We're not supposed to hang around the lobby without good reason, but Mrs McAllister does this every time anyone else has a visit, insisting that her son, Peter, will soon be here to take her home.

We hear a lot about Peter McAllister, not all of it entirely reliable. Already since I've been here, Peter has been a banker, a research chemist, a policeman, a fashion designer, a Navy commander and a teacher of Latin and Greek at St Oswald's Grammar School, although none of us, not even the oldest residents, recall ever having seen him.

The nurses have long since given up explaining to Mrs McAllister that her son died of prostate cancer seven years ago, and nowadays they allow her to sit by the door for as long as she likes, provided she doesn't get in the way.

This time, however, things were different. If someone else had been at the desk – Chris, for instance, or Helen – they would have let it go, but it was the new girl, Lorraine. Maureen chose her; and even though she hadn't been with us for very long, it was clear that she was firmly on the side of the management. A surly piece – except with Maureen herself, whose arrival invariably triggered a personality change and a burst of efficiency that was as surprising as it was short-lived. When Maureen wasn't there, Lorraine did as little as possible, took a break every ten minutes and spoke to us – when she spoke to us at all – with a sharpness verging on contempt.

Now to be fair, we have all, at some time or other, found Mrs McAllister annoying. She can't help it, poor old thing; at ninety-two, she's the oldest person here, and though she's more able-bodied than either Hope or myself, she's terribly confused. Things tend to vanish around her: chocolates; eyeglasses; clothing; teeth. Chris once told me that he found fourteen pairs of false teeth hidden under her mattress, plus two squashed doughnuts, a bag of Yorkshire Mixture, half a packet of chocolate digestives, a stuffed panda, some war medals belonging to Mr Braun, the German resident, and a green rubber ball belonging to the common-room dog.

Of course, Chris didn't say anything about it to the management. Instead, he just quietly restored the items to their original owners and made a note to check the mattress again from time to time. Lorraine, I sensed, would not have let it go. Nor did she in the case of Mrs McAllister's unsanctioned presence in the lobby.

'Now, dearie, you go back to your room,' she said. Her sharp voice penetrated even to the morning room where Hope and I were sitting, I in my wheelchair and Hope in one of the home's Shackleton high-seaters, eating Tom's chocolates and enjoying the sunshine. Chris was wiping the windows near by, whistling softly to himself.

'Go back *right now*,' we heard from the lobby. 'No one's coming to fetch you, and I can't have you sitting here all day.'

The reply was faint though audible. 'But Peter always comes on a Thursday' – it was a Sunday. 'He comes all the way from London. He's an account executive, you know. And today he's going to take me home.'

Lorraine's voice went up slightly in volume, as if she were talking to a deaf person. 'Now listen to me—' she began. 'We'll not have any more of this nonsense. Your son isn't coming to fetch you, no one's coming to fetch you, and if you don't go back to your room right now I'm going to have to take you there myself.'

'But I promised Peter—'

'Oh, for Christ's sake!' There came the sound of Lorraine's hand slapping down on the desktop. 'Your son's dead, don't you remember? He's been dead for years. How can he be coming to fetch you?'

In the morning room, Hope took a sharp breath. Chris stopped wiping the window and looked at me, his mouth turned down in an unhappy grimace.

There came, from the lobby, a silence worse than any sound.

Oh, Mrs McAllister can be annoying. She's the one who took my favourite scarf, the silk one with the yellow edging, and a whole box of pink-iced biscuits that Tom gave me for Christmas. I got the scarf back – eventually, and with a greasy stain on it that never came off – but I had to leave her the biscuits, because by then she was sure they had come from Peter, and I couldn't face having to explain everything to her all over again.

'He's such a *good* boy,' she kept repeating, looking fondly at my Christmas biscuits. 'He makes such wonderful cakes for that big restaurant of his. And do you know, he comes all the way from London?'

And so I left them. Tom's always giving me biscuits,

anyway – he thinks that's all old ladies ever eat – and I knew he'd buy me another box sooner or later. It's hardly a great price to pay, is it, and at least it kept her happy.

But now she came into the morning room and her face was grey and somehow caved-in-looking, like a very old apple that has started to rot. 'She says Peter's dead,' she quavered. 'My son's dead, and no one even told me.'

Hope's better at this kind of thing than I am. Maybe it's her Cambridge experience; maybe just her personality. In any case, she put her arms around Mrs McAllister and let her cry it out against her shoulder, from time to time patting her poor old humped back and saying, 'There, there, lovey, it'll be all right.'

'Oh Maud,' said Mrs McAllister. 'I'm so glad you're here. When can we go home?'

'Not just yet,' said Hope, gently. 'Come on now, sweetheart. Faith and I will get you a cup of tea.'

They say you never feel unfairness as strongly as when you're a child. Certainly, childhood episodes – with all their accompanying emotions – tend to remain in the memory for much longer than recent events. I still remember, when I was seven years old, how a girl from my school – her name was Jacqueline Bond – would lie in wait for me as I came home for lunch and punch me repeatedly between the shoulderblades, for no reason that I could discern, as her younger sister, Caroline, watched and laughed. I still remember how it felt: my helplessness and my rage. I had no words for my hatred of them. There was certainly nothing childish about it. Even now, seventy years later, I *remember* those girls, their mouse-brown hair and bony, inbred faces, and I hate them still, though they must be old now – that is, if they are still alive. I hope they are not. That's what unfairness does to you; and although the business is long done, the voice of the seven-year-old is still as strong as ever in my memory, protesting, *'Not fair! Not fair!'* long after births, deaths, marriage and other disappointments have receded and been forgotten.

My anger at Lorraine's casual cruelty to poor, confused Mrs McAllister was not quite of that magnitude. But for a while it came uncomfortably close. It was the *unfairness* more than anything else; the fact that Lorraine or any other member of the Meadowbank staff could believe they had the right to bully us without fear of complaint.

We tried, though – that very night, when Maureen came on duty – but by then Mrs McAllister was asleep, exhausted, in her room; Lorraine was on her best behaviour and Chris, who had stayed past the end of his shift to confirm our story, was looking decidedly uncomfortable.

In the staff kitchen, Lorraine was drinking coffee and pretending not to know what was going on. There was a smile on her pencilled lips, and maroon lip-marks all around the rim of her coffee cup. From the lobby desk, Maureen glanced at Lorraine, then looked back at Hope and me. She did not look at Chris, or comment on his presence.

Hope and I finished our account. Hope kept to the facts in her best cool-and-businesslike Cambridge manner, but I could not help but voice my indignation. 'It was downright mean,' I said, still watching Lorraine through the kitchen door. 'Mean and unnecessary. What does it matter to Lorraine if Mrs McAllister sits by the door? What harm does it do to indulge her a little?'

'I don't think you appreciate all the work Lorraine has to do,' said Maureen.

'Work?' I said. 'The only work she does is when you're around to watch her. The rest of the time she just sits in the staff lounge, smoking and watching TV.'

But this was territory into which Maureen refused to go. 'Now, girls,' she said with horrible archness, 'I hope you're not *telling tales*. Because, you know, if you can't say anything *nice*, then it's better not—'

'We're not at kindergarten,' said Hope. 'And this isn't just tittle-tattle. It's a complaint, which, if you prefer, we can put in writing.'

'I see.' Maureen's expression told me everything I needed to know about the complaints system, and the likelihood of any letter of ours ever reaching the Meadowbank governors. 'And what does Mr Er' – she fixed her eyes on Chris – 'what does *he* have to contribute to this?'

Chris explained that he too had overheard the conversation, and that he felt that Lorraine's behaviour had been insensitive.

Maureen peered at him in blue-shadowed silence. Then, at last, she nodded. 'All right. Leave it to me,' she said. 'I don't think you'll be having any more trouble.'

*

244

Of course, she was wrong. Lorraine continued unchastened – rather worse, in fact, than before. It took us some time to understand the extent of her spitefulness: by then she had contrived to ingratiate herself with the management in a number of small, significant ways, as well as cleverly undermining the very people who might have alerted Maureen to her activities.

Things disappeared. Little things at first; my own teacup, the one with the pink flowers around the rim. My new stockings. A little box of Turkish Delight that Tom had given me, and that I was saving for a special occasion.

This may not seem very important to you, but we're hardly allowed any possessions, here at the Meadowbank Home. Anything we bring is limited to what will fit in a small wardrobe and a three-drawer cabinet. I know they're only *things*; but in this place, where anything not stamped with the Meadowbank logo is rare, things are all we have to remind ourselves of who we are.

I still miss my own possessions. I know I couldn't have brought the piano, or my glass-fronted dresser with my mother's china in it. But some things, surely, could have been allowed? My little green-and-brown rug, perhaps; my rocking chair; my own bed. Maybe a painting or two to replace those cheap flower prints they seem so fond of. But rules are rules, they tell me. What they don't tell me is *why*.

Still, I manage. When small things are all you have, then small things become important, and it was astonishing how much I'd enjoyed my tea when I could drink it from my very own cup. Now I had to use a Meadowbank cup, and it tasted different; institutional, somehow, like the tea we'd had to make do with during the War, half sawdust and half dandelion.

Hope lost things too. When you have as few possessions as Hope does, that hurts; but it was the day she went to her cupboard and found that the shoe-box, with the little bundle of Priscilla's postcards, was gone, that we realized that this was not normal Meadowbank pilfering. It was personal.

Of course the first thing we did was to check on Mrs McAllister. But since learning once more of Peter's death she had been listless and unwell, staying in her room and hardly speaking to anyone. Hope and I had expected her to forget, as she usually did, but this time, perversely, the memory held. Little else did – meals, toilet stops, the few television shows around which she built her life. It was as if this one truth – her son's death, fresh in grief as in memory – had grown so large in her mind as to eclipse everything else.

'A mother should never outlive her son,' she repeated, when Hope wheeled me in to see her. 'Do you know they weren't even going to let me go to the funeral? They're like that in the army, you know, when someone goes missing in action. Thank God you're here, Maud.' (This was to Hope.) 'Now they'll *have* to let me go, now you're here to take me home.'

To which Hope always said, 'Not just yet, sweetie,' and wheeled me out again.

Compared with Mrs McAllister's loss, the loss of our few bits and pieces seemed trivial, and so we let it go for a while, especially as by then we were almost certain that Mrs McAllister had nothing to do with their disappearance.

It was nothing concrete, you understand. Just a look in Lorraine's eye when she went about her duties; the way she spoke to us, calling us *dearie* in that hard, contemptuous voice. It was the way her fingers dug into my shoulder and the small of my back as she lifted me from my chair on to the toilet. I'd try and keep it in if it was Lorraine's shift; wait until someone else came on duty, but sometimes it was inevitable, and at those times her fingers knew exactly where to go, searching and probing for the nerve spots like a prospector digging for gold. From time to time I'd give a yell, and she'd apologize, but I could tell she was grinning inside.

Once more, we tried to complain. Chris came with us again, but said nothing; and Maureen listened to us with an ersatz smile, and hinted that we might possibly be growing just a *teeny-tiny* bit forgetful. Our evidence – my flowered teacup, found broken in the kitchen waste bin – was disregarded. I might have dropped it there myself, said Maureen, and forgotten all about it. Anyhow, why would Lorraine do such a thing? And what would a girl like Lorraine want with Hope's old letters?

Of course, we couldn't tell her. But other things had disappeared too, insisted Hope.

'Valuables?' Maureen's eyes lit.

'Not exactly.' We're not allowed valuables at the home, though I have a little jewellery – my pearls, a brooch, a couple of rings and a bracelet – concealed in the seat of my wheelchair.

'Oh.' She seemed disappointed. 'Because if any *money* disappeared—'

'No,' said Hope firmly. 'I must have made a mistake.'

And at that she turned me round and began to wheel me briskly away. There was a time when I might have questioned that; but Hope sees more than I do, in spite of her blindness, and I knew that she had recognized something then in Maureen's voice that had alerted her to danger.

Of course I had noticed Maureen watching Chris. I knew she disliked him, too; but until then it had never occurred to me that she might suspect him of those thefts. *He* knew, though; that's why he was so quiet, and that's why he kept his distance afterwards, as if he sensed we might bring him – and that silly old criminal record – back under scrutiny. Lorraine knew it too; and by the second week she had become increasingly cocky. Hope's perfume disappeared; so did the *World's Best Grandma* pillow on my bed. She knew we wouldn't complain; if we did, we would simply bring more trouble on to our friend.

During the next few days, we noticed that Maureen was there less and less. She had taken over the administrative side of things, or so Lorraine told us, which meant that she was often away, leaving Lorraine to oversee the other carers. With terrifying speed, the Meadowbank way became Lorraine's way.

Our privileges, we found, were suddenly curtailed. Residents who toed the line were favoured; others were targeted for special attention. Thus it was that the flowers

Tom brought me were removed from my room 'for hygiene purposes'; that Hope's cassette player was confiscated as 'an electrocution hazard' and that Chris was demoted from his largely unofficial post of staff carer to window-washer and handyman, with strict orders not to gossip with the residents.

Soon after that, Mrs McAllister's cache under the mattress was discovered. There was nothing in it of value – biscuits, soap, toys, stockings and Mrs McAllister's perennial favourite, teeth – but Lorraine made a terrible fuss. As a result Mrs McAllister was to be shut up in her room for most of the day, with instructions to the staff to confiscate her dentures except at mealtimes. She made it *sound* perfectly sensible; obviously, Mrs McAllister couldn't be trusted with her own dentures, and Lorraine didn't see why Meadowbank staff should spend hours every mealtime looking for residents' teeth. It was ridiculous; they were busy; and anyway, it wasn't as if the old dear *needed* them for anything.

Sensible or not, it was a contemptible piece of bullying. Hope and I knew it; but by then we had learnt caution. Lorraine was out to get us, and we knew that the slightest bit of provocation might bring down her anger upon us. And so we endured; stoically at first, then with deepening misery.

Without Hope, I think I might have given up. But there's steel in Hope, under those Cambridge manners. We'd go to her room in the evenings (it was furthest from the lobby, and Lorraine), drink tea in the Meadowbank cups and talk. Sometimes I read aloud – Hope likes her books, and without the cassette player she was once more reliant on my reading – and sometimes we went through holiday brochures, which

I would describe to her in loving detail, and imagined the journeys we would make if we were free. Most of all, though, we talked about Lorraine.

'The worst part of it is the helplessness,' said Hope one night. 'I mean, children are helpless, aren't they, but at least they have something better to look forward to. Old people don't. They're not going to grow big and strong and face up to their bullies. Bully an old person, and they're yours for life.'

It was a depressing thought. Once more I remembered Jacqueline Bond.

'What happened to her?' asked Hope, and I realized she was thinking along the same lines. That happens, you know; like an old married couple, we read each other's thoughts.

'She left,' I said. 'One day she just wasn't there any more.'

'Sounds good to me,' said Hope. 'Was she expelled?'

'I don't remember.'

Hope thought about this for a time. 'It's a pity,' she said, 'that you never stood up to her. It would have been cathartic, and would have done you good. Still—' She gave one of her rare, sweet smiles. 'It's never too late for a bit of catharsis. Don't you agree?'

I did; but I didn't see what we could do about it. There was no point in complaining to Maureen; clearly something more drastic was required. But what could we do?

Over several days, we considered the possibilities. If Chris had been around, he would have noticed at once. *Hey, Butch!* he would have said. *Planning a jailbreak?* But Chris was looking uneasy from his place at the outer edge of things; Chris knew that a single step in the wrong direction might send him flying off. I could see it in his eyes as he brought Lorraine her tea in the morning; in his new, careful walk as he came and went.

But we *were* planning. We'd read once, in an old newspaper, the story of the pensioner who had held up a number of post offices unchallenged and at gunpoint, not even bothering to cover his face. To most people, one old man in a flat cap and muffler looks much like another, after all, and who would think to suspect a pensioner?

'Remember this, Faith. We only have one chance,' said Hope one night as we sat in her bedroom, talking. 'If we do anything to put Lorraine on her guard, she'll be on to us like a poultice. Whatever we do must be quick, clear and unequivocal.' She talks like that, you know; the Cambridge professor as was. 'And *public*,' she added, with a sip at her tea. 'Most of all, it must be public.'

All very well, I suppose; but what public did we have? We hardly left our rooms any more, except for meals, which were dull and unappetizing, and for our monthly check-up with the Meadowbank nurse. News of the outside world came from Tom, Chris and occasionally the staff hairdresser (who offers three approved styles, all of them identical, and a range of unappealing treatments such as corn removal and lymphatic drainage). We always have an Open Day in January, but at this rate of deterioration Mrs McAllister might not last the month, let alone till next year.

We racked our brains, but nothing came. Easter approached; Lorraine had a little party to celebrate her promotion to deputy supervisor; after which our movements became even more restricted, with long application forms to fill in for the most elementary requirement, special times of day allocated to visiting and all our favourite TV programmes forbidden on the grounds of unsuitability.

Then came my brainwave. I have to admit that I sat on it for a while, hardly daring to imagine we could carry it off. Hope was the one who should have thought of it, I told myself; clever Hope, with her BBC vowels and fierce independence. But in those last few days Hope had begun to fade. Not like poor Mrs McAllister, and not in any way that the others would have noticed; but I could see it. She retained her dignity, of course; she was calm as ever; talked to Mrs McAllister, who called her Maud and wept on her shoulder; always took care of herself; never wandered around in her dressing gown during the day, as so many of them do; but I could see that there was something missing in my old friend, that spark, perhaps; that cheery gleam of revolt.

Then it happened. I was watching Chris fix the smoke alarm (Lorraine had caught Mr Bannerman smoking in the toilets again). It was one of Maureen's days in the home, and Lorraine was on her best behaviour. So was Chris; working in silence, not looking at me; not even whistling. Usually he talks; about football; television; his little girl, Gemma; his mother-in-law; his ex-wife; his garden; his nights out with the lads. Today Lorraine's shadow was over him, and he started guiltily at the sound of my voice.

'Tea, Chris? You haven't had a break all day.'

'Sorry, Butch.' It sounded *almost* right; but I knew Chris, and I knew it wasn't. 'Work to do. Gotta test this when it's done.'

'The smoke detector?'

'That's right.'

'Good idea,' I told him. 'Don't forget the staffroom.'

He smiled at that, as I knew he would, but made no comment. Lorraine enjoys her Silk Cuts, and I was prepared to bet that some regulation or other would ensure she continued to enjoy them. As for the rest of us, if Lorraine could have installed pleasure detectors in every room, I reckoned she would have done it already, and cut off the supply. I said as much to Chris, and watched his smile turn into a grin.

'*You* might say that, Butch,' he said. 'I wouldn't dare.' And it was then – right then, on the word *dare* – that I had my brainwave.

The Meadowbank governors (great sticklers for rules) insist on a complete fire drill at least twice a year. It's just like school, really: the alarm goes; we line up on the grass; someone keys in a number code to the alarm box so that the fire brigade doesn't actually have to turn up and two of the duty staff run round the building checking all the rooms while Maureen stands by, 'reassuring' everyone in her most Wagnerian tones (*Now then, dearie, don't panic. It's just a drill, remember. I said it's JUST A DRILL!*), spreading confusion as a sower spreads seed.

It's quite funny, really; however much warning she gives, some people always forget; or they're not wearing their hearing aid; or they're on the toilet (and at our age, sweetheart, that takes *time*!) or they're watching TV and don't want to leave. Last year it took us nearly half an hour to clear the building, and that was with the best effort of every staff member on the team. Someone forgot to key in the code; with the result that the police *and* the fire brigade turned up, and we were all subjected to a lecture of nursery-nurse severity by Maureen, telling us that if there had been a *real* fire we would all have been burnt alive.

Now, with the installation of the new smoke detectors, there would have to be another fire drill. I guessed Lorraine had insisted upon it; it would be an excellent opportunity for her both to exercise her authority in front of Maureen and to cause as much disruption and unhappiness as possible among the residents of the home. It would be public, I told myself; and in the noise and confusion, maybe – just maybe – Hope and I would have our chance.

I suggested it to Hope later that evening. She had been with Mrs McAllister, who was having one of her bad days, and although Hope remained as patient as ever, I could see the strain beginning to show. But Lorraine was off duty – dim Claire was at the front desk, chewing gum and reading *Goodbye!* magazine – and we made a nice enough evening of it, with a stack of travel brochures (that week we were doing Italy), a couple of biscuits filched from the kitchens and a lot of imagination.

'Where to tonight?' said Hope, stretching her back so that it popped.

'I thought we might do Rome.'

She shook her head. 'I've had enough of antiquities for one day,' she said wryly. 'Give me something – *pastoral*.' And so

I obliged: planned routes – London–Paris–Milan–Naples – and then by boat to the islands – Sicily, Ustica, Pantelleria – to orange groves and bright misty mornings and fat purple olives and salted lemons and anchovy toasts and boisterous wines and lithe young men of heroic beauty and snowy egrets flying in that impossible sky. It's our kind of travel, and I have learned to describe it so that Hope can see it as clearly as I can myself. I don't suppose we'll ever really go to those far-off places; but we do dream. Oh yes, we dream.

Hope was lying on her bed, eyes closed, enjoying one of my best sunsets and an imaginary glass of Sicilian red.

'This is the life,' she said, but in such a wistful voice that I felt quite alarmed. Usually she joins our little game with great good humour, inventing outrageous details to amuse me (young men swimming naked on a deserted beach; a fat woman aquaplaning as a brass band plays a Souza march). This time she lay passive, not smiling, but straining – *wanting* so hard – to be there, and I knew she was thinking about Priscilla. Priscilla and the box of postcards – that last, broken link between herself and her vanished daughter.

'At least I know she's still all right,' said Hope, whenever she received one of those infrequent postcards. 'Imagine not knowing. Imagine losing her altogether, like Mrs McAllister's Peter—'

As if she wasn't lost already, I thought. Selfish, silly Priscilla, too lost in her own complicated affairs to think of anyone else. 'She's getting worse, you know. I saw it today. She's giving up, poor old thing.'

'Perhaps not.' I was thinking of my plan: the risks; the

timing; of what we'd lose if it didn't work. But my heart was beating fast; my breath caught; sixty years ago, dancing used to feel like this.

Hope picked up on it at once. 'Why?' she said, sitting up. 'Have you thought of something?' I told her; and little by little I saw her face change, come back into focus like a Polaroid, like a face on the water.

'Well?' I said. 'Do you think it might work?'

'Yes, Faith.' She nodded. 'I really think it might.'

It was the next morning that Lorraine announced the fire drill. We'd been awake most of the night, Hope and I, talking and planning like naughty schoolgirls; pillows in our beds arranged to look like sleeping bodies in case someone (Lorraine, who else?) came round and looked through the peephole.

Now, Lorraine addressed us all in her best official voice, announcing the drill for precisely two o'clock that afternoon. A few groans accompanied the announcement; it was the time when most of us would have been listening to *The Archers*.

Lorraine looked reproachful (Hope and I guessed she must have planned it this way) and treated us all to a little lecture on how selfish we were, how much work she did on our behalf, and how she was really the only one who cared enough about us to ensure our safety from smoke, fire and electrical hazards.

'Now Maureen has told me what a very *poor* response she got *last* time there was a fire drill,' she went on. 'I hope that this time you'll really make an effort, and evacuate the building in ten minutes or less. Otherwise' – and she gave that smile of hers, nothing but teeth, and false all the way up to the eyes – 'I might have to Take Certain Measures.' A Lorraine phrase, that, if ever there was one, and she was looking right at Chris as she said it.

Well, Hope and I both knew what *that* meant. Lorraine had been looking for an excuse to get at Chris ever since he complained to Maureen about Mrs McAllister. I could see he knew it too; his mouth tightened and he looked away. Ten minutes was an unfair, impossible time, and Lorraine knew it.

I looked at Hope, who was smiling serenely ahead, and Mrs McAllister, on my other side, sitting in one of the Meadow-bank chairs, her face all squashy-looking without her teeth.

'Now I expect anyone who can *walk* to be out of the building in the first five minutes,' continued Lorraine in her brisk voice. 'Then we'll handle the rest of you, just as we did last time. What I *don't* want to see is people trying to bring bags and coats and God knows what with them. Leave all personal possessions *in your rooms*. D'you hear? *In your rooms*. Don't worry. This *isn't* a real fire. Your things will be *perfectly* safe.'

I suppressed a little smile. My legs may be no good, but there's nothing wrong with my brain. I'd caught that look, the sideways glance towards me in my wheelchair. I knew what she was thinking, and I fingered the tapestry cushion in the small of my back, where I still keep my few remaining valuables.

Nothing much, you understand. A few pieces of jewellery,

too good for everyday wear, that I'm keeping for Tom's little girl. A small bundle of banknotes (we're not supposed to have money, but it's nice to have it from time to time). There's no real way to keep a secret, here at the Meadowbank Home, and I suppose most people know about the cushion by now, but they'd always turned a blind eye to it before – after all, what harm could it do to let me hang on to a few bits and pieces?

Lorraine was different, of course. I'd seen her eyeing up my wheelchair a few times before, though I'd never given her a chance to get a look at the cushion. This was her chance, though; the fire drill, the thinly veiled excuse about leaving personal items in rooms, and I could see that her little eyes fairly lit up at the thought that she might finally get her paws on something worthwhile.

'When you're all lined up outside, Chris and I will check the building. No one is to move until it's all been checked.'

She handed Chris a set of passkeys. That, too, was like her. Most of the time she never seemed to notice Chris at all; but now, with thieving on her mind, she wanted him near, a handy scapegoat if things went wrong, and a likely suspect if anyone complained of valuables going missing.

Hope reached for my hand and I felt the brief pressure of her fingers against mine. On my other side, Mrs McAllister was mumbling anxiously to herself, her old head nodding repeatedly as if to underline a point. I reached for her hand too, and felt it tighten on mine like a frightened child's.

'What's happening, Maud?' she whispered, her eyes red-rimmed.

'It's all right,' I said to her, hoping it was.

The minutes leading up to two o'clock were agonizing. It took all our patience to wait as if nothing unusual were about to happen. Maureen arrived at twenty to, and settled into her office for a cup of coffee and a cigarette. Lorraine joined her; I could see them through the glass door, talking and laughing like old cronies. Once they looked out, both together, and I was sure they were talking about Hope and me; but I pretended not to notice and they looked away again.

For twenty minutes we played chess (Hope always wins) and then we just waited in the common room, declining Chris's offer of tea (I'd have loved to accept, but when you get to my age an unscheduled toilet stop at a crucial moment can sometimes lead to disaster). Instead I listened to the wireless and tried hard not to worry. I already knew that a great deal would depend upon Chris's co-operation, and I'd gambled that it might be better not to tell him too much beforehand – he really needs this job, and he's wary enough of the management as it is.

Then it came – just as the theme tune for *The Archers* was coming on – and I felt a sting of excitement so powerful that it almost overrode my fear. A braying, whooping siren that set my teeth on edge. 'Time, Hope,' I whispered, and she stood up and felt carefully for the handles of my wheelchair.

I kept an eye on the office door. It was still closed. Maureen and Lorraine were taking their time, it seemed, which suited me just down to the ground. In any case, Maureen was here to supervise – I doubted whether she would take an active part in the proceedings – and Lorraine was too fond of her dignity to bother with the evacuation process. She left that to the orderlies – three per shift, in this case Chris, Denise and Sad Harry.

Ten minutes, she had said. I guessed twenty. Time enough, in any case, for Lorraine to have a good look round.

Chris was overseeing the mêlée. If he was nervous, there was no sign of it. His voice was pleasant, strong, not too shrill and without that hectoring note that Lorraine and some of the girls always seem to adopt. 'You know the drill, folks. Everyone out on the lawn. Ten minutes – it's a lovely day – Mrs Banerjee, do you *really* need that third overcoat? Come on, Mrs Swathen, if you think *that*'s loud, you should hear Metallica play at Wembley. This way, everybody – ten minutes – no, not you, sweetheart, *you* get *carried* over the threshold, how sexy is that?' It was nonsense, and most of us knew it. But *comforting* nonsense nevertheless; and even the oldest, most baffled ones reacted to it, moving gradually – the ones who could – towards the double doors and Chris's voice.

I was supposed to stay put. Hope was supposed to wait too, until the rest of them had gone, and someone was free to guide her out. Neither of us obeyed orders, however. As soon as Chris wasn't looking, Hope guided the wheelchair, swiftly and confidently, back up the corridor.

On the left, two doors before mine, there is an airing cupboard. It's a large cupboard, lined with shelves on which stacks of sheets, blankets and pillows are stored. Now, instead of going to my room, Hope stopped at the airing cupboard and opened the door.

I looked left and right. No one was watching. Chris was at the exit now, surrounded by residents. Denise was outside, forming a queue. Sad Harry was trying to explain to Polish John why the drill couldn't wait until *The Archers* was finished and Mrs McAllister was wandering vaguely about the common room, wailing – *Is there a fire?* – until one of the others (it was Mr Braun) took her arm and led her to the door.

'Coast's clear,' I said, and Hope pushed me into the airing cupboard, chair and all. Then she moved me out of my chair (I can help, when I want to, using my arms) and on to a pile of blankets, then she turned – manoeuvring the chair with difficulty between the stacks of shelves.

'Two doors on the right, remember,' I whispered.

Hope gave me her Cambridge look. 'You think I'm senile?' she said. 'I know my way about this place better than you do.' And at that she wheeled the chair – tapestry cushion and all – smartly out of the cupboard, closing the door behind her. The whole process had taken five minutes thus far – we're not fast, you know, but we do get there in the end – and I guessed that the lobby would be more or less clear.

By now only the residents who needed help in getting out – myself and Hope among them – should still be in the building, waiting patiently for someone to guide or carry us to the assembly point. Lorraine was on duty; Maureen would be observing, and the rest of them would be racing round to check the rooms, to ensure that no one had forgotten, or failed to hear, or decided to go for an unscheduled toilet break.

The siren – a kind of *whoop-whoop-whoop* electronic noise, not what you'd call a fire bell at all – had fallen silent. In the corridor I heard the clopping of footsteps on the carpet and recognized the sound of high heels. I held my breath – by rights Lorraine ought to check the cupboards as well as the rooms, but I was counting on Hope to divert her.

'Lorraine?' Good. Right on time. Hope's voice, muffled and uncharacteristically querulous, reached me through the thickness of the door.

'Good God, what are *you* doing here?' Lorraine's voice was needle-sharp.

'Lorraine? Is that you? Is there a fire?' said Hope, in a voice so like Mrs McAllister's that I had to bite the inside of my mouth to stop myself from laughing.

'No, you silly thing – where's the orderly? – oh, come with me,' said Lorraine impatiently, and I heard the sound of her high heels receding towards the lobby, with Hope's softer footfalls in pursuit.

I smiled. So far, so good. It would take Lorraine a few minutes at least to get Hope outside. Longer, perhaps; Hope was under instructions to delay Lorraine for as long as possible, and I was counting on her to be as imaginative as she could. That left Chris to check the rooms – and if only I could get to him before Lorraine came back, I was pretty sure I could make him listen.

If. I used the shelving to move myself towards the door, and, balancing on a pile of sheets, I managed to get it open without falling over. I looked out into the corridor. It was deserted.

I called softly. 'Chris? Are you there?'

No one came. I wondered how long Hope could hold Lorraine before my absence was noticed. I called again. This time I heard the sound of footsteps from the locker room across the hall; no clip of heels this time, but the soft, fast steps of someone wearing sneakers.

'Chris!' I waved my hand at him from inside the cupboard, and a moment later he was running down the passageway towards me.

'Hey, Butch?' He looked concerned. 'You OK?'

'In here. Quick. Before she gets back.'

For a moment he hesitated.

'*Please*, Chris!'

He cast a rapid glance up and down the passage. Then he sighed – OK – and stepped into the airing cupboard. 'You know, Butch, there are easier ways to get me to yourself. What is it?'

As quickly as I could, I told him.

When I got to his contribution, he shook his head. 'Oh no,' he said. 'If I do that I'm toast.'

'You're toast anyway,' I said, and told him about Lorraine and the tapestry cushion.

'You and me both,' said Chris, when I finished. 'Except you're too damn old to be dragged off to gaol, and nowadays all I have to do is sneeze—' He paused, pricking up his ears, then lowered his voice still further. 'It's OK,' he said. 'It's not too late. I'll just carry you out – tell Lorraine you needed the loo – and there'll be no trouble for either of us. She wouldn't dare go through your stuff anyway—'

'She would,' I said. 'She's done it before.'

'Really, Butch—'

'You know she has. She's been pinching stuff since she first arrived. Hasn't she?'

Chris turned away and said nothing.

'*Hasn't* she?' Pause. 'You know she has. And you know where she keeps it, don't you, Chris?'

Chris sighed. 'What is this?' he said. 'Some kind of inquisition?'

'Vee heff vays,' I said, sounding (I thought) rather a lot like Mr Braun.

Chris shook his head. Reluctantly, he grinned, though I noticed he still wouldn't look me in the eye.

'You've got to stand up to bullies,' I told him. 'You can't go around just hoping they'll tire of it and leave you alone. They never do. It makes them worse. You should never have let her get away with it the first time, Chris. We'd have stood up for you. Now she thinks she owns you. Thinks you'll do whatever she wants. But you're not like her, are you, Chris? I know you. And you're not a thief.'

He turned round at that, rather abruptly, and his usually open expression was bleak and complicated. 'But I *am* a thief,' he said in a flat voice. 'You know it, *she* knows it—'

'Rubbish,' I said. 'You don't judge a man on the mistakes he's made.'

'Then how the hell *do* you judge him?' said Chris, not caring who heard him now and furious, furious as I'd never seen him before. Oh, not with me – I could tell that from the look in his eyes. With himself, maybe; or with the world that reduces people to pages in a file, names on a list—

'Chris,' I said. 'I *don't* judge.' And in the silence that followed – rather a long silence – he put his face in his hands and just sat there on a pile of towels, breathing heavily, not talking, until I started to feel anxious about him and touched his shoulder to make sure he was all right.

'All right?' he said, looking up at last. 'Yeah, sure. I'm just fine.' He told me then what I'd suspected before. 'You were right, though, about my knowing where she keeps the stuff. She hides it right under my nose. It's her way of getting back at me for that complaint I made, you know, that time with Mrs McAllister.'

'But if you just help me,' I protested, 'then we can catch her red-handed. None of us will ever have any trouble from her again.'

He looked rueful. 'I haven't told you where she hides it.'

'Where?' I said.

'In my locker.'

Ah. Of course. I hadn't thought of that. Lorraine, of course, has the master keys, and with them, access to all the lockers in the staffroom. Easy for her to stash whatever she has stolen; easier still for her to plant something in Chris's locker to incriminate him.

'And she would, too,' Chris said when I told him. 'She's just dying for me to step out of line. She's got me snookered, Butch; I can't keep my eye on that locker all the time, and she knows it. All it would take is one spot check—'

There was another silence, punctuated only by the clacking sound of Lorraine's high heels in the corridor outside.

'There she is,' said Chris bleakly. 'Time's up.'

As I said, I don't have many things of my own any more. Possessions – even such trivial things as a book, a cup, a box of photographs – are doubly precious for being in short supply. And the things inside the tapestry cushion – my anniversary pearls (not real, of course, just cultured, but I love them so), my mother's little gold brooch, the engagement ring that has grown too small for my swollen fingers – are not just precious in the ordinary way. They are what's left of my life; proof, if you like, that I lived at all. And all this time I've kept them safe; for Tom; for the children; but most of all to keep some part of myself secret, private, in this place of routine intrusion and casual indifference.

But things, after all, are only things. If we confronted Lorraine with the truth, I'd keep my things, but I'd lose my friend. And if there's anything I've learnt in this place, it's this: that a good friend rates higher than pearls.

I smiled at Chris. 'Let's go,' I said. 'Our ten minutes must be nearly up.'

He looked surprised. 'You're letting her get away with it, then?'

'Don't worry.' I shrugged. 'It's mostly junk.'

He almost smiled. 'Butch,' he said. 'I never knew such a respectable old lady could tell such barefaced lies.'

I gave him a look. 'Quit soft-soaping me and take me outside.'

He picked me up then – not cheerily, but with ease – and carried me out into the corridor. Lorraine was there, checking bedroom doors. I saw that she was just two doors away from my own bedroom, and the expression on her face as she saw me was pure poison.

'What's this?' she said.

Chris shot her a nervous glance. 'Sorry,' he said. 'Wrong door. I think Faith just got a little confused. I'm taking her outside now, OK?'

Lorraine gave him a look of contempt. 'Hurry up,' she said in an icy voice. 'I need you here.'

It took Chris thirty seconds to get me out into the open. The others were already outside, sitting or standing on the grass; Mrs Swathen was complaining loudly about the disruption; Maureen was looking at her watch; Hope was reassuring Mrs McAllister.

'Gotta go, Butch,' was all Chris said before running back into the building, his passkeys rattling at his belt.

I saw Hope's face turn towards me.

'I'm sorry,' I whispered. 'It didn't work.'

Later, I would explain to her. I knew she'd understand. After all, the things we had lost – and they were, after all, only *things* – were of such little importance when set against our friend's dilemma. Things can usually be replaced. People, on the other hand—

Suddenly, the alarm went off again. Louder, this time; the *whoop-whoop-whoop* of the siren now joined by an urgent and unfamiliar wailing sound. It was the new smoke alarm.

We looked at each other in surprise (all except for grumpy Mr Bannerman, who just turned off his hearing aid and sat down on the grass).

Poor, dried-up Mrs McAllister, who had calmed down a little under Hope's influence, gave a squeal.

'Fire!' she shrieked, and I was about to point out (I'd lost count of how many times I'd already done so) that it was only a drill, and nothing to be worried about, when I saw the dim yellow flicker at one of the windows and knew that, somehow, Mrs McAllister had got it right.

'Good God,' said Mrs Swathen. 'I thought it was supposed to be a *drill*!'

A murmur of anxiety went through the assembled residents as Maureen, Sad Harry and Denise went around trying to reassure them. Mrs Swathen began to complain about all the things she had left in her room; Polish John said it was just like the war; Mr Braun observed that he always liked a nice fire; Mrs McAllister began to cry again and Hope and I held hands very tightly and whispered – *Chris!*

The flames were quite visible now through the passageway window, heating the frosted glass and turning it black. My room was on the other side, opposite the staffroom; difficult to tell from outside where the fire had started. There was still no sign of either Lorraine or Chris.

Sad Harry, ignoring procedure, ran for the main doors, but they wouldn't open. 'Must be jammed!' he yelled, punching at the entrance pad with no success.

'An electrical fault,' suggested Hope in her calm voice.

'Sabotage,' said Polish John with dour glee.

'Lorraine!' yelled Maureen in her most Wagnerian tone. 'Lorraine, can you hear me?'

From the far side of the building came a faint tinkle of breaking glass.

'Lorraine!'

'In here!'

Maureen moved with as much speed as her bulk would permit towards the source of the cry. For obvious reasons, Hope and I stayed put. A minute or two later, Chris came running out by a fire exit, looking sooty and dishevelled, but laughing silently, one of the Meadowbank fire extinguishers in his hand.

'Where's Lorraine?' I hissed at him.

Chris said nothing, but only grinned.

Later we pieced together the sequence of events; but for the present we could only speculate and listen.

Of course, you can't always trust an eyewitness account. If you'd believed some of the stories that went around afterwards, then you might have been forgiven in thinking that we had survived something in the nature of a Towering Inferno. In fact, by the time the fire brigade arrived, some five minutes later, the blaze, such as it was, had already been put out, leaving nothing but a few cracked windowpanes and some scorch marks up the walls to show that it had ever been.

It seems to have begun in the staffroom. A cigarette, said the fire chief, left to smoulder near a pile of newspapers, seemed to have been the source of the fire, which had spread quite rapidly to curtains and cushions on the sofa by the window. A small fire, certainly not large enough to account for the degree of panic shown by certain members of the Meadowbank staff, not least a Miss Lorraine Hutchens, care administrator, who was discovered hiding inside a wardrobe in the bedroom of one of the residents, having tried the door (or so she said) and found it jammed. Good thing the handy-man had been around; his quick thinking (and judicious use of a nearby fire extinguisher) had ensured that the fire failed to spread to other parts of the home.

'Anyway, love,' said the fire chief reassuringly, as Lorraine was escorted out of the building, 'that door's made of solid wood. There'd have had to be a real blaze to do any harm to it, and it's hardly even scorched the paint. I reckon you must have smelt the smoke and panicked. Happens all the time.'

Lorraine, still shaken but gaining resilience with every step, gave him a killer look. 'I never said the door was *jammed*. I said it was *locked*. There's a difference.'

Maureen's eyes narrowed. 'Locked?' she said.

Lorraine's cold gaze came to rest on Chris. He'd been standing quietly next to Hope and me, eyes on the ground. Now he glanced up, briefly, at Lorraine. The grin was gone from his face, to be replaced by an unmistakable expression of guilt.

Next to him, I saw Hope reach for his hand. There was a small sound of metal against metal that went unnoticed by all except Hope and me. Then Hope put her hands back into her lap. Again, that sound; and then she put her hand over one of mine, and I felt something cold and toothy press into my palm.

Meanwhile, Lorraine was speaking to Chris. 'I warned you,' she said. 'Did you think it was funny, eh? Did you really think you could get away with a stunt like this?'

Chris said nothing. So blessedly talkative in ordinary circumstances, he still clams up when anyone in authority addresses him. Instead, he shot a sideways glance at me, looking guilty and slightly sick. There was a smudge of soot on one of his arms, at which he rubbed nervously.

Lorraine took another step. 'I'm talking to you,' she said loudly. 'What was it, some kind of a joke? Or did you have something else in mind – what was it, going through lockers while I was out of the way? Looking for valuables in the rooms?'

That was more than Hope and I could take. 'You leave him alone,' I told Lorraine, and she turned and gave me one of her most poisonous looks.

'You keep out of this, dearie,' she said. 'That door was locked, and there's only one other person here who could have locked it. Isn't there?' She glared at Chris. 'You saw me give him the keys. Didn't you, Maureen?'

Maureen nodded.

'Only he could have locked the door.'

Once again, Maureen nodded as Lorraine's peculiar magnetism began to reassert itself. Her face hardened; her small eyes grew smaller. 'Well, did you?' she said.

There was a pause. Under Maureen's scrutiny Chris looked more wretched than ever.

Then Hope spoke up, not loudly, but in that Cambridge voice of hers that seems naturally to command authority. 'He couldn't,' she said.

'Why not?' said Lorraine with scorn. 'Because he's a friend of yours? Well, let me tell you—'

'No,' I told her. 'Because I've got his keys.' I pulled them out of my coat pocket. 'I saw him drop them when he carried me out,' I went on. 'I called after him, but he didn't hear me.' There was a pause, during which Maureen stared at Lorraine, Lorraine glared at Chris and almost everyone else looked at me with the keys still in my hand.

I held them out to Lorraine. 'Here you are,' I said with a smile. 'Oh, and Maureen—' Maureen was watching me now, her expression slowly veering from astonishment to a kind of grim understanding. 'I had a few things hidden in a little cushion, back in my room. I'm sure they're safe, but do you think we could check? I mean, I'd trust Chris with my life, of course—' I gave Lorraine my sweetest smile. '*Which* room did you say you were trapped in, dear? Now fancy that. What a coincidence. Well, I'm sure my things would have been perfectly safe with you. What's that?' Lorraine made an inarticulate sound. 'Oh, you've brought them with you. How very kind. And how clever of you to guess where I'd hidden them – my pearls, my engagement ring, my mother's brooch – oh yes, and the money. Two hundred pounds. What a relief. How nice to know that there are still some decent, honest people left in the world.'

Still smiling, I slipped my possessions into the pocket of my coat. I'd gathered quite a little audience by then;

Sad Harry with something suspiciously like a smile on his face; Claire almost forgetting to chew her gum in her astonishment; Mr Braun; Polish John; Mrs Swathen, who can be as clever as the next person when she really puts her mind to it, now staring at Lorraine as if she'd never really seen her before; Maureen, her doughy face frozen behind a furious smile; Chris, looking dazed; and behind him the firemen, five or six of them; young men, grinning; turning off the flashers on the unneeded fire engine, checking the building for stragglers, faults, electrical hazards, anything that might endanger the residents of the Meadowbank Home, now waiting quietly on the grass.

It took almost an hour for them to clear the building. It was a warm day, sunny and bright; there were daisies in the lawn and bumblebees in the azalea hedge alongside. Polish John started a game of cards with Sad Harry and Mr Braun; Mrs Banerjee took off one of her overcoats and Hope and I talked quietly while Lorraine and Maureen took their conversation (by now it was getting quite animated) to the car park by the main gates where they thought they couldn't be overheard. They could, though – at least in snatches – but we politely refrained from listening, except for the part when Lorraine told Maureen to stuff her effing job, it wasn't paying more than effing peanuts anyway, and who the hell wanted to spend their lives in a pit like the Meadowbank Home, you know what they call it in town, eh? The effing Morgue. How d'you like that, eh – *dearie*?

And so on. Worse than Mr Bannerman on one of his bad

days. Anyway, there was little doubt in my mind even then that that was the last we'd see of Lorraine. Across the grass, Chris was pretending not to overhear, but the smile on his face gave him away.

Of course I knew he'd locked her in. I was willing to bet he'd lit the fire in the staffroom, too; making it look as if one of Lorraine's eternal Silk Cuts had started the blaze. I guessed he had immobilized the front doors, and I was sure that it was he who had omitted to key in the fire-drill code, so that news of the emergency had been relayed straight to the fire station.

'Good thing too,' said the fire chief as he emerged from the building with the last of his men. 'Just goes to show you can never be too careful with those things around. Good job you had that smoke alarm.'

'Time to go in,' bugled Maureen from the car park. 'Is everyone here? Did everyone hear me? I said *time* to go *in*!'

A murmur, almost of protest, went through the residents on the lawn. Sad Harry stood up reluctantly from his game of cards. Denise looked up from the daisy chain in her lap. Mr Bannerman turned his hearing aid on again. Mrs Banerjee took off another of her coats and Hope said, 'Where's Mrs McAllister?'

For a second we all looked at each other. It was typical of Hope to have noticed the one thing that none of the sighted ones had taken in. Anxiously I scanned the grounds for signs of Mrs McAllister, imagining her lost and wandering, or worse, halfway down the busy main road in search of some place or person that hadn't existed since before the War.

'Mrs McAllister!' bellowed Maureen. 'We're going *in* now, dearie!'

Still, no sign of Mrs McAllister. I looked at Hope. I was beginning to get a bad feeling – a premonition, if you like – and imagined the old lady collapsed behind the angle of the building, toothless mouth caved in on itself, one hand flung out like a dry branch on the gravel path . . .

Well, it just goes to show that you can't trust those premonitions.

Just as I opened my mouth to speak she rounded the building, arm in arm with one of the firemen, a cheerful-looking young man of twenty-five or thereabouts, tall and dark and rather muscular in that understated way that firemen often seem to have (yes, I *know* I'm seventy-two, but that doesn't stop me noticing, does it?). Anyway, he must have said something hilariously funny, because Mrs McAllister was cackling away like a mad hen. I hadn't seen her this cheerful since that day in the lobby when Lorraine had told her Peter had died, and it brought a lump to my throat to see her this way; so old; so small; but clinging to the fireman's arm like a monkey and laughing fit to split.

'Where *have* you been?' said Maureen disapprovingly.

The young man grinned. 'Training for the fire brigade,' he said, detaching Mrs McAllister's hand (with some difficulty) from his arm. 'I'll give you this, Norah' – can you believe it, I never knew Mrs McAllister's first name was Norah – 'you're a hell of a sprinter.'

Mrs McAllister laughed again. She peered up into the young man's face (her own face was about level with his belt buckle) and took his hand in one of hers.

'I'm so glad you came,' she said brightly. 'Now you can meet all my friends. This is Faith – and this is Hope.' She waved at both of us, birdy-eyed with excitement. 'They've got me through some hard times; they've been very good to me, you know.'

'Don't be silly,' said Hope bracingly. 'Now – suppose you introduce us to your friend.'

'My friend?' Mrs McAllister laughed again. I don't think I'd ever seen her laugh as much; it made her young again. Her eyes shone; she skipped and danced; her toothless mouth was merry with wrinkles.

She took the young man by the hand and led him to the patch of grass where Chris and Maureen and Denise and Sad Harry were waiting to lead us back into the Meadowbank Home.

'This is my son, Peter,' she said. 'He's a fireman, you know.'

Road Song

Five years after 'River Song', I travelled to Togo with Plan UK. There I learnt all about the traffickers of children, who lure susceptible youngsters into slavery and prostitution with promises of wealth and fortune. This story is one of the many I collected when I was there.

There are so many gods here. Rain gods; death gods; river gods; wind gods. Gods of the maize; medicine gods; old gods; new gods brought here from elsewhere and gone native, sinking their roots into the ground, sending out signals and stories and songs wherever the wind will take them.

Such a god is the Great North Road. From Lomé by the Bight of Benin to Dapaong in the far provinces, it runs like a dusty river. Its source, the city of Lomé, with its hot and humid streets; its markets; its gracious boulevards; its beach and the litter of human jetsam that roams along the esplanade, and the shoals of mopeds and bicycles that make up most of its traffic. Unlike the river, even in drought the

277

Great North Road never runs dry. Nor does its burden of legends and songs; of travellers and their stories.

My current tale begins right here, outside the town of Sokodé. A large and busy settlement five hours' drive north of Lomé, ringed with smaller villages like handmaids to the greater town. All depend on the road for their existence, although many of these villagers have never been much further than a few dozen miles to the north or south. Often people walk up the track and sit and watch and wait by the side of the road for whatever flotsam it may bring: traders on cycles; mopeds; trucks; women on their way to the fields to harvest maize or to cut wood.

One of these watchers is Maleki, a girl from nearby Kassena. Sixteen years old; the eldest of five; she likes to sit in the shade of the trees as the road unwinds before her. Her younger brother, Marcellin, used to watch the sky for vapour trails, while Jean-Baptiste preferred the trucks, waving madly as they passed, but Maleki just watches the road, ever alert for a sign of life. Over the years she has come to believe that the road is more than just dirt and stones; it has a force, an identity. She also believes that it has a *voice* – sometimes just a distant hiss, sometimes many voices, compelling as a church choir.

And in the mornings at five o'clock, when she gets up to begin her chores, the road is already waiting for her; humming faintly; sheathed in mist. It might almost be asleep; but Maleki knows better. The road is like a crocodile; one eye open even in sleep, ready to snap at anyone foolish enough to drop their guard. Maleki never drops her guard.

As she ties her sarong into place; knots it firmly at her hip; ties the bandeau across her breasts; slips barefoot across the yard; draws water from the village well; hauls it back to the washing hut; as she cuts the firewood and ties it into a bundle, as she carries it home on her head, she listens for the song of the road; she watches its sly, insidious length and the dust that rises with the sun, announcing the presence of visitors.

This morning, the road is almost silent. A few bats circle above a stand of banyan trees; a woman with a bundle of sticks crosses from the other side; something small – a bush-rat, perhaps – rattles through the undergrowth. If they were here, Maleki thinks, her brothers would go out hunting today. They would set fire to the dry brush downwind of the village, and wait for the bush-rats to come running out of the burning grass. There's plenty of meat on a bush-rat – it's tougher than chicken, but tasty – and they would sell them by the road – gutted and stretched on a framework of sticks – to folk on their way to the market.

But Maleki's brothers are long gone, like many of the children. No one will hunt bush-rat today, or stand by the road at Sokodé, waving at the vehicles. No one will play *ampé* with her in the yard, or lie on their back under the trees watching out for vapour trails.

She drops the cut wood to the ground outside the open kitchen door. Maleki's home is a compound of mud-brick buildings with a corrugated iron roof around a central yard area. There is a henhouse, a maize store, a row of low benches on which to sit and a cooking pot at the far end. Maleki's mother uses this pot to brew *tchoukoutou*, millet beer, which she sells around the village, or to make soy cheese or maize porridge for sale at the weekly market in Sokodé.

Maleki likes the market. There are so many things to see there. Young men riding mopeds; women riding pillion. Sellers of manioc and fried plantain. Flatbed trucks bearing timber. *Vaudou* men selling spells and charms. Dough-ball stands by the roadside. Pancakes and *foufou*; yams and bananas; mountains of millet and peppers and rice. Fabrics of all colours; sarongs and scarves and *dupattas*. Bead necklaces, bronze earrings; tins of harissa; bangles; pottery dishes; bottles and gourds; spices and salt; garlands of chillies; cooking pots; brooms; baskets; plastic buckets; knives; Coca-Cola; engine oil and sandals made from plaited grass.

Most of these things are beyond the means of Maleki and her family. But she likes to watch as she helps her mother prepare maize porridge for sale at their stall, grinding the meal between two stones, then cooking it in a deep pan. And the song of the road is more powerful here: a song of distant places; of traders and travellers, gossip and news, of places whose names she only knows from maps chalked on to a blackboard.

The road has seen Maleki travel to and from markets every day since she could walk. Sometimes she makes her way alone; most often she walks with her mother, balancing the maize on her head in a woven basket. Until two years ago, she went to school, and the road saw her walk the other way, dressed in a white blouse and khaki skirt and carrying a parcel of books. In those days its song was different: it sang of mathematics and English and geography; of dictionaries and football matches and music and hope. But since her brothers left home, Maleki no longer walks to school, or wears the khaki uniform. And the song of the road has changed again; now it sings of marriage, and home; and children running in the yard; and of long days spent in the maize fields, and of childish dreams put away for good—

It isn't as if she *wanted* to leave. She was a promising student. Almost as clever as a boy, and almost as good at football, too – even the Chief has commented, though grudgingly (he does not approve of girls' football). But with a husband away all year round, and younger children to care for – all three with malaria, and one not even two years old – Maleki's mother needs help, and although she feels sad for her daughter, she knows that reading books never fed anyone, or ploughed as much as a square inch of land—

Besides, she thinks, when the boys come home there will be money for everyone; money for clothes, for medicine, for food – in Nigeria, she has heard, people eat chicken every day, and everyone has a radio, a mosquito net, a sewing machine—

This is the song the mother hears. A lullaby of dreams come true, and it sounds to her like Adjale's voice – Adjale, of the golden smile – and although she misses her boys, she knows that one day they will both come home, bringing the wealth she was promised. It's hard to send her children away – two young boys, barely into their teens – into a foreign city. But sacrifices must be made, so Adjale has told her. And they will be cared for very well. Each boy will have a bicycle; each boy will have a mobile phone. Such riches seem impossible here in Togo; but in Nigeria, things are different. The houses have tiled floors; a bath; water; electricity. Employers are kind and respectful; they care for the children as if they were their own. Even the girls are given new clothes, jewellery and make-up. Adjale told her all this – Adjale, with the golden voice – when the traffickers first came.

Traffickers. Such a cruel word. Maleki's mother prefers to call them *fishers of men*, like Jesus and his disciples. Their river is the Great North Road; and every year, they travel north like fishermen to the spawning grounds. Every year they come away with a plentiful catch of boys and girls, many as young as twelve or thirteen, like Marcellin and Jean-Baptiste. They smuggle them over the border by night, avoiding the police patrols, for none of them has a passport. Sometimes they take them over the river on rafts made of wood and plastic drums, lashed together with twine woven from the banana leaf.

Maleki's mother wonders if, on the day her sons return, she will even recognize them. Both will have grown into men by now. Her heart swells painfully at the thought. And she thinks of her daughter, Maleki – so clever, so young, with red string woven into her hair and the voice of a golden angel – still waiting, after all this time. And when the daily chores are done, and the red sun fades from the western sky, and the younger children are asleep on their double pallet in the hut, she watches Maleki as she stands perfectly still by the Great North Road, etched in the light of the village fires, singing softly to herself and praying for her brothers' return.

For Maleki knows that the road is a god, a dangerous god that must be appeased. Sometimes it takes a stray child, or maybe, if they are lucky, a dog – crushed beneath some lorry's wheels. But the traffickers take more than that: four children last year; three gone the year before. So Maleki sings: *Don't let them come; please, this year, keep them away* – and she is not entirely sure whether it is to God or Allah that she prays or to the Great North Road itself, the sly and dusty snake-god that charms away their children.

By night the road seems more than ever alive; filled with rumours and whisperings. All the old, familiar sounds from the village down the path – the chanting, the drumming, the children at play, the warble of a radio or a mobile phone from outside the Chief's house, where the men drink *tchouk* and talk business – now all these things seem so far away, as distant as the aeroplanes that sometimes track their paths overhead, leaving those broken vapour trails like fingernail scratches across the sky. Only the road is real, she thinks; the road with its songs of seduction, to which we sacrifice our children for the sake of a beautiful lie, a shining dream of better things.

She knows that most will never come back. She needs no songs to tell her *that*. The fishers of men are predators, with their shining lure of salvation. The truth is they come like the harmattan, the acrid wind that blows every year, stripping the land of its moisture and filling the mouth with a sour red dust. Nothing grows while the harmattan blows, except for the dreams of foolish boys and their even more foolish mothers, who send them off with the traffickers – all dressed in their church clothes, in case the patrols spot them and smell their desperation – each with a thick slice of cold maize porridge, lovingly wrapped up in a fold of banana leaf and tied with a piece of red string, for luck.

Money changes hands – not much, not even the price of a sackful of grain, but the baby needs a mosquito net, and the older one some medicine, and she isn't *selling* her children, Maleki's mother tells herself; she is sending them to the Promised Land. Adjale will look after them. Adjale, who every year brings news of her sons and tells her: *Maybe next year they will send a card, a letter, even a photograph—*

But something inside her still protests, and once again she asks herself whether she did the right thing. And every year Adjale smiles and says to her: *Trust me. I know what I'm doing.* And though it's very hard for her to see him only once a year, she knows that he is doing well, helping children along the road, and he has promised to send for her – *one day, very soon*, he says. *Just as soon as the children are grown. Four years, maybe five, that's all.*

And Maleki's mother believes him. He *has* been very good to her. But Maleki does not trust him. She has never trusted him. But what can one girl do alone? She cannot stop them any more than she could stop the harmattan with its yearly harvest of red dust. *What can I do?* she asks the road. *What can I do to fight them?*

The answer comes to her that night, as she stands alone by the side of the road. The moon is high in the sky, and yet the road is still warm, like an animal; and it smells of dust and petrol, and of the sweat of the many bare feet that pound its surface daily. And maybe the road answers her prayer, or maybe another god is listening; but tonight, only to Maleki, it tells another story: it sings a song of loneliness; of sadness and betrayal. It sings of sick children left to die along the road to Nigeria; of girls sold into prostitution; of thwarted hopes and violence and sickness and starvation and AIDS. It sings of disappointment; and of two boys with the scars of Kassena cut into their cheeks, their bodies covered in sour red dust, coming home up the Great North Road. The boys are penniless, starving and sick after two long years in Nigeria, working the fields fourteen hours a day, sold for the price of a bicycle. *But still alive*, Maleki thinks; *still alive and coming home*; and the pounding beat of this new song joins the beat of Maleki's heart as she stands by the road at Kassena, and her feet begin to move in the dust; and her body begins to lilt and sway; and in that moment she hears them all; all those vanished children; all of them joining the voice of the road in a song that will not be ignored.

And now she understands what to do to fight the fishers of children. It isn't much, but it *is* a start; it's the seed that grows into a tree; the tree that becomes a forest; the forest that forms a windbreak that may even stop the harmattan—

Not today. Not this year. But maybe in her lifetime—

Now *that* would be a thing to see.

Walking home that night past the fires; as Maleki walks past the Chief's hut; past the maize field; past the rows of pot-bellied henhouses; as she washes her face at the water-pump;

as she drinks from a hollowed-out gourd and eats the slice of cold maize porridge her mother has left on the table for her; as she lays out her old school uniform, the white blouse and khaki skirt and the battered old football boots that she has not yet outgrown; as she lies down on her mattress and listens to the sounds of the night, Maleki thinks about *other* roads; the paths we have to make for ourselves.

Tomorrow, she thinks, will be different. Tomorrow, instead of watching the road, instead of going to market, she will walk up to the schoolhouse wearing her khaki uniform; swinging her boots by the laces in time to the song only she can hear. Her mother will try to stop her, perhaps; but only with a half of her heart. And when her brothers come home at last, she will tell them: *Why did you leave? The Promised Land was always here. Inside me. Inside you.* And maybe, in time, she will make them hear this song she hears so clearly; and maybe their children will hear it too, and understand her when she says: *If the road doesn't take you where you want, then you must make your own road—*

There are so many gods here in this land of Togo. River gods; road gods; all of them, maybe, false gods. But the real power lies in the human heart; its courage; its resilience. This, too, is the song of the road, and through the voices of children it endures, and grows more powerful every day; sinking its roots deep into the soil, sending out its seeds of change wherever the wind will take them.

Acknowledgements

I owe a debt of gratitude to all the people around the world who have inspired these tales of mine: to children rescued from traffickers; children riding the rapids; actors who took time to chat at Stage Door; random encounters on the Tube; taxi drivers with stories to tell; book-group members in signing queues; elderly ladies with total recall of events that happened sixty years ago. To Twitterers; chocolatiers; people waiting in station cafés; bakers who send me cake through the post; young lovers on park benches. Also to those people who work so hard alongside me, especially Louise Page-Lund, my publicist; Anne Riley, my PA; Mark Richards, who maintains my website; my editor, Marianne Velmans and all my colleagues at Transworld, including: Larry Finlay; Kate Samano; Deborah Adams; Claire Ward; Suzanne Riley; plus all the reps, proofers, copy-editors and booksellers who continue to keep my books on the shelves – and, of course, to you, the readers, whose appetite for stories has kept the dream machine working for so long. And to Kevin and Anouchka, without whom there would be no dream machine at all.

The Little Book of Chocolat

Joanne Harris and Fran Warde

Try me . . . test me . . . taste me . . .

Rich, moist black-and-white chocolate cake; dark, gleaming truffles; spiced hot chocolate with *crème Chantilly* and chocolate curls; Aztec chocolate orange cake and chocolate pudding with salted caramel sauce . . .

Joanne Harris's bestselling *Chocolat* has tantalized readers with its sensuous descriptions of chocolate since it was first published. Now, inspired by the much-loved story of Vianne Rocher's deliciously decadent *chocolaterie*, Joanne Harris and Fran Warde have created the ultimate book of chocolate recipes to bring a touch of Lansquenet magic to your kitchen.

Coming soon from Doubleday